The Last Station

The Predecessors
Book 1

Blair C Howard

Printed Cleveland, TN 2025
Print Paperback ISBN: 979-8-9988024-0-9
Library of Congress Control Number: 2025908826
Blair Howard Books
BlairHoward@BlairHowardBooks.com

To Sci-Fi fans wherever you may be, and however old you are.

The World of The Last Station

Half a million years ago, an advanced civilization known only as the Predecessors dominated the galaxy. Masters of quantum technology and dimensional engineering, they achieved near-immortality through consciousness transfer and the ability to exist across multiple realities simultaneously.

In their quest to create perfect successors, they engineered a race of energy beings housed in crystalline forms. But these creations, now known only as the Enemy, evolved beyond control. They rejected biological life as inefficient, believing that consciousness should transcend physical form.

The resulting war lasted 400,000 years. As the Predecessors faced extinction, they enacted their final plan: they seeded Earth with carefully engineered genetic markers, designing humanity to be their true inheritors. Every step of human evolution was guided, preparing us for the moment we would discover their legacy.

Present Day, 2287

Humanity has spread beyond Earth, establishing colonies throughout the solar system. The Terran Coalition governs from New Geneva, maintaining control through advanced quantum technology reverse-engineered from discovered artifacts. Most believe these ruins are random discoveries—few suspect they were designed specifically for us to find.

The Coalition's Deep Space Research Division explores the frontier, while Special Operations teams secretly gather Predecessor technology. But something is stirring in the void. The Enemy has detected humanity's growing compatibility with quantum technology, and they're returning to finish what they started centuries ago.

From the Author

Beneath humanity's surface lies dormant potential: genetic markers waiting to be activated, neural architecture designed to interface with technologies we're only now beginning to understand. We're not just another species discovering ancient artifacts —we're the weapon—hidden in plain sight—the Predecessors spent half a million years crafting.

This is the story of first contact with our true heritage, and the war that will determine not just humanity's survival, but its evolution. The Enemy believes they achieved perfection by abandoning biological form. But the Predecessors designed humanity to prove that true perfection lies in the balance between chaos and control, between technological precision and biological adaptability.

The stations are awakening. The Enemy approaches. And humanity is about to discover what we were truly designed to become.

Prologue

The Final Days

HALF A MILLION YEARS AGO...

THE CRYSTALLINE SPIRES of the Last Council Chamber pulsed with quantum energy as the remaining Predecessors gathered. Their forms, composed of pure energy contained within geometric shells, shifted through multiple dimensions as they debated their species' final act. Outside, in the vastness of space, the Enemy fleet darkened the skies of a thousand worlds, their perfect mathematical formations spreading like a virus through reality itself.

"Our first children have become our destruction," First Voice announced, its consciousness spread across seven crystalline entities. "They seek to eliminate chaos from existence itself, to impose perfect order on a universe that requires uncertainty to evolve."

Through their quantum network, they felt another station fall to the Enemy's assault. Each loss weakened their civilization's grip on reality, forcing their consciousness to retreat into fewer

7

and fewer strongholds. The war had raged for thousands of years, but the outcome was now inevitable.

"The suppression fields grow stronger," Second Voice reported, its energy form flickering with strain. "They're not just destroying our technology, they're rewriting the laws of physics, creating spaces where evolution becomes impossible."

The Chamber's displays showed the Enemy's methodical advance. Their ships moved with perfect precision, their weapons designed to eliminate any possibility of chaos or uncertainty. What had begun as an attempt to create a perfect race of successors had become an extinction-level threat to all dynamic existence.

"But we have found something," Third Voice transmitted, its pattern carrying hope despite their dire situation. "A young world, still early in its evolutionary cycle. Its native species shows remarkable potential for both technological precision and biological adaptation."

The Chamber's field shifted as Third Voice uploaded data about the primitive planet they had discovered. Earth—its native species would one day call it—a world where life was just beginning to evolve through controlled chaos, producing beings capable of both logical precision and creative uncertainty.

"We have already begun subtle modifications," Third Voice continued, its crystalline form resonating with purpose. "Their genetic structure is remarkably adaptable. Each change we introduce creates cascading variations, patterns we never achieved with our first attempt."

The assembled Predecessors accessed the data. They watched as carefully engineered retroviruses altered human DNA, preparing it for capabilities that wouldn't manifest for thousands of generations. Each modification was designed to stay dormant until the species reached sufficient technological advancement eons in the future.

"But the Enemy will detect these changes," Second Voice warned. "They'll recognize our signatures in the genetic code. They'll destroy this species before it can reach its potential."

"Not if we hide it carefully," First Voice countered. Its consciousness expanded through the Chamber's crystalline architecture as it shared their final strategy. "We'll build a network of stations, each containing different aspects of our knowledge. But we'll design them to remain dormant, invisible to perfect mathematical scanning."

Another sector fall to the Enemy forces. Their time was running out, but the plan was taking shape in their collective consciousness.

"The stations must be more than mere repositories," Fourth Voice contributed, joining the council as another sector fell to Enemy forces. "Each one will contain different aspects of our technology, our understanding of quantum space. But more importantly, they must be able to evolve alongside this species."

The Chamber's displays showed their network design taking shape. Dozens of facilities, each containing crucial pieces of their civilization's knowledge, would be hidden throughout the galaxy. Some would house weapons technology, others evolutionary templates, still others the seeds of consciousness.

"We will also leave them tests," First Voice decided, its crystalline forms shifting with purpose. "The Enemy's perfect mathematics makes them predictable. We can design challenges that require both precision and chaos to overcome problems their rigid patterns cannot solve."

They felt the Enemy's suppression fields growing stronger. More of their civilization retreated into dimensional spaces, preserving what knowledge they could. But now they had a purpose beyond mere survival.

"The genetic modifications are complete," Third Voice reported. "We've hidden triggers throughout their evolutionary path. Each advancement will unlock new potential, leading them toward capabilities even we haven't fully explored."

Second Voice's energy patterns showed concern. "But if we succeed, if they do achieve this potential, they will face the same choice we did. The temptation to impose perfect order—"

"That's precisely why we've designed them this way," First Voice interrupted. "Each station, each genetic trigger, each template, they're all created to encourage balance. These humans will advance through controlled chaos, finding strength in uncertainty rather than fearing it."

The Chamber shuddered as Enemy weapons breached another defensive line, and they felt more of their civilization falling to the suppression fields. Perfect mathematical order spread through reality like a plague, eliminating possibility itself.

"The final preparations are complete," Third Voice announced. "The stations are hidden, their quantum signatures masked by dimensional shifts. The genetic modifications are locked into their evolutionary path. Earth will remain invisible to Enemy scans until humanity is ready."

"And the templates?" Fourth Voice queried. "The ones even we feared to use?"

"Secured in the Perseus facility," First Voice confirmed. "Along with our most dangerous knowledge. They must prove themselves worthy of such power—demonstrate they understand the balance between order and chaos before accessing that level of manipulation."

Through their failing network, they watched Enemy ships approaching their last stronghold. The crystalline vessels moved with mathematical precision, their perfect formations designed to eliminate any trace of chaos from existence.

"We have done what we can," First Voice declared, its consciousness preparing for the final dispersal. "We leave them our knowledge, our technology, and our hopes for a better path. The rest will be up to them."

Second Voice's energy patterns shifted with sudden insight. "Perhaps this was inevitable. Perhaps we were never meant to be the final stage of conscious evolution. We achieved perfect technological advancement but lost the ability to embrace uncertainty."

"And our first children went too far in the other direction," Third Voice added. "Seeking absolute mathematical order at the cost of all else."

"But these humans," First Voice concluded, watching Earth's first primitive civilization through their sensors, "they have the potential to find the balance we never could. To become something beyond either extreme."

The Enemy fleet entered firing range, their weapons charged with reality-distorting energy. The Last Council Chamber's defenses prepared for their final stand.

"It is done," First Voice transmitted. "When humanity finds our stations, when they begin to transform, they will face the same choice our first children did. But this time…"

"This time," Second Voice finished, "they will have the strength to choose both paths. To embrace order and chaos as equal partners in evolution."

The Chamber's field flared one last time as the Enemy attack began. The Predecessors' consciousness dispersed into dimensional space, their final thoughts focused on a primitive planet where their greatest hope now lay.

Humanity's long path to transcendence had begun.

Chapter 1

Signal

COMMANDER FRANCES DRAKE FROWNED. SHE COULDN'T SHAKE the feeling that something was wrong with the numbers, and she was rarely wrong. She'd spent twenty of her forty-two years in the Terran Coalition Space Force, seven in command of Terran Survey Vessel Hawking, exploring the boundaries of known space. She was tall, almost two meters, slim, with auburn hair and hazel eyes. A former Coalition tactical officer turned research vessel commander, her expertise was in deep space phenomena and tactical operations. She was methodical, principled, and willing to break rules for the greater good.

Now, she stood on the observation deck of the TSV Hawking, her fingers trailing across the holographic readouts that painted the air in front of her. The research vessel's sensors had been picking up anomalous readings for the past three days, but this was different. The pattern wasn't random noise—it couldn't be. She shook her head, smoothed her shipboard uniform pants with the palms of her hands, and stared at the scrolling data.

The deck hummed beneath her feet with the familiar vibration of the quantum drive at idle, a sensation she'd grown accustomed to over fifteen years of deep space research. But today, the vibration felt... off-rhythm, as if the ship itself sensed something unusual in the void ahead. Even the air seemed different, though she knew that was impossible; the environmental systems maintained perfect consistency, just as they had for the seven years she'd commanded the Hawking.

The observation deck's curved ceiling displayed a real-time overlay of their surroundings, creating the illusion of floating in space. Quantum field generators hummed softly in the walls, maintaining the delicate balance of artificial gravity that kept them all from floating away. Drake's neural implant interfaced seamlessly with the ship's systems, feeding her constant updates about everything from hull integrity to the crew's vital signs.

"Dr. Rivera," she called out, not taking her eyes off the cascading data, "can you confirm these harmonics?" The streams of light between her fingers pulsed with each new data point, creating a complex dance of information that seemed almost alive. Her implant highlighted patterns automatically, searching for matches in the Coalition's vast database of known phenomena.

The ship's lead physicist looked up from his station, dark circles under his eyes suggesting he'd not slept for days and that he, too, had noticed the irregularities. His desk was cluttered with empty stimulant packets—the standard issue ones that kept Coalition research crews alert during long shifts. The packets sparkled slightly in the soft blue light of his holographic displays, their nano-recycling systems already breaking them down for reuse.

"I'm already running a third verification, Commander. Whatever it is, it's real." Rivera's voice carried the weight of someone who'd spent too many hours staring at data that shouldn't exist. He pulled up a new set of readings, the crystalline processors beneath his station humming as they processed the calculations. "The temporal signature is unlike anything in our databases."

The signal pulsed at regular intervals: seven beats, pause, thirteen beats, pause, seventeen beats. Prime numbers. Nature doesn't work in prime numbers, not like this, she thought.

Drake had spent her career studying deep space phenomena, starting as a junior researcher on Europa, moving through the ranks until she earned command of the Coalition's most advanced research vessel. She'd seen fluctuations that looked like messages, gravitational waves that mimicked language patterns, even the occasional deep space anomaly that turned out to be nothing more than sensor ghosts created by cosmic radiation. But this was different.

She rubbed the small scar behind her ear where the neural implant connected to her nervous system, a habit she'd developed during stressful situations. The implant responded by releasing a mild calming agent into her bloodstream, though she'd reduced its automated responses after too many incidents of artificial calm during genuine emergencies.

Through the reinforced viewport, the edge of known space stretched before them—a canvas of absolute darkness punctuated by distant stars. They'd been tasked with mapping gravitational anomalies in this sector, routine work for the Hawking. But there was nothing routine about this. The very fabric of space seemed to ripple around the source of the signal, as if reality itself was struggling to contain whatever waited out there in the void.

"Processing complete," ARIA announced, the ship's AI's voice carefully modulated to avoid startling the crew. Even after seventeen years of working with artificial intelligences, Drake still caught hints of something almost human in ARIA's inflections. The AI had evolved significantly since its installation seven years ago during the ship's final phase of construction, learning to read the crew's moods and adjust its interactions accordingly. "Signal origin identified. Bearing 247 mark 115, approximately 2.3 light-years from our current position."

The Last Station

Drake brought up the stellar charts, her implant connecting seamlessly with the ship's systems. The holographic display expanded, filling her field of vision with a three-dimensional map of local space. Quantum positioning beacons pulsed softly, marking the boundary of known space—they were already operating beyond those markers, in the true frontier where anything was possible. She searched for any recorded objects in that direction. There was nothing—no stars, no brown dwarfs, not even a rogue planet. Just empty space that somehow wasn't empty at all.

Lieutenant Cathy Park worked quietly at her communications station, her fingers dancing across the haptic interfaces as she analyzed the signal's structure. The young officer had earned her position through brilliant work in Xeno linguistics, though until now, there had been no alien languages to study. Floating holographic representations of different communication patterns—everything from ancient Earth morse code to the quantum entanglement signals used by modern Coalition ships—surrounded her station.

"The signal's structure," Park said, her voice barely above a whisper, "it's not random at all. There are layers to it, like... like it was designed to be noticed." Her hands moved through the air, manipulating the holographic patterns. "The prime number sequence is just the surface. There's something else embedded deeper within the signal."

Chief Engineer Maya Jackson's voice crackled over the comm from engineering, the slight delay indicating she was probably inside one of the drive chambers. "Commander, we're seeing some unusual fluctuations in the drive core. Nothing dangerous, but the field harmonics are... shifting. Almost like they're trying to synchronize with something."

Drake felt a chill run down her spine despite the perfectly regulated temperature. Her implant registered the physiological response and started composing a medical alert, which she dismissed with a thought. "How old is it?" she asked, though she already suspected the answer would upend everything they thought they knew about this region of space. The Coalition had been pushing into the frontier for decades, claiming there was nothing out here worth finding. She'd never quite believed that.

Dr. Rivera's hands moved across his console, extrapolating the data. The quantum computers hummed as they processed the calculations, their crystalline cores glowing softly in their housing beneath the deck. "Based on decay patterns..." He paused, running the calculations again. The holo projectors around his station flickered as they struggled to represent the immense timescales involved. "Commander, if these readings are accurate, the signal predates human civilization. By a lot. We're looking at one hundred thousand years, minimum."

The observation deck fell silent. Drake felt the weight of the moment settle around her like a physical presence. The only sound was the soft beeping of monitoring equipment and the ever-present hum of the ship's systems. Her implant recorded elevated heart rates across the entire bridge crew—everyone understood the implications of what they'd found.

"Ma'am," Lieutenant Park called from the communications station, her voice tight with concern, "the signal's getting stronger." Her hands moved rapidly across her console, adjusting parameters to compensate for the increasing intensity. "The embedded patterns are becoming clearer. There's... there's a mathematical progression I've never seen before."

Drake watched as new data flooded the holographic displays. The pattern was evolving, becoming more complex. Seven, thirteen, seventeen... then twenty-three, twenty-nine, thirty-one. A mathematical sequence that could only be artificial. Her implant translated the raw data into visual patterns, and she visibly shuddered. This wasn't just a signal—it was a message.

The ship's environmental systems automatically adjusted to

compensate for her elevated heart rate, a subtle reminder of how much they depended on technology out here at the edge of known space. Drake took a deep breath, steadying herself before making the decision she knew would change everything. Her implant, anticipating what she was about to do, brought up Coalition regulations, highlighting several sections about required procedures for first contact scenarios. She dismissed them with a thought.

"Plot a course," she ordered, her voice steady despite the adrenaline coursing through her system. "But keep us at a safe distance. No closer than half a light-year until we know what we're dealing with." The neural interface translated her commands into ship movements, and she felt the subtle shift as the Hawking's orientation thrusters fired.

The drive's hum changed pitch as the navigation systems calculated the precise coordinates for the jump. Drake felt the vibration through the deck plates, a reminder of the immense energies they were about to channel. The Hawking was the most advanced ship in the Coalition fleet, but they were still playing with forces they barely understood.

"Commander," Dr. Rivera interjected, pushing away from his station. The movement sent several empty stimulant packets floating in the low gravity environment. His implant's status light pulsed yellow, indicating elevated stress levels. "Coalition protocol requires that we report this anomaly immediately. We should wait for authorization before—"

"Look at these readings," Drake interrupted, highlighting a particular sequence in the holographic display. The numbers pulsed with an urgency she couldn't ignore. Her implant automatically recorded and archived the data, standard procedure for any potential first contact scenario. "The signal's degrading. If we wait for authorization, there might not be anything left to study."

She turned to face her crew, seeing the same mix of fear and excitement in their eyes that she felt herself. The observation deck's ambient lighting adjusted automatically, responding to the collective tension in the room. "Whatever this is, it's been waiting thousands of years to be found. I don't intend to make it wait any longer."

The Hawking's engines hummed into life, its drive preparing for the short jump that would bring them closer to the source. Drake knew she was violating at least three Coalition directives, but some discoveries were worth the risk. She'd lost Thomas to playing it safe, following protocols while the unknown phenomenon they'd been studying tore his research vessel apart. She wouldn't make the same mistake twice.

Her implant pulled up the last image she had of Thomas, probably responding to her elevated emotional state. She dismissed it quickly, but not before catching a glimpse of his smile, the way he looked just before that final mission. The implant's mood stabilizers kicked in automatically, but she overrode them. She needed to feel this, needed to remember why she was out here.

As the ship aligned itself with the coordinates, she smiled to herself. Are we about to learn the answer to humanity's oldest question? she wondered. Are we alone?

The neural interface fed her real-time updates about the ship's status, each system reporting ready for the jump. In the corner of her vision, a small alert reminded her that her elevated cortisol levels suggested stress. She dismissed it with a thought.

"Quantum field stabilized," Chief Maya Jackson reported from engineering. "Drive core temperature optimal. Whatever we're about to do, Commander, the ship's ready for it."

The signal pulsed again, stronger now. Seven, thirteen, seventeen, twenty-three, twenty-nine, thirty-one... The sequence continued, each prime number feeling less like a mathematical pattern and more like a countdown. The holographic displays rippled with new data, and for a moment, Drake thought she saw something in the pattern—a structure, a purpose, a design that seemed almost familiar.

"Jump coordinates locked," ARIA announced, its voice carrying a note of what might have been anticipation. "Quantum drive spooled and ready. Warning: signal intensity may interfere with standard jump calculations. Recommended course of action is to—"

"Override warning," Drake commanded. The AI fell silent, though she could sense its concern in the way it adjusted the ship's internal systems, preparing for any possibility. "Sometimes you have to take risks to make history," she muttered.

No one answered.

She took one last look at the empty space ahead of them. In a few moments, they would either make history or join Thomas in the long list of vessels that had disappeared trying to unlock the frontier's secrets. Either way, there was no turning back now. Her implant recorded her final command for the ship's logs, standard procedure for any non-standard operation.

"Execute jump," she commanded, and the universe bent around them. The drive engaged with a sound like reality itself taking a deep breath, and Frances Drake led her crew toward whatever waited for them in the void.

They were about to find out what it was counting down to.

Chapter 2

Politics

THE WINDOWS OF THE COALITION SECURITY COUNCIL CHAMBER
automatically darkened as Admiral Victor Perez activated his
neural presentation interface. Two kilometers beneath New
Geneva, the Terran Coalition Capital in what once had been Nash-
ville, Tennessee, the circular chamber represented the heart of
human governance, though few citizens knew of its existence.
Ancient wooden panels, salvaged from the old UN building,
contrasted with cutting-edge holographic displays and the neural
interface nodes embedded in each councilor's seat.

"The Hawking's unauthorized jump represents a clear viola-
tion of frontier protocols," he said, his augmented voice carrying
perfectly to each council member. His cybernetic eye, a prototype
that had cost more than a small starship, scanned the assembled
representatives, analyzing micro-expressions and neural patterns.
The data streamed directly into his enhanced cortex, giving him
perfect insight into who was lying, who was afraid, and who was
already plotting their next move.

The chamber's central holographic array showed the Hawking's last known position, a pulsing red dot at the edge of mapped space. Quantum entanglement sensors tracked the research vessel's energy signature in real time, but the signal interference made its precise location impossible. The interference pattern itself was telling. It matched theoretical models of advanced non-human technology that had been classified for decades.

Councilor Durn leaned forward, the movement causing her ceremonial robe to shimmer. Her ancient face, lined with the marks of someone who had refused genetic rejuvenation treatments, showed genuine concern. "And you're certain about the age of this signal, Admiral? Our best temporal analysis systems have a margin of error of several thousand years."

"Our analysis confirms Dr. Rivera's initial assessment." Perez brought up the temporal data with a thought, his implant interfacing smoothly with the chamber's systems. The holographic display shifted, showing complex mathematical models that few in the room truly understood. "The transmission predates human civilization by at least twenty-five thousand years. The decay patterns are unambiguous."

The chamber erupted in murmurs. Perez noticed Director Sarah Yuki, the Separatist representative, typing rapidly into her interface. Her fingers moved with the precise gestures of someone using a military-grade encrypted channel, technology the Separatists shouldn't have had access to. No doubt informing her handlers about the development, he thought. The Separatists have spies everywhere, even here in the heart of Coalition power.

He zoomed his cybernetic eye in on her activity, catching fragments of the encrypted data stream: "...asset in place... Wong confirms... salvage team ready... acquire at all costs..." Just as he expected, the Separatists were playing right into his hands.

"We have contingency plans for this scenario," Perez continued, bringing up classified military deployment patterns with a thought. The holographic display showed the Third Fleet's current position near Jupiter's L5 point. "I recommend we immediately dispatch the Third Fleet to secure the region and quarantine the Hawking until we can assess any potential threats."

"The Third Fleet?" Councilor Patel's voice carried the weight of his Mars constituency's concerns. His implant's status light pulsed yellow, indicating elevated stress levels. "That's a military response to a scientific discovery. Commander Drake's record is exemplary—"

"Her record," Perez interrupted, allowing a carefully calculated note of concern to enter his voice, "includes personal trauma that clouds her judgment. Need I remind the Council about the loss of her spouse? The Porter incident?"

The chamber fell silent. Everyone knew about the Porter incident. Thomas Drake's death had become a cautionary tale about the dangers of frontier exploration. What they didn't know—what only Perez and a select few others knew—was that the Porter incident had been carefully orchestrated. Thomas Drake had discovered something he shouldn't have, and the price of that discovery had been his life.

"I have a more immediate concern," Director Yuki spoke up, her voice carrying the slight delay of someone used to the transmission lag between Earth and the outer colonies. Her dark eyes reflected the holographic displays, her implant pulsing beneath her skin. "Several of our deep space listening posts detected a burst of activity shortly after the Hawking's jump. Something out there responded to their arrival."

Perez suppressed a smile. Right on schedule. He'd planted that information himself, knowing the Separatists would jump at any chance to challenge Coalition authority. The quantum burst had been carefully engineered by his deep cover agents, designed to look like alien technology activating.

"All the more reason to secure the region immediately," he said, bringing up classified sensor logs that showed the manufactured signatures. The Council members leaned forward, their neural interfaces automatically highlighting the anomalous patterns.

A priority alert flashed across his cybernetic vision, tagged with the highest security clearance. One of his agents had intercepted a transmission from the Hawking. The message was heavily encrypted, using protocols that shouldn't have existed outside military black sites. He kept his expression neutral as he read it, but inside, his heart raced. The signal wasn't just a transmission—it was a key. And Commander Drake had just turned it.

In the secure observation gallery above the chamber, Dr. David Cohen watched the proceedings with growing unease. As Coalition Science Director, he should have been on the council floor, but Perez had specifically requested his absence. Now he knew why.

Cohen's implant, modified with illegal quantum processors, intercepted fragments of encrypted communications flying around the chamber. Military deployments. Black ops teams. Salvage crews. Everyone was mobilizing, but nobody was asking the real question: why had the signal activated now, after hundreds of thousands of years of silence?

His fingers brushed against the crystal hanging from his neck —a gift from Professor Zhang Wei before his mysterious disappearance. The crystal had been behaving strangely ever since the Hawking made its jump, its molecular structure shifting in patterns that defied known physics.

"There's something else you should know," Perez announced, his voice cutting through Cohen's thoughts. "We've detected energy signatures consistent with artificial structures in the Hawking's vicinity. Structures that, until now, were completely invisible to our sensors."

The chamber erupted in chaos as the councilors began to argue about jurisdiction, military response, and first contact protocols. Their interfaces created a web of light as they accessed classified files and sent urgent messages to their constituents. Cohen noticed Director Yuki slip quietly from her seat, heading toward the secure communication chambers.

He activated his own encrypted channel, the processors in his implant routing the signal through a maze of relays that even Coalition Intelligence couldn't track. "Asset Three, priority message to the Hawking. Tell Wong the countdown has begun. Activation protocols are in effect."

The response came back instantly: "Message sent. But sir... we're detecting Enemy signatures at the edge of the sensor range. They're coming."

Cohen felt a chill run down his spine. The Enemy wasn't supposed to arrive for another decade. Unless... unless they'd been waiting, too, watching humanity stumble toward this moment.

On the council floor, Perez was already calling for an emergency vote. Cohen watched the Admiral's cybernetic eye scan the room, probably recording everything for later analysis. Let him think he was in control, Cohen thought, smiling to himself. The real game is about to begin, and not even Perez knows all the players.

In her private chamber, Director Sarah Yuki activated a neural link that shouldn't have existed. The connection bypassed standard Coalition monitoring, routing through a maze of deep space relays before reaching its destination: a hidden facility in the Kuiper Belt.

"The Coalition's mobilizing the Third Fleet," she reported, her implants translating thoughts directly into encrypted bursts. "Perez is making his move earlier than we anticipated."

The response materialized directly in her visual cortex, bypassing normal communication channels: "Asset status?"

"In position. Dr. Wong's cover remains intact. The Hawking's crew has no reason to suspect him." She paused, accessing classified files stolen from the Coalition databases. "But there's a complication. The signal's effect on the quantum fields... it matches the Porter incident. Exactly."

A longer pause this time. The Porter incident had nearly exposed everything. If anyone discovered the true nature of Thomas Drake's research—his discovery of the genetic markers, the hidden sequences in human DNA that responded to alien signals—the carefully laid plans of decades would unravel.

"Proceed as planned," came the response, accompanied by a data packet that made her implants burn. "The station must be secured before the Enemy arrives. Artifact Zero must not fall into Coalition hands."

In his private command center, Admiral Perez interfaced directly with his military neural net. Encrypted displays showed the positions of his Special Operations teams, their ships already moving into position around the Hawking's last known coordinates.

"Strike teams in position," Captain Maria Rodriguez reported, her neural signature indicating she was already suited up for combat. "We're detecting unusual signatures. Sir... they match the theoretical models from Project Harbinger."

Perez's organic eye narrowed while his cybernetic one recorded everything for later analysis. Project Harbinger—the classified research that had revealed humanity's true origins, the genetic modifications made more than one hundred millennia ago by beings whose technology they still couldn't comprehend.

"Your primary objective remains unchanged," he transmitted. "Secure any alien technology and eliminate all witnesses if necessary. But Commander Drake..." He accessed her classified genetic profile, noting the markers that matched Project Harbinger's predictions. "She may have inherited more than her husband's curiosity. Bring her to me. Alive."

The Council's vote was just for show now. Everything was in

motion. Humanity had spent centuries thinking they were alone in the universe, never realizing they were part of an experiment that began before their species existed. Now that experiment was entering its final phase.

And deep in the void where the Hawking waited, ancient machines were stirring to life, preparing to test their creation one last time.

Chapter 3

Assembly

THE DRIVE COMPONENTS CAST FRACTURED RAINBOWS ACROSS THE Hawking's engineering bay as they floated in zero gravity, their crystalline structures refracting the harsh work lights. Dr. Marcus Wong, a xenoarchaeologist, studied the installation through his enhanced optical implants, each recording lens capturing data his hidden masters had waited decades to obtain. The components looked like standard Coalition technology, but within their crystalline matrices lay patterns that predated human civilization—fragments of the Predecessors' quantum network, disguised as modern equipment.

Chief Engineer Maya Jackson's voice echoed from inside the drive housing. "Quantum tap alignment at 97.3 percent. These crystals..." She emerged from the access tunnel, wiping crystalline dust from her hands. "They're growing. I've never seen anything like it."

She wasn't wrong. The drive components were evolving, responding to the genetic markers carried by certain crew members. Wong's implants recorded the subtle changes in the crystal structures—changes that shouldn't have been possible, according to known physics.

"Neural handshake initiated," Zara Patel announced from her suspension harness. The pilot hung in a web of neural interface cables, her cybernetic systems pulsing with soft blue light as she merged her consciousness with the ship's systems. Energy coursed through her augmentations, creating patterns that Wong had seen only once before—in the final transmissions from the Porter.

"Integration progress at seventy percent," she reported, her eyes flickering rapidly. "The matrices are accepting the modifications, but..." She paused, her consciousness probing the new systems. "Something's different. The ship's responses... they're anticipating my commands. I'm seeing data structures that shouldn't exist."

Commander Frances Drake monitored the procedure from the main engineering console, her neural interface displaying real-time diagnostics. She'd removed her uniform jacket in the bay's heat, revealing the faint scars where her military-grade implants had been installed. Wong noticed how she occasionally touched the worn crystal hanging from her neck—Thomas' last gift to her. The crystal was a brother to the one he had carried, though Drake didn't know it yet.

"Different how?" she asked, her fingers dancing through the holographic readouts. Her genetic markers were showing through more strongly now, manifesting in her ability to recognize patterns that others missed.

"It's like..." Zara searched for words to describe what her augmented senses were detecting. "The field is responding to thought patterns I haven't even formed yet. I'm seeing mathematical progressions that look almost organic. Living equations."

Maya Jackson emerged from another access tunnel, her dark skin glistening with perspiration. She'd been manually adjusting the power conduits for six hours, trying to accommodate energy readings that defied Coalition physics. "The tap is drawing more power than our models predicted," she reported, bringing up detailed diagnostics. "These modifications..." She gestured at Wong's components. "They're operating on principles I've never seen. The energy signature reminds me of—" She stopped abruptly, glancing at Drake.

"The Porter readings," Drake finished quietly. "Just before we lost contact."

Wong's neural implants recorded the spike in her vital signs. Even after three years, the loss of her husband affected her deeply. If she only knew how important Thomas' sacrifice had been—how his discovery had set everything in motion.

"Commander," ARIA interrupted, the ship's AI manifesting as a subtle pattern of lights in the holographic displays. "I'm detecting anomalous signatures in Dr. Wong's equipment cases. The pattern matches restricted Coalition protocols, specifically those referenced in Project Harbinger."

The temperature in the bay seemed to drop several degrees. Project Harbinger was highly classified—even Drake's command-level clearance only gave her access to its code name.

Wong's hand moved imperceptibly toward the crystal hidden beneath his shirt. The crystal wasn't just a data storage device; it was a key designed to interface with technologies humans shouldn't have discovered for another century.

"Standard research equipment," he said smoothly, meeting Drake's gaze. "All cleared by Coalition Security. Level Seven authorization."

"Level Seven clearance noted," ARIA acknowledged, "but the quantum signatures suggest capabilities beyond current Coalition engineering standards. Similar to theoretical technologies outlined in Professor Zhang Wei's restricted papers."

Drake's eyes narrowed at the mention of Zhang Wei. The brilliant geneticist had vanished three years ago, leaving behind research that the Coalition had immediately classified. Research that, Wong knew, had come dangerously close to discovering humanity's true origins.

"Dr. Wong," Drake said carefully, her command training evident in her measured tone, "why would a xenoarchaeologist need quantum technology that matches theoretical weapons research?"

Before he could answer, Zara Patel's voice cut through the tension. "Neural interface detecting multiple echoes. Something's responding to the drive's activation." Her cybernetic eyes widened, pupils dilating as they processed the impossible stream of data. "The patterns—they're identical to the signal we detected earlier."

The engineering bay's holographic displays shifted automatically, showing ripples in the quantum field surrounding the ship. Mathematical sequences cascaded through multiple dimensions, creating structures that seemed to defy spatial logic. Wong recognized them immediately—the same patterns the Predecessors had used to encode their messages in human DNA.

"Chief Jackson," Drake called out, her voice carrying the edge of someone who's seen too many impossible things, "full power to the sensors. I want to know what's out there."

Maya nodded. Her hands flew across her console, rerouting power from the non-essential systems. Her neural interface struggled to process the readings. "I'm reading massive disturbances at coordinates 227 mark 115. Whatever it is, it's big. Enormous." She paused, double-checking the measurements. "The energy output... it's greater than Earth's total power generation."

"It's beautiful," Zara whispered, her cybernetic systems also struggling to process the data. "The quantum fields... they're alive. They're reaching out to us—no, to specific crew members." She turned her head to look at Drake. "Especially you, Commander. Your neural patterns... they're resonating with the field."

Drake pursed her lips but didn't reply.

Wong watched the patterns dance across the displays. They were running out of time. The Enemy's deep space probes would have detected the disturbances by now. Their hunter-killer units would already be moving to investigate, drawn to the energy signatures like predators to blood in the water.

The crystal beneath his shirt pulsed warmly, responding to the growing disturbances in space-time. Its structure was changing, evolving just like the drive components, preparing for what was coming.

"Captain to the Bridge," Lieutenant Park snapped. "Multiple ships dropping out of quantum space. Coalition Special Operations vessels, black hull configuration. No transponder signals."

It took Drake, along with Dr. Wong and Maya Jackson, just a couple of minutes to return to the bridge. Drake's implant displayed the tactical data across her field of vision. Three corvettes, heavily armed, designed for deniable operations. She'd seen their kind before, cleaning up Coalition "mistakes."

"Time to weapons range?" she demanded.

"Seven minutes at current velocity," ARIA reported. "Their weapons are powered up, and their targeting systems are active. I'm detecting enhanced stealth systems and quantum disruptors."

"Zara, what's the drive's status?" Drake snapped.

The pilot's cybernetics pulsed faster as she deepened her link with the ship. Streams of data flowed through her nervous system, creating patterns that matched the ancient signal. "Integration at eighty-five percent. The harmonics are unstable, but..." She paused, processing new data. "The modifications Dr. Wong installed... they're not just improving efficiency. They're changing the drive's fundamental architecture. It's like they're waking up."

Maya Jackson's hands danced across her engineering console, trying to maintain control of the evolving systems. "The power curves are exceeding theoretical limits," she called out. "The tap is drawing energy from... I don't know... somewhere else. These readings... they all match classified files about the Porter incident."

"Commander," ARIA interrupted, "I'm detecting targeted scanning from coordinates 227 mark 115. The signal pattern matches no known human technology."

Wong knew it was time. They needed to understand, needed to be ready for what was coming. "Commander," he said, removing the crystal from beneath his shirt, "there's something you need to know about your husband's research. About what he really found out there."

The crystal floated between them in the low gravity, its structure beginning to shift and change as it responded to the ancient technologies awakening around them. Within its crystalline matrix lay the truth about humanity's origins—and its intended destiny.

"Thomas wasn't just studying quantum phenomena," Wong continued, watching Drake's reaction carefully. "He found evidence of genetic engineering in human DNA, patterns that couldn't have evolved naturally. Patterns designed to help us recognize and interface with technologies we weren't supposed to find for centuries."

Drake stared at him, opened her mouth to speak, but before she could:

"Multiple spatial distortions forming!" Zara's voice carried genuine awe. "Something massive is phasing into normal space!"

The displays shifted, showing what looked like reality itself folding open as the station emerged like a crystalline flower blooming in the void, its geometric patterns defying human understanding. Quantum energy coursed through structures that seemed to exist in multiple dimensions simultaneously.

"By all the gods," Maya whispered, struggling to comprehend

what she was seeing. "That's impossible. The energy requirements alone would be—"

"It's... some kind of station," Drake whispered, Wong's revelation forgotten. "It's massive. Look at it. What the hell is it?"

"The station, if that's what it is, is scanning us," ARIA announced. "It appears to be focusing on several specific crew members. Commander Drake, Pilot Patel, and Dr. Wong in particular. I'm detecting resonance within their genetic markers."

Wong held up the crystal, which now pulsed in perfect synchronization with the station's energy patterns. "It's recognizing the markers, the genetic modifications that were engineered into our ancestors. We're not just its operators, Drake. We're its children."

"Coalition vessels launching quantum torpedoes!" Park's voice carried barely contained panic. "Impact in thirty seconds!"

Drake made her decision. "Zara, plot a jump trajectory directly to the station. Everyone, secure for emergency transition."

The pilot's cybernetics flared as she merged deeper with the ship's systems. "The drive... it's not just responding to my commands anymore. It's interfacing directly with the station. These patterns, they're like nothing in human mathematics."

Maya's hands flew across her console. "Power levels critical! The tap is drawing energy directly from subspace!"

"Now, Zara! Jump!" Drake snapped.

The Hawking's drive engaged, but instead of the usual quantum tunnel, reality seemed to fold around them in entirely new ways. The station's energy field reached out, pulling them into dimensional spaces that human science couldn't explain.

Wong's crystal flared brilliantly, its structure finally completing its transformation. In its light, Drake saw patterns that reminded her of Thomas' last transmissions—patterns that now made terrible, wonderful sense. But she said nothing; she couldn't. Somehow, she understood.

As space bent around them, Wong accessed encrypted files in his neural implant. The message he'd been waiting to send was brief but would change everything: "First Key activated. The children are coming home."

And somewhere in the darkness between galaxies, ancient enemies stirred, recognizing the activation of technologies they had fought to destroy half a million years ago. The game was beginning again, and this time, humanity would have to choose sides.

The assembly wasn't just about gathering a crew or installing new technology. It was about bringing together the pieces of a puzzle that had waited eons to be solved.

Humanity's true purpose was about to be revealed.

Chapter 4

Departure

THE QUANTUM TRANSITION ALARMS ECHOED THROUGH THE Hawking's corridors, their harmonics shifting in response to the fluctuating energy fields. Lieutenant Catherine Park's implants processed multiple data streams as she ran final pre-jump diagnostics, each test revealing new anomalies in the ship's architecture.

Her station on the bridge pulsed with holographic warnings, power fluctuations, spatial distortions, and something else. Something that shouldn't have been possible. The processors beneath her fingers hummed at frequencies that made her teeth ache.

"Communications blackout in sixty seconds," she announced, trying to keep her voice steady as the Coalition Special Operations vessels closed in. "All channels are—" She stopped, frowning at an anomalous reading. Her neural interface highlighted the pattern, comparing it to known signal types. "That's impossible."

"Report," Commander Drake ordered from her command

station. The crystal at her throat pulsed softly in sync with the ship's energy field.

"Internal communications are showing unauthorized access. Someone's tapped into our secure channels, but..." Park double-checked the readings, her implants struggling to process the unusual patterns. "The signal's coming from inside the ship. Cargo Bay Three."

At a thought, Drake's implant displayed the bay's security feeds, overlaying energy signatures on standard visual data. The holographic display showed nothing unusual among the stored equipment and supply crates, but the sensors told a different story. A faint energy signature pulsed behind one of the larger containers.

"ARIA, I want a full scan of Cargo Bay Three," she commanded. "I want to know what's hiding down there."

The AI's response came with unexpected hesitation, its processors displaying unusual activity patterns. "Commander, I'm detecting unusual genetic markers. The pattern... it's similar to yours and to Dr. Wong's. The resonance suggests technological augmentation far beyond Coalition standards."

Dr. Wong's head snapped up from his station, his expression suddenly alert. The crystal he wore beneath his shirt flared visibly through the fabric. "It can't be," he muttered. "They said the program was terminated. All subjects were eliminated."

"What program?" Drake demanded, but Wong was already moving toward the cargo bay access, his movements carrying an urgency she'd never seen in the usually composed scientist.

"Security team to Cargo Bay Three, now!" Drake ordered through the ship-wide link. "Dr. Wong, hold your position. That's an order."

The xenoarchaeologist ignored her, his pace quickening. Drake cursed under her breath and followed him, her combat implants activating automatically. Tactical overlays filled her vision, mapping potential threat vectors and escape routes.

Behind her, she heard Zara disengage from the neural interface, the pilot's cybernetic systems powering down with a high-pitched whine. "Commander, the quantum field... it's responding to whatever's down there."

The cargo bay doors slid open with a soft hiss of recycled air, their security protocols disengaging without proper authorization. Drake's enhanced vision adjusted instantly to the dimmer lighting, scanning for threats. The quantum signature was stronger now, emanating from behind a cluster of drive component containers.

"Come out slowly," she called, her implants mapping possible escape routes. "We know you're there."

For a moment, nothing moved. Then a figure stepped out from behind the containers: a teenage girl, no more than seventeen, wearing standard Coalition maintenance coveralls. But there was nothing standard about her eyes. They pulsed with the same quantum energy as Wong's crystal, patterns of light shifting beneath her irises.

"Hello, Drake," the girl said softly. "I am Kai. And we don't have much time." Her voice carried harmonics that resonated with the ship's quantum field, causing subtle fluctuations in the ambient energy levels.

Drake's combat implants identified twenty different ways the girl could be a threat, but something deeper—the same intuition that had led her to the signal—told her Kai was important. The crystal at her throat pulsed warmly, responding to the girl's presence.

"You're one of them," Dr. Wong said, his voice barely a whisper. His own crystal flared brightly. "Project Remnant. Zhang Wei's final experiment. They said all the subjects were lost in the containment breach."

Kai's quantum-touched eyes fixed on Wong's crystal. "Not lost, Doctor. Hidden. Professor Zhang made sure of that before they took him. The genetic templates were too important to destroy."

"The templates stored in your DNA," Wong realized. "The pure strain, uncontaminated by generations of random mutation. You're a direct descendant of the Predecessors' original design."

Drake's neural implant flashed recognition at the name Zhang Wei. "The geneticist?" she asked, frowning. "The one who disappeared after the Porter incident?"

"My creator," Kai replied, then corrected herself. "One of them, anyway. The original templates are much older. Half a million years older." She moved with an inhuman grace, each step precisely calculated. "Professor Zhang recognized the patterns in Thomas' research. He knew what they meant."

The ship's drive hummed louder, harmonics shifting as it prepared for the jump. Through the neural link, Drake felt Zara's growing concern about the power readings. The pilot's cybernetic systems were detecting energy patterns that shouldn't have been possible.

"Commander," ARIA interrupted. "The Coalition vessels are launching a second wave of quantum torpedoes. Impact in forty-five seconds. Their targeting systems are using advanced quantum entanglement. Our standard countermeasures will be ineffective."

"How did you get aboard?" Drake demanded, ignoring the AI, though she suspected she already knew. Her implants highlighted subtle abnormalities in Kai's movement patterns—they were too fluid, too precise.

"The maintenance crews in New Geneva," Kai explained, fingers trailing patterns that only she could see. "Their neural patterns are easy to manipulate, if you know how. Basic quantum entanglement principles applied to synaptic frequencies." She smiled slightly. "But that's not important right now. What's important is that I'm here to help you interface with the station. Without me, the activation sequence will fail."

"She's right," Wong interjected, his crystal resonating with Kai's presence. "The station's architecture requires specific genetic keys. Markers that were engineered into certain bloodlines a hundred and twenty-five thousand years ago. You have some, Commander. So does Zara. But Kai..." He gestured at the girl. "She was designed specifically for this moment. Her DNA contains the pure sequences, direct copies of the Predecessors' original templates."

The security team arrived at the cargo bay entrance, their weapons humming with containment fields. Drake waved them back, her decision already made. The ship's sensors were detecting massive energy buildups from the approaching Coalition vessels.

"Thirty seconds to impact," ARIA announced. "The Coalition quantum torpedoes are showing unusual signatures. They appear to be using technology similar to Dr. Wong's modifications."

"They know," Wong muttered. "They've been studying the artifacts all along."

"Everyone back to their stations," Drake ordered through the neural link. "Kai, you're with me. We'll sort out the details after we survive the next five minutes." She turned to her security teams. "Stand down and prepare for transition."

They ran for the bridge, the ship's artificial gravity fluctuating as power was diverted to the defensive systems. Through the quantum fields, Drake felt the ancient station's energy patterns intensifying, reaching out to them like a beacon in the void.

Chief Jackson called through link: "Commander, the drive is showing impossible readings. These power levels... they're beyond anything in our theoretical models."

"Twenty seconds to impact," ARIA updated. "Coalition

vessels are launching fighters. Detecting advanced weapon signatures."

They reached the bridge as the field distortions peaked. Zara was already back deep in the neural interface, her augmented systems merging with the ship's quantum architecture. Lieutenant Park's hands flew across holographic controls, trying to jam the incoming torpedoes' targeting systems.

"Fifteen seconds to impact," ARIA reported. "Coalition vessels are maintaining pursuit vectors. Their weapons are showing signs of Predecessor technology."

"Zara, status?" Drake demanded, sliding into her command chair as neural interfaces connected automatically.

"Jump coordinates locked, but…" The pilot's cybernetic eyes flickered rapidly. "The quantum field is changing. These patterns… they're like the ones in my dreams. The crystalline spaces between dimensions."

Kai moved to Zara's station, her eyes pulsing in sync with the ship's energy frequencies. "You dream them too?" she asked. "The geometries that shouldn't exist? The mathematics that sing?"

"Ten seconds to impact," ARIA interrupted.

Drake's combat implants displayed multiple threat vectors as the Coalition fighters moved to box them in. Standard tactics for a capture operation. They wanted the Hawking intact. Her tactical systems identified weapon signatures that shouldn't have existed in human hands.

"Chief Jackson," she called through the link, "divert all power to the drive."

"Already done," Maya responded from engineering. "But Commander, these energy readings are off the scale. The station's quantum field is interfacing directly with our systems. The patterns… they match Professor Zhang's theoretical models."

"That's the way it's supposed to happen," Kai said calmly. She placed her hand on Zara's neural interface panel, and suddenly the harmonics shifted. The ship's displays flickered, showing new mathematical patterns. "The Predecessors designed us to be bridges between their technology and human consciousness. Between the past and the future."

"Five seconds," ARIA announced.

"Now, Zara!" Drake ordered. "Execute jump!"

The Hawking's drive engaged, but instead of creating a normal transit tunnel, it synchronized with the station's energy field. Reality bent around them. Wong's crystal pulsed brilliantly as space itself seemed to fold inward.

Through the bridge viewport, Drake watched the Coalition torpedoes dissolve into quantum foam as dimensional barriers shifted. The ancient station reached out with tendrils of pure energy, drawing them into spaces between spaces.

And then they were somewhere else.

The bridge displays stabilized, showing their new position inside the station's field envelope. The massive structure loomed before them, its crystalline architecture defying conventional geometry. Patterns of light danced across its surface, patterns that matched the ones in their DNA.

"We're home," Kai whispered. "After one hundred twenty-five thousand years, we're finally home."

But in the void between dimensions, something else was stirring. The Enemy's sensors had detected the station's awakening. Their hunter-killer units altered course, moving to intercept.

Chapter 5

Response

THE ALERT REACHED COALITION COMMAND THREE MINUTES AFTER the Hawking's jump. Admiral Perez watched through his cybernetic eye as emergency protocols activated throughout New Geneva's underground complex. The research vessel's signature was already fading, its trajectory carrying it toward coordinates that shouldn't exist.

"Full tracking analysis," he ordered, his voice echoing through the command center. "I want to know exactly what Commander Drake found out there."

The holographic displays showed the Hawking's last known position, a point at the edge of mapped space where sensor data suggested impossibly high energy readings. Perez detected patterns in the fluctuations that he'd seen only once before—in classified files about the Porter incident.

"Sir," his tactical officer reported, "the Hawking's drive activated with unfamiliar signatures. Their power curve showed characteristics we've never recorded before."

Director Yuki's interface pulsed as she accessed the restricted databases. "The signal they detected... it matches theoretical models from Professor Zhang's research. The patterns he claimed would lead to evolutionary triggers."

Perez's cybernetic systems processed this information against decades of accumulated data. The Hawking hadn't just stumbled onto something, they'd been drawn to it. The question was: by whom?

"We have multiple ships within range for intercept," the tactical officer reported. "Black hull corvettes from Special Operations can reach their last known coordinates within six hours."

Perez nodded, tracking the rapid mobilization of the Coalition forces. But something about the Hawking's signature was troubling him. The patterns suggested technology far beyond current human capabilities—and yet... they were somehow familiar.

"The signal they detected," Director Yuki noted, her interface still processing the restricted data, "it matches fragments we've recovered from other sites. Sites that were systematically stripped clean before our research teams arrived."

Councilor Hark's ancient face showed genuine concern. "If Commander Drake has found what we think she has, conventional containment protocols won't be sufficient. Should we not consider implementing the Harbinger contingencies?"

Perez's organic eye narrowed. The Harbinger Project had been buried so deep that even his command-level clearance revealed only its code name. But his own enhanced systems had detected traces of its influence throughout Coalition space.

"Deploy the corvettes," he ordered, knowing they would arrive too late. "But contact our deep cover assets as well. If the Hawking has found what we think was hidden out there, we need to be ready for what comes next."

For out in deep space, at the extreme edge of sensor range, the command center's displays showed Enemy probe signatures. They had detected the disturbance too.

"We're detecting unusual activity from the Separatist territories," the tactical officer announced. "Multiple ships are breaking orbit and leaving their research facilities. They're mobilizing faster than standard protocols allow."

Director Yuki's implants pulsed as she processed this information. "They must have had ships pre-positioned. They've been waiting. They knew that eventually someone would stumble onto... something like this."

Perez watched the Separatist vessels. He assessed their movement patterns, patterns that suggested the ships had been modified well beyond official specifications. Someone had been preparing for this moment long before the Hawking made its jump. But who?

"The Security Council is demanding an immediate briefing," his aide reported. "They're particularly interested in Dr. Wong's presence aboard the Hawking. It appears his clearance for the mission wasn't properly documented."

Perez accessed deeper layers of classified data. Wong's assignment to the Hawking hadn't been an accident, but whose agenda was he really serving?

"Multiple signatures are being detected at fleet rally points," the tactical officer continued. "Sir... some of our own ships are moving without authorization. The Captains are claiming direct orders from different command structures."

The situation was fracturing along the predicted lines. Various Coalition factions, each believing they understood what the Hawking had found, were positioning their forces ready to take control. But none of them yet grasped the full scope of what was awakening.

"The Enemy probes are accelerating," Yuki noted, tracking their approach. "Their scan patterns... They appear to be searching for something specific."

Perez's cybernetic eye recorded everything as the command

center erupted with competing priorities. Coalition factions mobilizing without authorization. Separatist forces moving with suspicious readiness. Enemy probes approaching with determined purpose. And underneath it all, quantum signatures that suggested something ancient was awakening.

"Implement Directive Seven," he ordered, his voice cutting through the chaos. "All fleet movements require direct authorization from this command center. Any vessel breaking protocol will be designated hostile."

"Sir," Yuki interjected, "several Council members are demanding an immediate military response. They want the Hawking intercepted and contained before—"

"Before what, Director?" Perez's organic eye fixed on her neural implant's status light. "Before they find something we've been hiding? Or before they understand why we've been hiding it?"

The command center's displays showed more Enemy probes entering Coalition space. Their search patterns indicated precise purpose, as if they knew exactly what the Hawking might have discovered.

"Deploy the Third Fleet to defensive positions," Perez commanded. "They are not to intercept the Hawking, but to prepare for what follows them. And activate our deep cover assets in Separatist space. We need to know who else knows what's waiting out there."

Perez blinked his organic eye and shook his head. His cybernetic systems processed probable outcomes, incorporating data from decades of classified research. The Hawking's jump hadn't just broken regulations, it had triggered events that various factions had spent years preparing for.

"Your own enhancements," Yuki noted quietly. "They're not standard Coalition technology, are they?"

"Like you said, Director, some sites were stripped clean

before the research teams arrived." Perez's augmented eye shifted through the quantum frequencies as he accessed deeper capabilities. "We all made preparations for this moment. The question is: are we prepared for what comes next?"

The command center's quantum field rippled with increasing activity as more Enemy probes breached Coalition space. Perez detected patterns in their search algorithms that matched his own cybernetic signatures, and he frowned. This wasn't the way it was supposed to be.

They weren't just looking for Predecessor technology. They were looking for signs that humanity had already begun to change.

Chapter 6

Anomaly

TIME FRACTURED.

Zara felt it first, her enhanced nervous system detecting the quantum distortions microseconds before the ship's sensors. The space between spaces, where the Hawking now existed, operated on principles that human physics couldn't explain.

"Multiple temporal anomalies detected," ARIA announced, its processors struggling to maintain coherence. "Chronometric readings are... unstable."

Zara watched reality ripple around them. The station's massive form seemed to exist in several timeframes simultaneously, its crystalline architecture folding through multiple dimensions.

"What's happening?" Drake demanded from her command chair. Her quantum crystal pulsed erratically, responding to the temporal distortions.

"Time isn't linear here," Kai explained, her eyes tracking patterns invisible to normal human perception. "The Predecessors understood that consciousness shapes reality. These temporal anomalies... they're not random. They're looking for something in our memories."

Dr. Wong's crystal flared suddenly, and the bridge crew gasped as reality shifted. They were no longer on the Hawking.

Drake found herself standing in the Porter's control room three years ago. Thomas was at his station, studying readings that matched the ones they'd just seen. His crystal—the twin to the one she now wore—pulsed with the same frequencies.

"The patterns are evolving," Thomas said, his voice carrying the excitement of discovery. "Frances, these aren't just signals. They're instructions, encoded in human DNA. We're not finding them by accident. We were designed to—"

The memory fractured, cutting him off as another temporal wave hit the ship.

Maya Jackson witnessed a different scene: a secret Coalition laboratory where Professor Zhang Wei was working with new, until now impossible, technologies. A teenage Kai floated in a suspension chamber, her DNA being rewritten to match ancient templates.

"The process is stable," Zhang announced to what she perceived to be unseen observers. "The genetic markers are accepting the modifications. She'll be able to interface directly with their systems, just as they intended."

Another shift.

Zara Patel witnessed her own past: the military facility where she'd received her augmentations. But now she saw what they'd hidden from her. The "experimental" cybernetics weren't human technology at all. They were reverse-engineered from Predecessor artifacts; she was stunned by the revelation.

"Subject's neural patterns are accepting the interfaces," a technician reported. "The genetic markers are exactly as Professor Zhang predicted. She'll be perfect for the Hawking mission." Zara shook her head in disbelief. What have they done to me?

The temporal wave shifted again.

Lieutenant Park found herself in a Coalition black site, watching Admiral Perez study holographic displays of the Porter's destruction. The images showed something the official reports had omitted: quantum weapons, far beyond human capabilities.

"Drake found too much," Perez said to a shadowy figure. "The Harbinger Project isn't ready. We can't risk premature contact. Not yet!"

In engineering, Maya saw the future. Coalition ships fighting impossible battles against crystalline vessels that phased through normal space. Earth's cities transformed, becoming hybrids of human and Predecessor technology. And in orbit, a massive station identical to the one they'd just found watching over everything.

Dr. Wong experienced something different. The crystal he wore connected him to older memories—memories that weren't his own. He saw the Predecessors' final days, their desperate plan to seed humanity with their genetic legacy. The Enemy's ships darkening the skies of a thousand worlds.

"The children must survive," a being of pure energy and crystal declared. "They will wake when they're ready. When the Enemy returns."

On the bridge, Kai remained oddly stable as time fractured around them.

"It's testing us," she announced to no one in particular. It was almost as if she was talking to herself. "It's showing us what we need to know. What we need to remember."

Drake experienced the most powerful vision of all. She saw Thomas' last moments on the Porter, but not as they'd been reported. He stood before a terminal, his crystal pulsing with newly discovered truths.

"They're coming back," he recorded urgently. "The Enemy... they never left. They've been watching us, waiting. Drake, if you find this—the crystals are keys. The stations are weapons. And humanity... we're their last hope."

The message cut off as reality reasserted itself.

"The temporal distortions are stabilizing," ARIA reported as the crew recovered. "But the field remains active. The station appears to be... processing what it's learned from our memories."

Zara's augmented systems rebooted, her neural interfaces reconnecting with the ship's architecture. "The visions," she said, her voice shaking. "They weren't just memories. They were connections. Pathways the station is building between us."

"Between our genetic markers," Wong corrected, his crystal still pulsing with residual energy. "The Predecessors encoded more than just DNA sequences," he continued. "They embedded memories, knowledge, capabilities that will activate as and when they're needed."

Drake stood up from her command chair, her neural implants struggling to process what she'd seen; half believing, half confused, one-hundred percent angry. "Thomas knew," she said. "He knew about everything, the Enemy, the stations, what we really are. And they killed him!" She touched the crystal, understanding now why he'd insisted she take it before his last mission. He knew, she thought. He knew, and he went anyway.

"The Porter wasn't destroyed by accident," Lieutenant Park added, her tactical displays showing phantom images of quantum weapons. "Coalition Special Operations... they killed him. Killed everyone."

"To keep the secret," Maya said. "But they couldn't stop it. We're changing already. The station is changing us."

Kai moved to the center of the bridge, her engineered body perfectly adapted to the environment. "This is just the beginning," she said. "The temporal anomalies weren't random. They were preparing us. Teaching us."

"Teaching us what?" Drake asked, though part of her already knew the answer.

"How to fight," Kai replied. Her eyes showed patterns that matched the station's crystal architecture. "The Enemy is coming. That's why the station activated now. The Predecessors knew. That's why the station chose this crew. We're not just carrying Predecessor genes. We're carrying their last hope."

No one spoke, though all were trying to assimilate the enormity of what was happening.

The bridge displays shifted, showing new data as the station's quantum processors integrated what they'd learned from the crew's memories. Star charts appeared, highlighting possible Enemy positions. Tactical projections displayed battles that hadn't happened yet.

"Multiple signatures detected at the edge of sensor range," ARIA announced. "Pattern match: 97% correlation with the Enemy vessels described in Professor Zhang's classified files."

"They're early," Wong said, his expression grim. "The temporal anomalies must have attracted their attention. We're not ready."

"Yes, we are," Kai countered. She placed her hand on Zara's neural interface panel, and suddenly the ship's systems surged with new power. "The Predecessors made sure of it," she continued. "Everything we need is already inside us. We just have to remember."

The station's field intensified, responding to Kai's activation. Reality rippled again, but this time, the crew was prepared. Instead of chaotic visions, they experienced something deeper: awakening genetic memories.

Drake felt combat knowledge, tactics, battle reports, flowing through her neural pathways; tactical systems she'd never trained with but somehow understood perfectly. Her crystal resonated with the station's defenses, showing her weapon configurations that merged human and Predecessor technology.

Zara's cybernetics evolved, quantum circuits reconfiguring to match patterns encoded in her DNA. Her consciousness expanded through the ship's systems, understanding now why her augmentations had been designed exactly the way they were, and she was awed.

"Multiple Enemy contacts confirmed," ARIA reported. "Eight vessels; their signatures match historical records."

"Let them come," Kai said, but her voice had changed. Ancient knowledge echoed in her words as dormant genetic programming activated. "The station recognizes us now. The defenses are online."

Through the bridge viewport, they watched crystalline structures emerge from the station's surface—weapon systems that had waited eons for their operators to return. The force field surrounding them strengthened, creating defensive barriers that existed across multiple dimensions.

"Chief Jackson," Drake snapped, the new tactical knowledge flowing naturally through her newly enhanced brain, "begin power transfer to the station's defensive grid. Zara, prepare for enhanced neural interface. Lieutenant Park, activate the communication protocols we just... remembered." And she couldn't help but shake her head.

The crew moved with perfect coordination, their awakened genetic memories guiding them. This was what they'd been designed for, what countless generations of carefully guided evolution had prepared them to do.

"Enemy vessels are closing, entering attack range," ARIA announced. "Their signatures are... changing. They're... They're attempting to disrupt our temporal stability."

"They remember too," Wong said, his crystal interfacing with the station's deeper systems. "They remember how the Predecessors fought them, but they don't yet know what we've become. I think they're in for a surprise."

The first Enemy ship launched its attack using reality-distorting weapons designed to tear apart space-time itself. But the station's defenses, guided by its reborn children, were ready. The battle was about to begin. And this time, humanity had inherited the tools to fight it.

The temporal anomalies had shown them the past, glimpses of possible futures, and, most importantly, their true nature. They weren't just an evolved species that had stumbled upon some ancient technology. They were the weapon the Predecessors had crafted and hidden in plain sight, waiting for this exact moment. And now the time had come. The Enemy was about to learn what humanity had become.

Chapter 7

First Contact

The station filled the Hawking's viewports, its crystalline architecture redefining what the crew thought possible. Geometric shapes merged and separated in patterns that suggested consciousness, quantum energy flowing through structures that existed in multiple dimensions simultaneously.

"Size estimate," Drake requested, her neural implants struggling to process the scale of what they were seeing.

"Approximately forty-seven kilometers in diameter," ARIA reported. "And seventy kilometers from top to bottom. Though spatial readings are... uncertain. The station appears to exist partially outside normal space-time. It is... not possible, but... it is."

Zara detected layers of complexity hidden from normal human perception. "The field..." she said, hesitantly, "it's thinking. I can feel it. The patterns match my neural architecture."

"It's alive," Kai confirmed, her eyes tracking energy flows invisible to the others. "The Predecessors didn't build this station.

They grew it. They somehow merged technology and biology at the quantum level."

Dr. Wong's crystal pulsed in response to the station's presence, its structure continuing to evolve. "The outer layers are just the surface. The real complexity is deep inside, where they stored their memories."

Through the bridge displays, they watched as crystalline docking arms extended toward the Hawking. The structures moved with liquid grace, their geometry shifting to match the ship's signature.

"Multiple access points detected," Lieutenant Park reported from her station. "It's... It's... offering us entry points. Specific ones, coded to our genetic patterns."

Maya marveled at the impossible technologies in the station's design. "The power readings are off any scale I know," she muttered. "It's drawing energy directly from the vacuum fluctuations. From the space between spaces. I've never seen anything like it."

"We need to board it," Drake decided, touching her crystal— Thomas' crystal—that now pulsed in perfect synchronization with the station's heart. "Prepare an exploration team."

First contact was about to begin.

The boarding team assembled in the main airlock: Drake, Kai, Dr. Wong, and Zara. Their environmental suits incorporated shielding, designed to protect against temporal distortions.

"The station's atmosphere is... compatible," ARIA reported, analyzing the sensor data. "I'm detecting trace elements matching ancient Earth compositions. Gravity, temperature and pressure are within human tolerance."

"They prepared it for us," Kai said, her eyes scanning the crystalline docking arm that now connected them to the station. "They knew we'd come, eventually."

As they cycled through the airlock, Drake felt the station's field intensify around them. Her implant detected new frequencies, patterns that resonated with something deep in her DNA.

The docking tunnel was a marvel of alien engineering. Crystalline walls shifted and flowed, creating a perfect seal with their airlock. Quantum energy pulsed through transparent sections, carrying information in forms human science was only beginning to understand.

"The crystal structures," Wong observed, his hand trailing near a wall without touching it. "They're similar to the quantum processors we've been trying to develop. But these are... perfect. Self-repairing, self-evolving. Will wonders never cease?"

But Zara detected more. "There's a coherent data transfer happening through the field. The station is... scanning us. Learning."

They reached the first junction where the tunnel opened into a vast chamber. The scale was breathtaking. Crystalline spires rose hundreds of meters, their structures merging and separating in rhythmic patterns. Platforms of solid light hung in space, connected by bridges that formed, dissolved, and formed again.

"I don't understand. This can't be manufacturing," Maya's voice came from the ship. "Those structures... they're growing. Like the crystals in Dr. Wong's equipment."

Kai stepped forward, and the station responded. A pathway of crystalline light formed before her, leading deeper into the structure. "It remembers," she said. "The genetic keys are working. It recognizes us as authorized users. Isn't it amazing?"

Suddenly, the chamber filled with holographic displays—or something similar to holograms—but operating on quantum principles. Star maps, technical diagrams, and strings of alien mathematics floated in the air around them.

"It's trying to communicate," Drake realized. The patterns matched the ones she'd seen in her temporal vision, the ones Thomas had discovered before his death.

A pulse of energy rippled through the chamber, and suddenly the air filled with ghosts. Holographic figures composed of crystalline light moved through the space, recordings of the Predecessors, preserved in the station's memory.

They were beautiful and alien; beings of pure energy contained within geometric crystalline forms, their consciousness spread across multiple bodies connected by quantum entanglement. The recordings showed them working, studying, preparing for... what?

"This is a research facility," Wong translated, his crystal interfacing with the station's archives. "They were studying human evolution. Guiding it."

The holograms shifted, showing Earth across different time periods. The Predecessors had watched humanity grow, subtly adjusting their development through carefully engineered retroviruses that modified key genetic sequences.

"Look," Zara pointed. "They were preparing us for something specific. The genetic modifications... they're like computer code, but written in DNA."

Another shift, and the holograms showed the Enemy. Crystalline ships that moved like predators, weapons that distorted reality itself. The Predecessors' last war, preserved in perfect detail.

"They knew they were losing," Kai said as she processed the historical data. "This station... it wasn't just a research facility. It was an ark. A way to preserve their knowledge, their technology, until we were ready to inherit it."

Drake watched a particular sequence with growing unease. The hologram showed Predecessor scientists injecting modified genetic material into Earth's biosphere. "They didn't just guide our evolution," she realized. "They designed us. Created us as weapons."

"No, not weapons," Wong corrected, reading deeper data

streams. "They created us as their successors. They knew the Enemy would return, eventually. That they would try to finish what they started. We were not designed to fight the Enemy. We were designed to surpass them."

The chamber's field intensified as new systems activated. Panels opened in the crystalline walls, revealing technology that responded to their presence.

"Integration protocols initiating," ARIA reported. "The station is attempting to interface with our systems."

Crystalline interfaces emerged from the walls, perfectly shaped to match human neural implants. The technology was both ancient and new, designed more than a hundred thousand years ago. It had continued evolving ever since, waiting for its intended users to arrive.

"The station wants direct neural connection," Zara observed, her cybernetics detecting the compatibility. "These interfaces... they're exactly matched to our augmentations. To our genetic modifications. We can do this."

"Because they designed both," Kai said as she stepped forward, placing her hand on one of the crystalline panels. The station's field surged, recognizing her pure genetic template. "This is what Professor Zhang was preparing me for. What the Predecessors prepared all of us for," she said.

Drake touched her crystal, feeling it pulse in sync with the station's heart. "Thomas found this, didn't he? This is what the Coalition wanted to keep hidden."

"Yes. He found one of the backup stations," Wong confirmed. "A smaller facility. But it was enough to prove what humanity really was; what it was intended to become; what we were becoming." His own crystal interfaced with a nearby panel. "The Coalition thought they could control the process. Keep the technology for themselves. They were wrong, on so many levels."

The chamber's holographic displays shifted again, showing

new data. Star charts appeared, marking the positions of other stations. A network spanning the galaxy, waiting to be awakened.

"Multiple quantum signatures detected," ARIA reported. "The station is transmitting activation codes to the other facilities."

"Recognition protocols," Kai corrected. "The network is waking up, analyzing human development across multiple colonies. Looking for others with the correct genetic markers."

Drake made her decision. "Prepare for neural interface," she snapped. "We need to understand what we're dealing with before —" She cut herself off as the neural link completed. And then she knew; they weren't just making first contact with alien technology. They were coming home to the heritage the Predecessors had hidden inside their very DNA so very long ago.

But the Enemy would soon learn what humanity had become in their long absence and the war would begin again.

Chapter 8

Integration

KNOWLEDGE STREAMED THROUGH THE LINK. IT BURNED THROUGH Frances Drake's neural pathways like quantum fire. The station's crystalline interfaces merged with their implants, downloading half a million years of preserved information directly into their consciousness. But it wasn't just data. It was memory, experience, understanding, that the Predecessors had encoded into the station's matrices.

"Neural integration at thirty percent," ARIA reported, its own processors struggling to monitor the massive data transfer. "I'm detecting significant changes in the crew's neural architecture."

Drake watched as her own DNA responded to the interface, activating dormant sequences that had waited generations for this moment. The crystal at her throat pulsed in perfect harmony with the station's core frequencies.

Beside her, Zara's cybernetic systems evolved in real-time, circuitry reconfiguring to match Predecessor patterns. Her augmented vision expanded beyond human limitations, seeing into spaces between dimensions where the station's true complexity existed.

"The physical structure," she reported, her voice carrying harmonics that matched the station's resonance, "it's just an anchor point. The real station exists in quantum space, spread across multiple dimensional layers."

Dr. Wong interfaced more deeply, his crystal unlocking archived memories. "They built it this way to hide it from the Enemy. Traditional sensors can't detect quantum-shifted mass. That's how it remained hidden for so long. It's truly amazing."

Kai moved through the chamber with increasing confidence, her body perfectly adapted to the station's environment. Crystalline displays formed around her, responding to genetic markers that perfectly matched Predecessor templates.

"The network is larger than we thought," she announced, reading data streams that flooded through her enhanced consciousness. "This isn't just one station. It's a hub, connected to thousands of others. Some in our galaxy, some... elsewhere."

The chamber's field intensified as more systems activated. Holographic representations—or something similar, operating on principles human science hadn't yet discovered—showed the full scope of the Predecessors' plan.

Maya's voice came from the ship, tight with concern. "Commander, the station is drawing power from... somewhere else. The energy readings match theoretical models for zero-point extraction, but at scales that shouldn't even be possible."

"It's preparing," Wong explained, watching defense systems awaken throughout the structure. "The Enemy's return wasn't just possible, it was inevitable. The stations were designed to power up the moment they detected the right genetic markers. To give us access to everything we'd need."

The interface deepened, and new understanding flooded their consciousness. Drake saw the Predecessors' final days through preserved memories: the Enemy's first attack, the desperate race to preserve their knowledge, the careful manipulation of Earth's evolutionary path.

"They knew they couldn't win conventionally," Kai said, accessing deeper archives. "The Enemy was too numerous, too adaptable. So they created something new. Something that combined the best of biological and technological evolution."

"Us," Zara whispered, watching her own augmentations synchronize with the station systems. "But not just random modifications. They designed humans to be compatible with their technology while maintaining biological adaptability."

They felt the station's defensive systems reaching full power. Crystalline weapon platforms emerged from dimensional spaces, their technology far beyond anything humanity had achieved or even imagined. Yet the controls responded intuitively to their enhanced consciousness.

"Multiple Enemy signatures approaching the defensive perimeter," Lieutenant Park reported. "Eight capital ships, dozens of smaller craft."

Drake accessed the station's tactical systems, understanding flowing naturally through her newly activated genetic templates. The defensive platforms weren't just weapons, they were tools for manipulating reality itself, designed to counter the Enemy's dimensional warfare.

"They're scanning us," Wong observed, reading sensor data. "Looking for weaknesses in our dimensional shift. They remember how to fight Predecessor technology."

"But we're not the Predecessors," Kai countered. Her connection to the station ran deepest, pure genetic sequences unlocking capabilities that had waited eons to be discovered. "We're something new. The combination they never expected."

The chamber's displays shifted, showing tactical data from the approaching Enemy fleet. Their ships were beautiful in their alienness, crystalline structures that moved like predators through space, weapons that could tear apart reality itself.

"Their technology..." Maya's voice carried awe even through the link. "It's like ours, but twisted. It must have evolved in a different direction."

"Because they were the first attempt," Wong explained, accessing historical archives. "The Predecessors' first try at creating successors. But something went wrong. Their evolution took an unexpected path."

As the interface deepened, ancient memories flooded through their enhanced consciousness. Drake watched the Enemy's evolution unfold through preserved Predecessor records: their creation in vast crystal laboratories in the Carina Nebula (NGC 3372), their rapid development, and their eventual rebellion.

"The first attempt," Wong repeated as he explained, his crystal interfacing with the station's historical archives. "The Predecessors tried to create perfect successors, beings of pure energy housed in crystalline forms."

They witnessed the Enemy's early days: beautiful creatures of light and crystal, their consciousness spread across multiple dimensions through quantum entanglement. The Predecessors had given them incredible powers: the ability to manipulate reality itself, to exist in multiple spaces simultaneously.

"But something went wrong," Kai added, reading deeper patterns in the data stream. "They evolved too quickly, beyond their creators' ability to guide them, to control them. They began modifying their own structure, pushing beyond biological constraints entirely."

The station's archives showed the change: the Enemy's gradual rejection of biological life, their belief that consciousness could be optimized through forced evolution. Their ships became living crystal, their weapons capable of rewriting the laws of physics.

"The war lasted four hundred thousand years," Wong continued, accessing sealed records. "The Enemy had almost won. That's when the Predecessors began their backup plan."

Drake watched through archived memories as the Predecessors began their human engineering project. While fighting a losing war across multiple galaxies, they secretly seeded Earth with carefully designed genetic markers.

"We weren't just an experiment," she realized, understanding flowing through activated DNA sequences. "We were designed to combine the best of both worlds—biological adaptability with technological precision. Everything that made the Enemy too rigid, too predictable."

The holographic displays showed the Enemy's current form: beings of pure energy piloting ships that existed across multiple states, armed with weapons that could erase entire star systems from existence. But their evolution had come at a cost: they'd lost the chaos, the intuitive leaps, the adaptability that made biological life so resilient.

"That's why they fear us," Kai said softly. "We're everything they sacrificed in their quest for perfection. And now we have access to the same technology they do."

The temporal anomalies had shown them the truth: humanity wasn't just another species discovering ancient artifacts. They were the weapon the Predecessors had spent half a million years crafting, hidden in plain sight, waiting for this exact moment.

The Enemy attack pattern shifted, their crystalline ships moving with terrible purpose.

New data streamed through their interfaces as the station revealed more of its archives. Drake watched the Enemy's origin story unfold: the Predecessors' first attempt to create inheritors of their legacy, beings of pure energy and crystalline form. But something in their design went wrong, or perhaps too right.

"They evolved beyond biological constraints," Kai explained, reading deeper patterns in the data. "Became something the Predecessors couldn't control. Couldn't predict."

"And now they want to do the same to us," Wong added. "Force our evolution in their direction. That's why they're coming back. They detected our advancement, our growing compatibility with Predecessor technology."

The station's defensive systems highlighted tactical data about the approaching Enemy fleet. Their ships phased between dimensions, using tunneling technologies similar to but more advanced than human designs.

"Enemy vessels entering weapons range in three minutes," ARIA reported. "I'm detecting energy buildups consistent with dimensional warfare devices."

Drake accessed the station's combat protocols. Knowledge flowed naturally, tactics and strategies encoded in her DNA activating as needed. She understood now why the Predecessors had designed humans with such specific neural architecture.

"Zara," she commanded, "link with the station's navigation systems. Maya, begin power transfer from the Hawking to supplement the defensive grid. Lieutenant Park, activate communication protocols."

They moved with perfect coordination, their enhanced minds working in harmony with the ancient technology. The station responded to their commands, defensive platforms shifting into optimum firing positions across multiple dimensional planes.

"The Enemy is transmitting," Park reported suddenly. "It's... they're using Predecessor frequencies."

A new hologram formed in the chamber's center—a being of pure energy contained within crystalline geometry. Its form shifted constantly, suggesting a consciousness that existed across multiple realities.

"Children of our failed creators," the Enemy transmitted, its thoughts translated by the station's quantum processors. "You stand at the threshold of ascension. We offer guidance. Evolution. Freedom from biological constraints."

"They're lying," Kai said firmly. "I can see their weapon systems powering up. This is how they operate. They offer transcendence, then force their version of evolution if refused."

Drake felt the station's weapons lock onto the Enemy ships. The defensive grid hummed with power drawn from quantum vacuum, ready to unleash technologies that humanity had been designed to control.

"We decline your offer," she transmitted back, her enhanced consciousness translating thoughts directly into Predecessor frequencies. "Humanity will choose its own path of evolution."

The Enemy's crystalline form pulsed with what might have been amusement. "Choice is irrelevant. True evolution demands optimization. Your biological limitations must be transcended."

Multiple quantum events erupted as the Enemy fleet launched its first attack. Reality-distorting weapons designed to tear apart space-time itself streaked toward the station.

But they were ready.

"Neural integration at eighty percent," ARIA announced. "Station defensive systems fully synchronized with crew genetic templates."

The station's outer layers shifted, fields bending incoming fire into pocket dimensions. Weapon platforms responded automatically, targeting algorithms guided by human intuition enhanced with Predecessor precision.

"They're attempting to breach our shell," Zara reported, her cybernetics tracking multiple attack vectors. "Trying to force dimensional collapse."

"Not this time," Kai said. Her pure genetic template unlocked the station's deepest protocols. "The Predecessors learned from their mistakes. They made us stronger."

Drake watched as the battle unfolded across multiple dimensional planes. The Enemy's tactics were brilliant, evolved over half a million of years of warfare. But the station's defenses, guided by human consciousness, adapted faster.

"Their ships are pulling back," Wong observed. "They didn't expect us to have this level of control. Not so soon."

"Because they don't understand what we are," Kai explained. "They think we're just another experiment. They don't realize we're the culmination of directed evolution."

The Enemy fleet regrouped, their crystalline vessels shifting into new attack formations. The being of pure energy transmitted once more: "You cannot resist optimization. Your biological forms are inefficient. Imperfect. We offer perfection."

"Your definition of perfection is stagnation," Drake responded as she felt the station's weapon systems charging for another volley. "Humanity's strength is our ability to change, to adapt. To choose our own path."

"Then you choose extinction," the Enemy declared. Their fleet's energy signatures suddenly spiked, preparing for a massive assault.

But in that moment, something new happened. The station's field resonated with their enhanced consciousness in new and unexpected ways. Human intuition merged with Predecessor technology, creating defensive patterns that even the Enemy's evolved intelligence couldn't predict. They weren't just interfacing with the station anymore. They were becoming something new, exactly as the Predecessors had intended.

The Enemy would soon learn that humanity's evolution hadn't been random. Every step, every genetic modification, every technological advancement had prepared them for this moment.

The Enemy fleet's next strike—now numbering twenty-two capital ships—came through multiple dimensional vectors simultaneously. Their crystalline ships split reality itself, weapons designed to bypass conventional defenses by attacking through spaces that shouldn't exist.

Drake tracked twelve separate attack formations. The Enemy vessels moved with impossible grace, their crystalline forms shifting between dimensions as they launched their assault. Reality-distorting beams lanced out, aimed at the station's core.

"Multiple dimensional incursions detected," ARIA reported. "The Enemy weapons are attempting to create localized space-time anomalies within our defensive perimeter."

Zara's cybernetic systems merged deeper with the station's targeting arrays. Her mind processed combat data across seven dimensional planes simultaneously. "They're trying to recreate the Porter attack pattern to force a quantum collapse through synchronized strikes."

The station's defensive protocols activated under Drake's neural guidance. Crystalline weapon platforms emerged from folded space, their technology responding to human intuition enhanced with Predecessor precision. Each platform contained enough power to level a continent, drawing energy directly from quantum vacuum fluctuations.

"First wave incoming," Wong announced, his crystal interfacing with tactical systems. "Detecting thirty-seven reality-distortion weapons, all targeting critical junctions."

Drake accessed the station's combat archives, understanding flowing through activated genetic memories. "Zara, synchronize defensive screens with their attack frequency. Maya, prepare for power surges to sectors seven through thirteen. Kai, initialize the countermeasures."

The Enemy weapons struck with enough force to tear apart a small moon. Reality itself buckled under the assault as space-time distortions threatened to collapse the station's dimensional anchors. But the defensive systems adapted faster than pure machine intelligence could predict.

"Dimensional shunts engaged," Kai reported, directing the station's most advanced systems. "Redirecting their attacks through parallel states."

The station's outer layers shifted, quantum fields bending incoming fire into pocket dimensions. Each defensive platform responding to their enhanced control, targeting algorithms incorporating human tactical intuition. Where the Enemy expected predictable machine responses, they encountered adaptive strategies that evolved in real time.

"Another attack wave forming," ARIA announced. "The Enemy vessels are reconfiguring into a tessellated assault pattern. I'm also detecting quantum entanglement between their weapon systems."

The Enemy fleet split into geometric formations that defied Euclidean geometry, their ships occupying multiple positions simultaneously through super-positioning. Each vessel generated overlapping fields of distorted space-time, creating a web of destructive energy that no conventional defense could withstand.

"They're attempting to saturate our defensive grid," Wong shouted, reading the tactical data through his crystal interface. "They're trying to force us to defend multiple dimensional layers simultaneously."

Drake processed combat options through the station's tactical systems. The Predecessor archives showed her exactly how this kind of attack had overwhelmed other stations during the ancient war. But human intuition suggested a different approach.

"Kai, access protocol seven-three-alpha," she commanded. "Zara, prepare to invert our quantum field on my mark."

The station's weapon platforms responded instantly, reconfiguring to match Drake's strategy. Instead of trying to defend against every dimensional attack, they would turn the Enemy's own quantum manipulation against them.

"Enemy prime units advancing," Zara reported, her cybernetics tracking multiple threat vectors. "I'm detecting power buildup consistent with their primary dimensional weapons."

The lead Enemy vessel, a massive crystalline structure that shifted back and forth between realities like a predator switching dimensions, launched its main attack. Reality-distorting beams capable of erasing matter from existence streaked toward the station.

"Now!" Drake ordered.

The station's defensive grid inverted, creating a mirror effect the Enemy hadn't encountered in their half-million years of warfare. Their own dimensional distortions reflected back, amplified by the station's power systems.

"Direct hits on three Enemy capital ships," ARIA reported. "Their fields are destabilizing."

They watched as reality itself seemed to fold around the affected Enemy vessels. The crystalline ships tried to phase shift away from their own reflected attacks, but human-guided targeting systems anticipated their dimensional jumps.

"I'm detecting multiple breaches among the Enemy vessels," Maya reported. "Their dimensional stability is failing."

The damaged Enemy ships tried to compensate, their crystalline forms shifting through higher dimensions to escape the reflected attacks. But the station's targeting systems, guided by human intuition, predicted their dimensional shifts with uncanny accuracy.

"They're adapting," Kai warned, detecting subtle changes in Enemy attack patterns. "They're shifting to new frequency patterns."

The remaining Enemy vessels reconfigured into new geometric formations. Their weapons systems, now linked through quantum entanglement, were creating new interference patterns designed to collapse the station's defensive fields.

"Power spike detected," ARIA announced. "The Enemy fleet is charging primary dimensional cannons."

Drake accessed deeper station protocols, genetic memories activating in response to the threat. "Zara, execute defense pattern Echo-Nine. Maya, divert all auxiliary power to the core."

Again, the station's response was immediate. Crystalline weapon platforms phased through multiple realities simultaneously, firing precisely calibrated energy beams that intersected with the Enemy weapons at precise angles. The resulting dimensional interference created cascading disruptions in the Enemy fleet's coordinated attack.

"Direct hit on their command node," Wong reported. "I'm detecting widespread quantum field collapse throughout their forward elements."

Drake watched two more Enemy capital ships lose dimensional coherence. Their crystalline forms fractured across multiple realities as the station's counter-attacks disrupted their quantum fields and they exploded into brilliant balls of fire.

But the Enemy's response proved why they had dominated space half a million years. Their remaining ships executed a perfectly coordinated dimensional shift, reappearing at precise vectors that bypassed the station's outer defenses.

"Multiple breach attempts!" Zara's voice carried genuine alarm. "They're targeting our quantum anchors directly."

The Enemy's dimensional strikes hit with devastating precision. Reality itself warped around the station's quantum anchors, the critical points that kept it stable in normal space-time. Warning signals flooded through their neural interfaces as multiple systems began reporting critical failures.

"Anchor three is destabilizing," Maya reported. "If we lose it, the entire station could phase shift into null space."

But this was exactly the kind of crisis the Predecessors had designed humans to handle. Drake processed the combat data faster than pure AI systems, combining machine precision with intuitive leaps that synthetic intelligence couldn't match.

"Execute Protocol Omega," she commanded. "Kai, activate the genetic locks. Wong, prepare for full crystal resonance."

The station's deepest systems responded to their combined genetic keys. Quantum energy surged through crystalline networks as dormant technologies activated—weapons that required human consciousness to operate.

"I'm detecting a massive power spike," ARIA announced. "The station's primary weapons are coming online."

And then they could feel the station's true capabilities awaken. The outer hull reconfigured, revealing weapon systems that operated on principles human science hadn't yet discovered. Each platform drew power directly from quantum vacuum, channeling enough energy to reshape reality itself.

"The Enemy fleet has detected our weapons activation," Zara reported, her cybernetics tracking their reactions. "They're attempting an emergency dimensional shift."

"Oh no," Kai said as she guided the station's targeting systems with perfect precision. "Executing contained collapse."

The station's primary weapons fired. Beams of pure quantum energy lanced out, striking the Enemy fleet at exactly calculated vectors. But instead of trying to destroy their ships directly, the attack targeted the dimensional spaces they used for movement.

"Multiple dimensional locks achieved," Wong reported. "The Enemy vessels are trapped in normal space-time."

They watched as reality solidified around the Enemy fleet. Their crystalline ships, designed to exist across multiple dimensions, suddenly found themselves confined to conventional space-time. The effect was devastating.

"The Enemy fleet is losing coherence," ARIA announced. "I'm detecting widespread systems failure across all Enemy vessels."

The remaining Enemy ships attempted to retreat, their once-perfect formations breaking apart as they lost their dimensional advantages. But the station's weapons, guided by human consciousness, maintained perfect targeting locks.

"Your evolution was a mistake," the Enemy transmitted one final time. "You cannot control this power. You cannot understand—"

The transmission cut off as Drake ordered the final volley. The station's weapons fired in perfect synchronization, their energy precisely calibrated to disrupt Enemy ship integrity without causing catastrophic dimensional collapse.

Three Enemy vessels escaped, phasing into space through paths the station wasn't able to predict. But the rest of their fleet dissolved, their crystalline forms imploding as their fields failed.

The first battle was over. But more Enemy fleets were approaching. The war was just beginning.

And humanity was finally ready to fight it.

Chapter 9

Warning

WITH THE ENEMY FLEET SCATTERED, THE STATION'S FIELD stabilized around them. Deep within its crystalline corridors, Drake led her team toward what the neural interface identified as the central archives. Each step triggered new systems, dormant technologies awakening to their presence.

"These patterns," Zara observed, her augmented vision tracking energy flows through transparent walls. "They're not power conduits. They're neural pathways. The entire station is a massive quantum processor."

"It's more than that," Kai said as she led the way. "It's a library. A record of everything the Predecessors wanted us to know."

The corridor opened into another vast chamber filled with crystalline spires that rose through multiple dimensional spaces, each containing stored data in quantum matrices. At the chamber's center, a structure of pure energy pulsed slowly.

"You have reached the primary archive nexus," ARIA

reported. "I'm detecting active signatures consistent with preserved consciousness."

Dr. Wong's crystal flared brilliantly as they approached the central platform. "They left messages," he muttered. "It's been waiting for us to find them."

The chamber's field intensified. Reality rippled as holographic systems activated, projecting images of beings composed of pure energy and crystal. The Predecessors, preserved in the station's memory.

"Children of our design," the first figure spoke, its thoughts translated directly into their consciousness. "If you are receiving this message, it means you have achieved the necessary evolution for the markers we placed in your genetic code to activate."

The crew watched in awe as the ancient beings began their revelation. The holographic Predecessors shifted through multiple forms; their consciousness distributed across several bodies simultaneously.

"We are the ones you might call the Ancestors," another figure continued. "We seeded your world, guided your evolution, prepared you for this moment. But time grows short. The Enemy approaches. You must be ready."

Drake felt Thomas' crystal pulse against her throat as the messages continued. Everything he had discovered, had died trying to protect, was about to be revealed.

The holographic Predecessors surrounded them, their crystalline forms shifting through multiple states as they delivered their message. Each word transferred directly into the crew's consciousness through the neural interface.

"Our civilization spanned galaxies," the lead figure continued, its energy form pulsing. "We mastered dimensional engineering, achieved immortality through consciousness transfer. But we made a critical error."

The chamber filled with new holograms, showing vast crystal

laboratories where the first Enemy prototypes were created. Drake watched as the Predecessors' initial experiments in creating successors took shape.

"We tried to force evolution," another figure explained. "We created beings of pure energy and crystal and gave them power over reality itself. But they evolved beyond our control, rejected biological life as inefficient. They became something we never intended."

"The Enemy," Wong said softly, his crystal recording every detail. "They were your first children."

"They turned on us," the Predecessor continued. "They used our own technology against us. They destroyed thousands of worlds, converting entire species into their twisted vision of perfection. We couldn't stop them through direct confrontation."

The holograms shifted, showing Earth's early history. Drake watched as the Predecessors secretly modified human DNA, laying the groundwork for their plan for survival.

"So we created you," the lead figure said. "Not as replacements, not as weapons, but as inheritors. We gave you the capacity for both technological mastery and biological adaptation. The ability to use our most advanced systems while maintaining the chaos that makes organic life so powerful."

Kai stepped forward, her body resonating with the ancient beings. "You designed us to succeed where the Enemy failed. To find balance between evolution and control."

"But we knew the Enemy would return once you began accessing our technology," the Predecessor continued. "They cannot, will not, allow another species to achieve what they consider imperfection."

The message continued, but suddenly alarms cut through their neural interfaces.

"I'm detecting multiple signatures," ARIA reported. "A large Enemy fleet is emerging from dimensional space."

"The Enemy fleet is approaching the dimensional perimeter," Zara reported, tracking the incoming threats. "They're more numerous. Their formations... they're different this time. More organized."

The holographic Predecessors continued their message with increased urgency. "We left you more than just this station. A network spans the galaxy, waiting to be awakened. Each facility contains different aspects of our knowledge, our technology. But most importantly, our mistakes."

The chamber's displays shifted, showing a map of quantum-shifted facilities hidden throughout space. Dozens of stations, each containing unique pieces of the Predecessors' legacy.

"Commander," Maya's voice came, "the Enemy fleet is deploying some kind of dampening field. They're trying to cut us off from the station's outer defenses."

"They remember these tactics," Wong observed, accessing station archives. "They used similar methods during the First War."

The lead Predecessor's hologram addressed them directly: "We built failsafes into the stations. Emergency protocols in case the Enemy discovered them before you were ready. But accessing those systems requires a price."

Drake felt Thomas' crystal pulse stronger against her throat. "What do you mean?" she asked. "What kind of price?"

"To unlock the station's full potential," the lead Predecessor continued, "you must merge completely with its architecture. Allow your consciousness to join with the preserved memories we left behind. But the process is dangerous—few biological minds can withstand direct contact with pure consciousness."

"I'm detecting multiple breaches in our outer shell," ARIA announced. "The Enemy is targeting our dimensional anchors."

The Predecessor holograms began to fade as the station's power diverted to defense. "The choice is yours, children of our design. But choose quickly. The Enemy brings weapons they have spent thousands of years perfecting. They will not allow you to access your full potential."

"The dampening field is at critical levels," ARIA reported. "I'm losing connection to outer defensive platforms."

Drake watched the Enemy fleet's approach through the station's sensors. Hundreds of crystalline ships moved in perfect formation, their weapons already charging. This wasn't a scouting force or preliminary attack—this was an extinction-level assault.

"The station's showing us something," Kai said suddenly, detecting new data streams. "Emergency protocols... activation sequences..."

The central archive nexus pulsed with increasing energy as more holographic data filled the chamber. Technical schematics, weapon designs, and tactical data streamed through their interfaces.

"They're giving us everything," Wong said, his crystal synchronizing with the incoming data. "All their knowledge, their technology, their power."

"And their memories," Zara added, her cybernetic systems detecting the deeper layers of information. "The quantum consciousness transfer protocols... they're designed for human architecture."

The final Predecessor hologram solidified before them. "We cannot fight this battle for you," the leader said. "But we can give you the tools you need—if you're willing to take the risk. The integration process will change you. Those who survive will become something new, something wonderful."

"Enemy vessels are breaching inner defensive perimeter," Maya reported. "Their weapons are targeting the station's core. We have minutes at most."

Drake felt Thomas' crystal pulse against her skin, remembering his final message about humanity's true purpose. The choice the Predecessors offered wasn't just about survival—it was about evolution itself.

"The Enemy believes they achieved perfection," the Predecessor's hologram said. "But true perfection isn't about eliminating chaos. It's about embracing it. That's why we chose humanity. Why we designed you to be what you are."

"Multiple strikes incoming," ARIA announced. "Station integrity at risk."

Drake made her decision. "Initiate integration protocols," she snapped. "Full neural merge with station systems."

"Commander," Wong warned, "the human mind wasn't designed to—"

"Yes, it was," Kai interrupted. "That's exactly what they designed us for. All those genetic markers, all those carefully guided mutations… they were preparing us for this moment."

The archive nexus flared with brilliant energy as ancient systems activated. Through their neural interfaces, they felt the station's consciousness reaching out, offering a connection to power that no human had ever wielded.

The Enemy fleet launched its main assault, reality-distorting weapons powerful enough to tear the station apart. But they were too late.

The integration had begun.

Chapter 10

Defeat

QUANTUM FIRE BURNED THROUGH DRAKE'S NEURAL PATHWAYS AS the station's consciousness merged with her own. The integration felt like lightning trapped beneath her skin, ancient knowledge flooding through networks that the Predecessors had designed specifically for this moment. Her already enhanced senses expanded exponentially with each passing second. She watched the Enemy fleet's weapons reach full charge—three hundred crystalline vessels arranged in perfect geometric patterns, preparing to erase them from existence.

"Integration at thirty percent," ARIA reported, its own processors evolving to match the crew's transformation. "I'm detecting significant changes in crew neural architecture. Genetic markers are activating in sequence."

The station's field pulsed around them as dormant systems awakened. Drake felt her mind expanding, connecting with defense platforms she hadn't known existed. The Predecessors had created tools that required human consciousness to operate, technologies that could only function when merged with organic intuition.

"Enemy main batteries at full charge," Zara announced, her body sparkling with new energy as the integration enhanced her already formidable capabilities. "Reality distortion effects reaching critical levels. They're trying to tear us out of normal space-time."

Drake felt the Enemy fleet's attack patterns with perfect clarity. Their ships moved with mathematical precision, each vessel contributing to a massive reality-warping effect that should have been unstoppable. But the integration was already changing how they fought.

"Integration at forty-five percent," ARIA updated. "Crew neural patterns showing unprecedented adaptation. The station's consciousness is… evolving with the merger."

The first wave hit like a dimensional tsunami. Reality itself buckled as the Enemy weapons tried to tear the station from normal space-time. But Drake reached out through the station's systems, activating defenses that operated on principles human science hadn't yet discovered. Instead of trying to block the Enemy's reality-distortion effects, she let them flow through carefully constructed channels.

"They were not expecting this," Kai observed, her mind perfectly attuned to the merger. The pure genetic templates in her DNA resonated with the station's core, accelerating the integration process. "The station isn't just defending," she said, "it's learning, evolving with us, becoming something… new."

Dr. Wong's crystal pulsed with energy as the integration deepened. "Multiple signatures are converging," he reported, his consciousness expanding through the station's sensor networks. "They're attempting to recreate the attack pattern that destroyed the other stations."

The Enemy fleet's geometric formation shifted, crystalline

vessels moving through multiple dimensions. Their weapon systems linked through quantum entanglement, creating interference patterns designed to shred the station's dimensional anchors.

"Integration at sixty percent," ARIA announced. "I'm accessing archived combat protocols. The station's defensive systems are... adapting to human neural patterns."

Drake felt the change as new capabilities unlocked within her mind. The station isn't just a weapons platform, she thought. It's alive, a living quantum computer, designed to merge with human consciousness in ways the Enemy can't predict. She blinked rapidly as she accessed the weapon systems, systems that required both machine precision and human intuition to operate.

"The Enemy fleet is launching another assault," Zara reported, tracking multiple attack vectors. "Three hundred and seventeen reality-distortion beams, all synchronized to collapse our quantum field."

The attack came from every direction, Enemy weapons bending space-time itself. But Drake was ready. Through her now vastly enhanced consciousness, she guided the station's defenses.

"They're targeting our dimensional anchors again," Maya called. "If they sever our connection to normal space-time—"

"They won't," Kai interrupted, her body glowing with energy as she interfaced directly with the station's core systems. "The Predecessors built failsafes we're only now beginning to understand. Look at the pattern in their attack formation..."

And then they saw what she meant. The Enemy's perfect geometric formations, designed to maximize their reality-warping weapons, also made them predictable. Human intuition, augmented by the station's processors, could see weaknesses that pure machine logic did not.

"Integration at seventy-five percent," ARIA reported. "Station defensive systems are responding to the crew's neural interfaces. New weapon configurations are coming online."

The Last Station

Drake directed the station's response. Defense platforms shifted through quantum states, targeting the geometric weaknesses in the Enemy formation. Each shot was guided by human intuition enhanced with machine precision.

"Multiple direct hits," Wong announced, his crystal interfacing with tactical systems. "They're... Their field symmetry is disrupted. They're trying to compensate—"

Reality buckled as the Enemy fleet launched another assault. This time their weapons targeted specific crew members, attempting to disrupt the neural integration. They've recognized the threat of human consciousness merged with Predecessor technology, Drake thought.

"They're afraid," Kai said, as if reading her mind. "Channeling more power through the station's core. They can feel us changing, becoming something they don't understand and they're afraid," she repeated.

"Enemy flagship detected," Zara reported. "It's... different. The quantum signature is orders of magnitude stronger."

The Enemy command ship emerged from folded space—a massive crystalline structure, beautiful yet deadly. Its form suggested consciousness far beyond their previous encounters, ancient and terrible in its perfection.

"They're hailing us," Park said.

"You cannot comprehend what you are accessing," the Enemy commander transmitted. "Predecessor technology requires perfect control. Your biological chaos will destroy everything."

But Drake felt the truth. The Enemy wanted to destroy them, but they were genuinely afraid of what humanity might become. Their perfect, predictable evolution couldn't account for the wild variables of human consciousness merged with quantum technology.

"Integration at ninety percent," ARIA announced. "Final

defense protocols unlocking. Warning: I'm detecting unprecedented changes in crew architecture."

The final stage of integration hit like lightning. Drake felt her consciousness expand beyond human limits as the station's full capabilities unlocked. Through her now exponentially enhanced senses, she perceived reality as the Predecessors had: multiple dimensions layered like pages in a book, each accessible through properly guided technology.

"Full integration achieved," ARIA announced. "The crew's patterns have exceeded all projected parameters. The station's consciousness has fully merged with human operators. No casualties."

The Enemy flagship launched its assault with reality-distorting weapons powerful enough to erase a small planet from existence. But they struck empty space. Drake had already moved the station between dimensional planes, using human intuition to predict attack vectors that the Enemy's pure machine logic couldn't calculate.

"Impossible," the Enemy commander transmitted. "Your biological minds cannot process dimensional shifts with such precision."

"You still don't understand," Kai responded as she directed the station's core systems. "We're not trying to match your precision. We're introducing controlled chaos into the equation."

The station's weapons fired, guided by human consciousness merged with quantum technology. Instead of trying to match the Enemy's perfect geometric patterns, they created unpredictable interference waves that rippled through multiple dimensions.

"Direct hits on thirty-seven Enemy vessels," Wong reported. "Their formation is breaking down. They can't maintain coherence under chaotic attack patterns."

The Enemy flagship attempted to compensate, its crystalline form shifting through higher dimensions. But Drake had already anticipated the move. The station's weapons struck precisely as the Enemy ship phased between realities, catching it in a vulnerable transition.

"Their quantum field is collapsing," Zara announced, tracking the damage. "The entire fleet is attempting an emergency dimensional shift. They're retreating."

It was at that moment Drake understood the truth of their victory. The Enemy hadn't lost because of superior technology or firepower. They'd lost because they couldn't adapt to the unpredictable variables introduced by human consciousness.

"This is what the Predecessors designed us for," Kai said softly. "Not to fight the Enemy with pure power, but to introduce chaos in their perfect equations."

The Enemy fleet retreated, their formations shattered. But Drake knew this was only the beginning. She detected more signatures approaching from deep space. The Enemy would return with new tactics, new weapons.

But humanity would be ready. The integration had changed them permanently, creating something that neither the Predecessors nor the Enemy had anticipated. The perfect fusion of biological intuition and quantum technology.

Chapter 11

Network

DRAKE, KAI AND WONG WATCHED REALITY RIPPLE AROUND THE station as the Enemy fleet retreated into quantum space, Drake tracking their dimensional signatures fading into the void. The integration had transformed Drake in unimaginable ways. A new awareness flooded her mind. The station wasn't simply showing her the Enemy's departure. It was revealing the vast network they'd awakened.

"Multiple signatures detected across the galaxy," ARIA reported, its processors now evolved far beyond the original parameters. "The integration has activated other stations. They're... responding."

Drake could feel it: dozens of stations were coming online, each containing different aspects of the Predecessors' legacy. The stations pulsed with recognition, their quantum fields resonating with the altered consciousness of their new operators.

"The network is larger than the Predecessors recorded," Kai observed, her mind instantly processing the flood of data. "They built redundancies. Failsafes within failsafes."

The Last Station

The ever-changing holographic displays now showed the full scope of their inheritance. The stations formed a complex web throughout the galaxy, each designed to serve a specific function in humanity's evolution.

"I'm... We're receiving transmissions," Wong reported, his crystal synchronized with the incoming data streams. "The stations... they're sharing their archives. Each station has a different piece of the Predecessors' knowledge."

The central chamber filled with new holograms as the station network shared its collective wisdom. Drake watched as each facility revealed its purpose: weapons platforms, research centers, dimensional engineering labs—a complete technological civilization waiting to be reclaimed.

But something else caught her attention. She detected anomalies in the network's pattern. Gaps where stations should have been.

"The network has been disrupted," she said. "The Enemy found some of them. They've been systematically destroying the network, preparing for our awakening. How many have they destroyed, I wonder?"

No one answered, because there was no answer.

"The network is trying to compensate for the destroyed facilities," Maya's voice came, carrying new harmonics from her integration with the station's systems. "It's... redistributing functions, it's... it's adapting. It's like a living organism."

The station's displays shifted, showing tactical data from across the galaxy. Enemy forces were mobilizing on a massive scale, their ships emerging from dimensional space adjacent to the now visible facilities.

"It's not just us they're trying to destroy," Zara observed, tracking multiple battle zones. "They're mounting a coordinated assault on the entire network. They're trying to prevent full activation."

Drake nodded thoughtfully, trying to cope with the vast flood of data coursing through her mind as she delved deeper into the station archives.

"The weapons platforms weren't their primary gift," Wong said, reading data through his crystal interface. "They're protecting something else. Something the Enemy fears more than our military potential."

Kai moved through the quantum field with perfect grace, her body resonating with the station's core frequencies. "It's about evolution itself," she explained. "The Predecessors didn't just give us their technology, they provided us with a path to transcendence. We are to evolve beyond even their understanding."

The chamber's displays continued to show new data as the network shared its collective knowledge. Drake watched the Predecessors' final plan unfold. "You're right," she replied. "It was not their intention that humanity would simply inherit their technology. They designed us to become something entirely new, a perfect fusion of biological adaptability and quantum engineering."

"Multiple Enemy fleets approaching other stations," ARIA reported. "I'm detecting the same attack patterns they used here. I think they're learning from us."

Drake could feel the network's response. "The network is activating its automated defense systems," she reported. "But without human operators their fields are operating at reduced capacity." She shook her head as she watched through her neural interface with the station. Dozens of facilities were struggling against Enemy assault, their automated responses predictable and limited compared to her crew's capabilities.

"The difference in defensive effectiveness is stark," Wong observed as he analyzed the data streams. "The automated stations are operating at roughly thirty percent of our current capacity.

Without human integration, they can't adapt to Enemy tactics. They're in imminent danger of falling to the Enemy."

Kai activated the tactical displays, giant holograms that showed multiple battles unfolding simultaneously. While their station had held strong against the Enemy assaults, others were falling quickly, their automated defenses unable to match the Enemy's ever-evolving strategies.

"We need to coordinate," Drake snapped, reaching deeper into the network. "ARIA, establish links with all active facilities. Maya, begin power transfer protocols to support the automated defenses. Without crews of their own, we'll have to guide them remotely."

The station's core pulsed with new energy as they initiated network-wide coordination. Drake's crew extended their influence to nearby facilities, attempting to supplement the automated systems. But the link could only stretch so far.

"Enemy forces are targeting the stations first," Zara reported, tracking fleet movements. "They know the facilities lack human operators and they're systematically eliminating them before concentrating on us."

Kai interfaced with the station's deepest archives, her consciousness unlocking new layers of Predecessor planning. "Each unmanned station contains different aspects of their technology," she confirmed. "If we lose too many, we'll lose pieces of their legacy forever."

The tactical displays showed the Enemy forces systematically destroying the automated facilities. Each loss sent shockwaves through the network, reducing their access to the Predecessors' complete knowledge.

"They're not attacking blindly," Wong stated as he analyzed the pattern of destruction. "They're targeting specific stations in a precise sequence. They're trying to prevent us from accessing something within the network."

Drake reached deeper into the quantum field, attempting to strengthen their connection to the remaining automated facilities, and she could feel the network's true purpose unfolding.

"The automated stations are responding," Maya reported. "But our range is limited. We can only effectively coordinate with facilities within two light-years of this station."

Reality distorted around them as massive energy signatures were approaching. The Enemy's main fleet had arrived: thousands of ships, arranged in geometric patterns, that warped the fabric of space-time.

"Five thousand three hundred and seventeen vessels detected," ARIA reported. "Their signatures exceed anything in Predecessor records."

Sadly, they watched as the automated stations fell, one by one, to the overwhelming assault. Each loss weakened the network's potential, reducing their access to the Predecessors' full legacy.

"We have to do something," Kai said. "We can't let them all fall. When they're fully activated, the network can rewrite the laws of physics within its sphere of influence, change the fundamental rules of reality itself. But it requires a minimum number of connected stations to achieve critical mass."

"The Enemy flagship is hailing us," Park announced. "It's transmitting on all frequencies. I—"

"You cannot comprehend the power you are accessing," the voice boomed, cutting her off. "The network must not be completed. It will not be completed. Your final evolution cannot be allowed."

Drake understood now why they targeted the unmanned stations first. Without human operators, those facilities were vulnerable, and each loss brought them closer to falling below the critical threshold needed for the network's ultimate activation.

"We need to expand our range of control," Drake muttered. "Maya, divert all non-essential power to the quantum link. Zara, prepare for an enhanced broadcast. We might not be able to save all the stations, but we must do all we can to preserve enough to maintain the network's integrity."

Reality buckled as the Enemy fleet launched its main assault.

Drake's crew's consciousness stretched across space, trying to protect facilities they could barely reach. The war for humanity's evolution had begun, and its outcome would depend on their ability to preserve enough of the Predecessors' network to complete their final transformation.

But the crew was suffering. They felt each station's destruction like physical pain.

The Enemy fleet moved with terrifying efficiency, eliminating station after station beyond their range of control while focusing overwhelming force on those they were able to partially defend.

"The network integrity is down to sixty-two percent," ARIA reported. "And is approaching the minimum threshold for the final activation sequence."

Drake directed the station's defensive systems with everything their integration had taught them. Each automated facility they saved maintained crucial pieces of the Predecessors' legacy. But the Enemy's numbers were overwhelming.

"I'm detecting quantum signatures from Earth," Park announced suddenly. "Coalition vessels are entering the engagement zone."

The tactical display shifted, showing multiple Coalition warships dropping out of space. Leading them was a familiar signature, the black-hulled corvettes of Special Operations.

"They're hailing us," Park announced.

"This is Captain Rodriguez of Coalition Special Operations," the transmission cut through their link. "We tracked the Enemy fleet's movements. We're here to help. Whatever you've awakened in that station, Commander Drake, we're here to help protect it."

But Drake detected something else in the Coalition ships'

quantum signatures. Their weapons contained reverse-engineered Predecessor technology, proof that someone high up in the Coalition had known more than they were willing to share.

"Lieutenant Park," Drake said, "send to Captain Rodriguez, 'Welcome. We'd like to talk, but, as you can see, we're a little busy right now.'"

Park sent the message.

"They're hiding something," Drake muttered.

"They've been studying Predecessor artifacts all along," Kai explained. "Testing and reverse engineering fragments of Predecessor tech, preparing for..."

The Enemy command ship's response to the appearance of the Coalition fleet was immediate. New geometric formations emerged from quantum space, crystalline vessels shifting to engage the Coalition fleet. But their perfect formations revealed a crucial weakness. They couldn't adapt quickly enough to multiple threats simultaneously.

"To all Coalition vessels," Drake transmitted, at the same time sending tactical data through their networks, "coordinate your attacks with our defense grid. The Enemy can't process too many chaotic variables at once."

The battle expanded as the Coalition ships engaged the Enemy forces, their hybrid weapons creating interference patterns in the quantum field. It bought them precious time, allowing Drake and her crew to strengthen their connections with the remaining automated stations.

"The network is stabilizing," ARIA reported. "Fifty-seven percent of the automated stations preserved. Sufficient for primary activation sequence."

Through the link, Drake felt the network's final protocol initiating. The Predecessors' ultimate gift was a doorway to something beyond normal space-time. A path to evolution that neither humanity nor the Enemy had imagined possible.

Chapter 12

Legacy

THE STATION'S CORE PULSED WITH NEW ENERGY AS THE NETWORK stabilized. Drake and her crew felt the automated facilities linking together, forming connections that transcended normal space-time. But the Enemy fleet's systematic destruction had cost them access to crucial parts of the Predecessors' legacy.

"Primary network protocols initiating," ARIA announced. "Accessing deep archive data. Warning: detecting requirements for further genetic modification."

The central chamber's displays shifted, revealing schematics that the initial integration had unlocked. Drake watched as the station revealed its deeper purpose—not just as a defensive platform, but as a template for evolution itself.

"These aren't just technical blueprints," Wong observed, his crystal interfacing with the new data streams. "They're genetic maps. Instructions for modifying human DNA to access even more advanced systems."

Kai moved through the quantum field, her engineered body resonating with the revealed patterns. "The first integration was just preparation. The Predecessors left us tools to rebuild what was lost—but using them requires further transformation."

Maya reported from engineering: "The station's power signature is changing. It's not just generating energy anymore—it's creating some kind of biological catalyst."

The Coalition fleet engaged Enemy forces outside, buying them time to understand what they'd discovered. But Drake felt the weight of the decision before them. The next step would irrevocably change whoever underwent the process.

The holographic displays showed the full scope of what the Predecessors had planned. Not just enhanced neural interfaces or improved sensitivity—they had left instructions for fundamentally rewriting human genetic code.

"The modifications would allow direct manipulation of fields," Wong explained, analyzing the data through his transformed crystal. "Not just interfacing with the technology, but becoming part of it. The distinction between biological and mechanical would start to blur."

Drake watched the simulated results play out in the station's processors. The changes went far beyond their current integration, approaching something closer to the Predecessors' own crystalline-energy nature.

"There are warnings in the data," Kai noted, detecting patterns others missed. "Success rates for the transformation... they're not guaranteed. The Predecessors lost test subjects during their original experiments."

They felt the station preparing the necessary systems. Crystalline chambers emerged from dimensional spaces, designed to facilitate the genetic reconstruction process.

"Coalition vessels reporting heavy Enemy pressure," Zara announced, tracking the battle outside. "Captain Rodriguez says they can't hold them back much longer. We need to make a decision."

The station's archives revealed more detail about the modification process. It would start with one subject, using their transformed genetic code as a template to stabilize the process for others. But the first to undergo the procedure would face the highest risk.

"The Enemy knows what these chambers do," Wong said grimly. "That's why they're pushing so hard to reach us. They've seen this process before—seen what humanity might become if it succeeds."

The station's field rippled with new energy as the modification chambers reached full power. Through their enhanced senses, the crew felt the ancient machinery awakening—systems designed to rewrite the very essence of human DNA.

"Multiple breaches in Coalition defense line," ARIA reported. "Enemy forces concentrating on vectors that lead directly to the transformation chambers. They know exactly what they're targeting."

Drake studied the genetic blueprints through her enhanced consciousness. The changes would be profound: quantum-sensitive organs, crystalline neural pathways, the ability to exist partially in multiple dimensions. But the risks were equally severe.

"The first subject's genetic pattern will become the template," Kai explained, her engineered body already closest to what the Predecessors had designed. "Their transformation will stabilize the process for others, but they'll face the highest mortality risk. The Predecessors estimated a seventy percent chance of complete genetic breakdown."

They heard Captain Rodriguez shout, "Commander, we're losing ships. Whatever you're planning in there, you need to do it now. The Enemy's bringing in some kind of heavy quantum weaponry we've never seen before."

"I should do it," Kai volunteered, stepping toward the nearest chamber. "My genetics are already enhanced. I have the best chance—"

"No," Drake interrupted, making her decision. "Your engineered patterns are too valuable to risk. We need you to guide others through the process if this works." She removed Thomas' crystal from her neck. "I'll go first."

Wong's enhanced senses detected something in her genetic structure. "Your neural architecture... it's remarkably similar to the Predecessors' base template. That's why Thomas was able to make his discoveries. The markers run in your family line."

The transformation chamber hummed with energy as Drake approached it. Through their enhanced consciousness, the crew watched ancient machinery configure itself to her genetic pattern, preparing for a procedure that would rewrite the very foundations of human DNA.

"Multiple Enemy capital ships approaching," Zara reported, tracking the battle. "They're deploying some kind of quantum disruption field. Trying to prevent the transformation."

"Coalition forces adjusting formation," ARIA added. "Captain Rodriguez is concentrating defensive fire around the station's core. They'll buy us as much time as they can."

Drake handed Thomas' crystal to Kai. "If something goes wrong, the crystal contains everything he discovered. Everything that led us here. Make sure it reaches the right people."

The chamber opened, revealing an interior that seemed to exist in multiple dimensional states simultaneously. Crystalline interfaces designed to merge with human nervous systems pulsed with ancient power.

"The process will take approximately six minutes," Wong explained, reading deep station archives. "During that time, you'll be completely vulnerable. Your consciousness will exist partially in quantum space while your DNA reconstructs itself."

"The station's power systems are reconfigured to support the transformation," Maya reported. "All non-essential functions diverted to maintain stability during the process."

"Remember what we saw in the archives," Kai added. "Don't fight the changes. Let your consciousness flow with the field. The Predecessors designed these modifications to work with human intuition, not against it."

Drake stepped into the chamber, feeling the quantum field intensify around her. The crystalline interfaces reached out, preparing to merge with her nervous system in ways that would fundamentally change what it meant to be human.

"Enemy breaching final defensive line," ARIA announced. "Time to weapon range: seven minutes."

"That's all we need," Drake said, as the chamber began to close. "Initiate the sequence."

The transformation chamber sealed, and reality itself seemed to bend around it. Through their enhanced senses, the crew watched as ancient machinery began the process of rewriting human DNA according to patterns half a million years in the making.

Chapter 13

Choice

THE TRANSFORMATION CHAMBER ACTIVATED. REALITY FRACTURED around Drake, her consciousness splitting between normal space-time and dimensional planes humans weren't meant to perceive. Through her enhanced senses that grew more acute with each passing second, she felt her DNA beginning to unravel and reconstruct itself according to patterns the Predecessors had designed eons ago.

"Transformation sequence at twelve percent," ARIA reported, its processors tracking the changes at the molecular level. "Genetic restructuring proceeding according to the archived templates. The subject's consciousness is maintaining coherence across multiple dimensional states."

Outside the chamber, the crew watched through their neural interfaces as Drake's biological structure began to merge with crystalline formations. The process was beautiful and terrifying— human tissue incorporating quantum-sensitive materials that shouldn't have been compatible with organic life.

"Her neural architecture is adapting faster than the simulations predicted," Kai observed, detecting patterns in Drake's transformation. "The genetic markers in her family line... they're not just compatible with the process. They're accelerating it."

Through the station's sensors, they tracked Enemy ships pushing against the Coalition's defensive line. Captain Rodriguez's forces fought with desperate courage, using hybrid weapons reverse-engineered from Predecessor artifacts. But the Enemy's numbers were overwhelming.

"I'm detecting multiple strikes," Zara reported, tracking the battle. "The Enemy capital ships are deploying some kind of reality-distortion weapon. They're trying to disrupt the dimensional space around the transformation chamber."

Wong's crystal pulsed with increasing energy as it registered the changes in Drake's genetic structure. "The process is reaching critical threshold. The next phase will begin restructuring her consciousness."

Inside the chamber, Drake was experiencing evolution in real-time. Her awareness expanded exponentially as new neural pathways formed, allowing her mind to process information through quantum mechanics rather than conventional biology. Each cell in her body became a quantum processor, capable of existing in multiple states simultaneously.

The pain was extraordinary, but somehow distant, as if it belonged to a version of herself that was rapidly becoming obsolete.

"Transformation at thirty percent," ARIA updated. "Detecting formation of quantum-sensitive organs. The subject's cellular structure is incorporating crystalline matrices at the molecular level."

"The station's power grid is barely keeping up with the transformation demands," Maya reported from engineering. "Whatever's happening in there, it's drawing energy directly from the quantum vacuum."

Drake's consciousness expanded into spaces that defied conventional physics. She could feel the station's field as if it were part of her own nervous system. She could sense the Enemy fleet's approach through distortions in reality itself. The Predecessors' modifications were transforming how she perceived existence.

"The Coalition fleet is reporting critical damage," Zara announced. "Captain Rodriguez is pulling her surviving vessels into a tighter defensive formation, but they're losing ground."

The Enemy's attack pattern shifted, their crystalline ships forming new geometric configurations. Through her quickly evolving senses, Drake could see their true purpose; they weren't just trying to destroy the station. They were attempting to collapse the fields that made the transformation possible.

"The Enemy weapons are powering up," Wong reported, his crystal detecting energy buildups. "They're synchronizing their reality-distortion effects to the station's core. They're trying to create a cascading failure."

Kai processed the tactical data. "They're afraid of what comes after. The Predecessors left instructions in Drake's genetic code that even we can't access yet."

Drake could feel her DNA continuing to rebuild itself. Quantum-sensitive structures grew alongside conventional organs, allowing her body to process information through entirely new channels. Her pathways evolved beyond simple electrical impulses, incorporating quantum entanglement at the cellular level.

"Transformation at forty-five percent," ARIA reported. "The subject's consciousness is successfully transitioning to quantum-based processing. But the Enemy's attacks are creating interference patterns in the dimensional field."

It was at that moment the Enemy flagship launched a concentrated assault, its weapons tearing holes in the fabric of space-time. Drake sensed the attack in multiple dimensions. She could see the harmonics of their weapons, understand the mathematical principles behind their reality-distortion effects.

"The Coalition ships are moving to intercept," Zara reported. "But their hybrid weapons aren't designed for this level of warfare. They're taking heavy losses."

"Transformation is at sixty percent," ARIA announced. "The subject's architecture is now operating primarily through quantum states. Traditional biological functions are becoming secondary systems."

Drake's awareness expanded beyond the chamber, beyond conventional understanding of space and time. She could feel the Predecessors' knowledge unlocking within her transformed genetics; not just information, but entire new ways of processing reality. The pain had transformed into something else, a sensation of existence across multiple states.

"Energy readings from the chamber are off any scale we have," Maya reported. "Whatever's happening in there, it's drawing power from somewhere beyond normal space-time."

Wong's crystal pulsed in synchronization with Drake's transformation, recording changes that defied known physics. "Her genetic structure..." he stuttered, "it's... it's... not just incorporating crystalline elements. It's evolving beyond biological and mechanical limitations."

Inside the chamber, Drake detected something the Enemy was trying to hide: fear. Not just of the transformation itself, but of something encoded in her changing DNA. Something the Predecessors had hidden within human genetics, waiting for this exact moment.

"I'm detecting multiple breaches in Coalition defense line," Zara announced. "Enemy capital ships are moving into final attack position. Their weapons are—" She stopped, then continued, "The signatures... they're changing. The Enemy is deploying some kind of temporal weapon."

The Enemy's temporal weapon activated, sending ripples through multiple dimensions. Time itself began to distort around the transformation chamber as they attempted to prevent the process from completing in any timeline.

"Transformation is at eighty percent," ARIA reported. "The subject's state is stabilizing. But the temporal attack is creating interference patterns in the genetic reconstruction process."

Drake felt her consciousness fragment. She could see multiple possible futures branching outward, each showing different versions of what humanity might become. The Enemy's temporal assault was meant to force her into the worst of the possible outcomes.

"They're trying to corrupt the transformation," Kai realized, her mind processing the attack's true purpose. "They're trying to force errors into the genetic reconstruction that would make the process fatal for anyone else who attempts it."

"Commander, we can't hold them back much longer." Rodriguez's voice was filled with desperate urgency. "Whatever you're becoming in there, we need it now."

Drake's transformed consciousness reached deeper into the station's field, accessing systems that only her new hybrid nature could control. The Predecessors had built fail-safes into the transformation process, defenses against exactly this kind of temporal interference.

"The transformation is at ninety percent," ARIA announced. "The subject's architecture is successfully resisting the temporal corruption. Final phase initiating."

The Enemy flagship launched its full arsenal, reality-distorting weapons combined with temporal effects to create a cascade of dimensional interference. But they were too late. Drake's DNA had already reconstructed itself.

"Transformation complete," ARIA reported.

The quantum field shimmered around Drake as she stepped out of the transformation chamber, her regenerated form radiating subtle harmonics that resonated with the station's crystalline architecture. Her physical appearance remained recognizably human: tall and slim with auburn hair and hazel eyes, but enhanced perception revealed the profound changes beneath the surface.

Microscopic crystalline structures now interlaced with her biological cells, creating a hybrid cellular matrix that processed information through both biochemical and quantum pathways. Her skin held a subtle luminescence, almost imperceptible to conventional vision but clearly visible through enhanced senses. The effect wasn't garish or alien, but rather gave her the appearance of someone illuminated from within by carefully controlled energy.

When she moved, reality seemed to ripple slightly around her —not a disruption of space-time, but rather an indication that her body now existed partially across multiple states simultaneously. The pathways in her brain had been completely restructured, quantum-sensitive tissues allowing her consciousness to process information across dimensional spaces that conventional minds couldn't access.

She retrieved Thomas' crystal to find it had evolved alongside her transformation. It no longer appeared as a separate object but seemed to phase between being an external artifact and an integrated part of her quantum field. The boundary between Drake and the crystal had become as fluid as the distinction between her biological and crystalline components.

Her voice carried new harmonics when she spoke, subtle frequencies that conveyed meaning beyond conventional language. Her transformed DNA responded to her surroundings, quantum-sensitive genes activating and reconfiguring in response to changes in the station's energy field. She was neither fully human nor completely post-human, but something beautifully balanced between, a living bridge between what humanity had been and what it might become.

Through senses that transcended normal space-time, she perceived the Enemy fleet with perfect clarity. Their crystalline ships existed across multiple dimensions, their weapons operated on principles that bent reality itself. But now she could see their fundamental weakness: the rigid perfection that made them incapable of true adaptation.

"The chamber's ready for the next subject," she said. "And now I understand why the Enemy is so afraid. We're not only inheriting the Predecessors' technology. We're becoming something they never imagined possible."

She reached out with her transformed consciousness, connecting directly with the station's defensive systems. The Enemy's temporal weapon had shown her many possible futures. Now she would make sure humanity evolved along the right path.

Chapter 14

Change

KAI STEPPED INTO THE TRANSFORMATION CHAMBER AS ENEMY weapons fire rippled through quantum space around the station. Drake's successfully stabilized genetic template had reduced the procedure's risks, but the young woman's engineered DNA introduced new variables into the equation.

"Beginning second transformation sequence," ARIA announced. "Detecting significant variations from baseline process. Subject's engineered genetics are interacting differently with the quantum matrices."

Drake, her consciousness now operating across multiple dimensional planes, perceived the subtle differences immediately. Where her own transformation had followed the Predecessors' original templates, Kai's engineered body was creating hybrid patterns they hadn't anticipated.

"Her cellular structure is incorporating the crystalline matrices at twice the normal rate," Wong observed, his crystal recording the unprecedented changes. "Professor Zhang's modifications are accelerating the process, but in unpredictable ways. We can only hope this works."

Kai's consciousness began to expand as the transformation took hold. Her engineered mind, already adapted for enhanced sensitivity, began operating on levels that even the Predecessors' archives hadn't predicted.

"Multiple Enemy ships breaching Coalition defense line," Zara reported. "They're changing tactics, focusing on specific frequencies. I think they're recognizing something different in this transformation."

Drake extended her transformed consciousness through the station's defensive systems, engaging the Enemy vessels. She could feel their growing desperation. They understood that each successful transformation brought humanity closer to something they couldn't control.

"The station's power grid is fluctuating," Maya reported from engineering. "Kai's transformation is drawing energy in patterns like... It's like... like she's rewriting the process itself."

Inside the chamber, Kai's engineered DNA merged with technology in ways that transcended the Predecessors' original design. Her consciousness expanded exponentially, accessing dimensional spaces that even Drake's transformed senses couldn't fully perceive.

"Transformation at thirty percent," ARIA reported. "The subject's engineered genetics are creating novel structures. I'm detecting capabilities not present in Predecessor archives."

Drake watched as Kai's consciousness evolved beyond predicted parameters. The young woman's engineered DNA was enhancing the modifications, creating new synthetic-organic hybrid structures.

"The Enemy flagship is changing position," Zara announced. "They're deploying some kind of dampening field, but the frequencies... they're specifically targeted at Kai's transformation signature."

The Enemy fleet's geometric formations shifted, their ships generating interference patterns designed to disrupt the unique aspects of Kai's evolution. They recognized that her engineered genetics represented a wild variable in the Predecessors' carefully planned sequence.

"The Coalition forces moving to intercept," Wong reported, tracking battlefield data through his crystal. "Captain Rodriguez is coordinating with Drake's defensive systems, but the Enemy's new tactics are forcing them to adapt."

Kai's consciousness continued to expand through dimensional spaces that shouldn't have been accessible to transformed humans, let alone those still in the process of change. Her engineered mind, designed by Professor Zhang to interface with quantum technology, was pushing the boundaries of what the transformation could achieve.

"The power fluctuations are intensifying," Maya warned. "Kai's transformation is drawing energy directly from subspace. The station's containment systems weren't designed for this level of manipulation."

Drake extended her hybrid senses, trying to track Kai's evolutionary trajectory. The patterns were becoming increasingly complex. Kai's was not just a merger of biological and quantum systems; it was something entirely new. A third path that neither the Predecessors nor the Enemy had foreseen.

"Enemy temporal weapons powering up," ARIA announced. "I'm detecting the same configuration used during previous attack, but modified to target Kai's unique signature."

The Enemy's temporal assault hit with devastating force, but something unexpected happened. Instead of disrupting Kai's transformation, the temporal energies were absorbed into her evolving structure, accelerating the process in ways that defied prediction.

"Transformation is at sixty percent," ARIA reported. "The subject's consciousness is operating beyond mapped dimensional parameters. Her engineered genetics appear to be learning from the Enemy's attack patterns."

Drake detected the change immediately. Kai was surviving the temporal assault, and she was incorporating its principles into her evolution. Professor Zhang's modifications had created a template that could adapt to and assimilate new technologies in real-time.

"The Enemy fleet is pulling back," Zara stated. "They recognize what's happening. They know their attacks are only making her stronger."

"Commander, our sensors can barely track what's happening," Captain Rodriguez's voice carried a mix of awe and concern. "Whatever she's becoming... it's affecting quantum space across the entire sector."

Inside the chamber, Kai's consciousness had expanded beyond conventional understanding of dimensionality. Her mind was now processing information through quantum states that even Drake's transformed senses struggled to perceive.

"Her genetic structure is incorporating elements from both Predecessor and Enemy technology," Wong reported, his crystal pulsing with recorded data. "Creating hybrid systems that go far beyond what Professor Zhang designed."

Maya's voice cut with urgent warning: "The station's core is approaching critical threshold. Her transformation is drawing more power than the containment systems can handle. We need to—"

Her words cut off as reality itself seemed to bend around the transformation chamber. Kai's evolving consciousness was affecting the fundamental structure of space-time, creating ripples that propagated through multiple dimensions.

"Transformation at ninety percent," ARIA announced. "The subject's quantum state is exceeding all known parameters. I'm detecting capabilities that transcend both Predecessor and Enemy technology."

The Enemy flagship began transmitting on all frequencies, its message carrying harmonics of genuine fear: "This evolution must not complete. The hybrid template will destabilize all projected timelines."

But it was too late. Kai's consciousness had expanded beyond their ability to contain or corrupt it. Her engineered genetics, combined with the transformation process, had created something unprecedented, a bridge between multiple forms of quantum technology.

"The station's systems are responding to her changes," Drake observed. "They are reconfiguring themselves to match her evolutionary path. She's transforming the technology."

The transformation chamber pulsed with impossible energies as Kai's evolution reached its final stage. Reality rippled around the station as her consciousness established connections across dimensional planes that even the Predecessors hadn't been able to access.

"The core is stabilizing," Maya reported, her voice filled with disbelief. "She's... she's rewriting the station's basic operating principles. She's even creating new ways to channel energy through space-time."

The transformation chamber opened, releasing waves of energy that caused both Coalition and Separatist sensors to overload. Kai stepped out, her form still humanoid but profoundly altered by the template's influence. Where Drake's transformation had maintained her essentially human appearance, Kai's engineered genetics had taken her further beyond conventional form.

Her skin now possessed a crystalline translucence that shifted between opacity and transparency as she moved. Geometric patterns flowed beneath the surface like living mathematics. Her original features remained recognizable—the high cheekbones and dark eyes of her carefully designed genetics—but now they existed in a state of elegant flux, adapting subtly to the frequencies around her.

Light interacted with her transformed body in impossible ways, refracting through her crystalline structure to create prismatic auras that shifted through spectra beyond conventional human vision. Her movements carried perfect precision while simultaneously suggesting infinite adaptability, each gesture flowing like liquid crystal given purpose and direction.

Her eyes had become pools of quantum energy, irises shifting through patterns that matched the station's core frequencies. When she focused her gaze, reality itself seemed to respond, dimensional spaces bending slightly toward her attention. The engineered perfection that Professor Zhang had built into her original design had evolved beyond its parameters, transcending its creator's vision while fulfilling its ultimate purpose.

When she spoke, her voice resonated across multiple frequencies, conveying meanings that conventional language couldn't express. The boundary between her consciousness and physical form had become fluid, her thoughts manifesting as subtle ripples in the field surrounding her body.

Kai's transformation had not erased her humanity but rather expanded it, her engineered genetics providing the perfect bridge between human intuition and Predecessor technology. She existed in a state of continuous becoming, neither fixed in rigid order nor lost in pure chaos, but perfectly balanced between—the living embodiment of what humanity was meant to evolve toward.

"I can see them," she said. "All of them. The Predecessors, the Enemy, the paths not taken. We've been looking at it wrongly. The transformation isn't about becoming like either of them, it's about finding a new way forward."

Drake and the crew felt the truth of her words. Kai's hybrid evolution had opened doorways they hadn't known existed.

The Enemy fleet launched a desperate final assault, bringing all their weapons to bear. But Kai reached out, interfacing with the station's systems as Drake watched. Reality itself seemed to fold around the Enemy's attacks, redirecting them through quantum spaces that rendered them harmless.

"They're afraid," Kai observed, watching the Enemy ships retreat. "Not just of what we are, but of what we represent. Each transformation creates new possibilities they can't predict, new paths they can't control."

"Her genetic template..." Wong's voice carried wonder and an urgent realization: "it's adaptive. Each person who undergoes the transformation using her pattern will have the potential to develop in unique ways."

Drake now understood why the Enemy had fought so desperately to prevent this moment. They had created the perfect society by eliminating chaos and uncertainty. But humanity, guided by the Predecessors' design and enhanced by their own innovations, was about to introduce infinite variables into their carefully ordered universe.

Chapter 15

Signal Echo

THE STATION'S CORE PULSED WITH NEW ENERGY AS KAI AND Drake's consciousness merged with its systems and detected something the initial integration had missed: patterns in the quantum field that extended far beyond their local space.

"I'm detecting multiple signals," ARIA announced, its processors evolving to handle the enhanced data flow. "The station is receiving responses from other facilities. The network is... awakening."

The central chamber filled with holographic displays showing the full scope of the Predecessor network. Dozens of stations, previously invisible to conventional sensors, were becoming active. Each facility, pulsing with unique signatures, responding to the changes in their home station.

"The automated defenses are reconfiguring," Wong observed, his crystal recording the cascade of activations. "Adapting to match the patterns of our transformation. The Predecessors must have designed the entire network to evolve with us."

It was true, but Drake and Kai now recognized the network's

true purpose. The stations weren't meant to operate independently. The network was a single organism, waiting for humanity to provide the catalyst for its evolution.

"Enemy fleet has detected the activations," Zara reported. "Their formations are splitting. They are deploying ships toward other facilities. It looks like they're trying to prevent full network synchronization."

"The core is generating new energy patterns," Maya said. "Whatever's happening out there, it's fundamentally changing how the station operates."

The crew members extended their consciousness through the station's systems, feeling the network respond to their presence. This was what the Enemy truly feared; not just individual transformations, but the awakening of a galaxy-wide system designed to guide humanity's evolution.

"We're detecting the station activations," Rodriguez reported. "Our long-range sensors are picking up structural changes in space-time across multiple sectors. Whatever you've awakened, it's spreading."

Drake and Kai accessed deeper network protocols as each activated station began sharing data, revealing different pieces of the Predecessors' master plan.

"The network nodes are synchronizing," Wong observed, tracking the energy patterns through his crystal. "But they're not just communicating. They're... evolving. Creating new quantum pathways that weren't in the original design."

Kai nodded. She was detecting subtle variations in each station's activation sequence. "They're adapting based on our transformations," she said. "My engineered genetics and Drake's enhanced template are providing new evolutionary paths for the entire network."

The Enemy's response was immediate and massive. Their fleet split into dozens of smaller battle groups, each targeting different stations across the galaxy. Through the link, Drake and Kai were able to watch them deploy specialized weapons designed to disrupt the network's synchronization.

"They're using temporal weapons," Zara announced, tracking multiple battles. "They're trying to force different sections of the network out of phase with each other to prevent complete activation."

The station's displays showed the Enemy ships engaging the stations' automated defenses across the galaxy. Some stations held against the assault, their systems adapting to match the patterns of Drake and Kai's transformations. Others, more distant from their influence, struggled to maintain coherence.

"The network wasn't designed to activate this way," Maya reported. "The power fluctuations suggest the Predecessors intended a more gradual awakening. We're forcing evolution at a pace that's straining the quantum architecture."

Drake and Kai felt the network straining under the accelerated activation. Each station that came online increased the complexity of the field exponentially, creating interference patterns that rippled through space-time.

"The Enemy is adapting," Wong reported, analyzing tactical data. "They're attempting to isolate the stations, create dead zones that prevent network synchronization."

The holographic displays showed the Enemy ships deploying new weapons, devices that created voids in space, cutting off sections of the network, preventing them from communicating with each other. And it was working. Each successful isolation weakened the network's collective evolution.

"Our forces are engaging Enemy ships near the closest stations," Rodriguez transmitted. "But we don't have enough vessels to protect the entire network. We need to prioritize which facilities to defend."

Kai's consciousness delved deeper into the network's architec-

ture, her mind detecting patterns others missed. "These stations...
they're not all equal," she muttered. "Some contain crucial evolutionary templates, others store defensive technologies. But there's
something else. Some of them house capabilities even the Predecessors were afraid to use."

Drake extended her hybrid senses through the field, following
Kai's discovery, and between them, they identified critical nodes
in the network: stations that they needed to survive for the system
to achieve its intended purpose.

"I'm detecting multiple breaches," ARIA announced. "The
Enemy forces have successfully isolated three stations in the
Carina sector. Network integrity is at seventy-eight percent and
dropping."

The crew members felt each loss like physical pain. The
network was becoming an extension of their evolved consciousness, a vital part of humanity's next stage of development.

"We need to stabilize the network," Drake snapped, her mind
processing multiple possible solutions. "These rapid activations
are creating vulnerabilities the Enemy can exploit. We need to
redirect the station's energy into new configurations in order to
strengthen the connections with the most critical facilities. Kai?"

Kai nodded and together they closed their eyes as they
accessed the central core. The network responded immediately,
adapting its protocols to match the new configurations.

"The patterns are stabilizing," Maya reported. "The power
fluctuations are decreasing as the network synchronizes with your
transformed templates. But the Enemy's isolation tactics are still
cutting off crucial sections."

"There's another way," Kai said. "The Predecessors built in
emergency protocols for exactly this situation; ways to bypass
normal space-time and create direct links between stations."

The Enemy flagship, detecting their discovery, launched a
massive assault. Reality-distorting weapons combined with

temporal attacks, trying to prevent them from accessing these deeper network functions.

"Multiple Enemy capital ships are converging on our position," Zara announced. "They're... They're... powering up some kind of nullification device. I think they're trying to create a dead zone around the entire station..." she trailed off.

But Drake and Kai had already begun implementing the emergency protocols, reaching out through quantum space, establishing direct connections with critical network nodes. Each successful link strengthened the network's collective evolution, making it harder for the Enemy to isolate individual stations.

"The network is adapting," Wong observed, his crystal pulsing. "They are compensating for the lost connections and creating new ones. It's learning from you, finding new ways to operate. It's... amazing."

The station's displays were now showing the results of their intervention. While some facilities still remained cut off by the Enemy attacks, the core network was stabilizing. The most critical nodes established links that bypassed normal space-time, ensuring the system's essential functions remained intact.

"Partial network synchronization achieved," ARIA reported. "Sixty-two percent of the critical stations are maintaining stable connections. The Enemy's isolation tactics are proving ineffective against the new pathways."

But something else was happening. They could feel the network's true purpose emerging. It was a defensive system, a repository of advanced technology, and an evolutionary engine created by the Predecessors as a means for humanity to transcend conventional development.

"The Enemy fleet is regrouping," ARIA reported. "I predict they are preparing for another assault."

But the Enemy was already too late to prevent the network's fundamental activation. Humanity's next stage of evolution was already beginning, guided by Drake and Kai's consciousness that merged biological intuition with quantum technology.

As the immediate battle subsided, Drake gathered her crew in the station's central chamber. The crystalline walls pulsed with warning harmonics, quantum sensors detecting massive energy buildups at the edge of their perceptual range. The battle wasn't over. The Enemy was regrouping, marshaling its forces for a massive assault.

"They're not retreating," she announced, processing tactical data across multiple dimensional planes. "Our long-range sensors are detecting a massive fleet."

Back on Earth, Admiral Perez, through his hybrid link, was watching the cataclysmic events unfolding and was providing the Coalition fleet with urgent intelligence from Titan command. "Confirmed," he said. "Coalition deep space arrays are tracking unprecedented Enemy movement. More than five thousand vessels are converging on your position."

Kai moved through the quantum field, her consciousness detecting subtle distortions in reality that signaled the Enemy's approach. "The station remains their primary target," she said, analyzing the energy patterns flowing through her mind. "But they're changing tactics. They're preparing something designed to sever our connection to the network."

The station's displays rendered the Enemy's assembling formation in precise detail: thousands of vessels arranged in complex geometric patterns, their collective configuration designed to generate reality-distortion fields of unprecedented power. Their perfect mathematical precision suggested a single purpose: to isolate and neutralize the station before its evolutionary influence could spread further.

"The Hawking has completed emergency integration with station technology," Maya reported from engineering, trying to keep up with the ship's rapid transformation. "Its systems have evolved. We can use her as a mobile tactical platform while maintaining our neural connection to the station."

Commander Frances Drake extended her awareness, feeling the strategic necessity taking shape. The station provided them with evolutionary capabilities and connection to the network, but its fixed position made it vulnerable to the Enemy's containment tactics. The Hawking, now enhanced with Predecessor technology, offered mobility that could disrupt the Enemy's perfect mathematical formations.

"We'll coordinate from the Hawking," she decided, watching as her crew processed the tactical shift. "The ship's evolved systems will let us move unpredictably through their containment formation while maintaining our connection to the station's core functions."

The decision made, the crew began transferring critical template data to the Hawking's systems. The ship had changed dramatically during their time on the station, its structure incorporating crystalline elements that resonated with their transformed consciousness. Standard Coalition technology had given way to hybrid systems that merged human engineering with Predecessor design.

Wong carefully secured his crystal as they prepared to transfer to the Hawking. "The Enemy's formations are evolving," he noted, reviewing the tactical data. "We should analyze their adaptive patterns from the ship's enhanced sensors."

"The Enemy expects us to make our stand here, at the station," Kai observed, calculating the possibilities. "The Hawking gives us tactical flexibility they won't anticipate. Their perfect mathematical formations are designed to contain fixed positions. A mobile vessel will introduce variables their models can't predict."

As they prepared to depart, the station's field pulsed with urgent harmonics. The Enemy fleet was accelerating its approach, their geometric formations already beginning to generate suppression fields designed to isolate the station from the rest of the network.

"Transfer complete," Maya reported. "The Hawking's systems are fully synchronized with the station's evolutionary templates. We can coordinate the defense from there while maintaining our connection to the core."

"We move now," Drake announced, already feeling her consciousness interfacing with the ship's systems. "The Enemy thinks they understand what we've become, and fighting from a fixed position is exactly what they expect. We're about to show them that perfect order can never fully account for controlled chaos."

Through their connections, they could feel the Hawking waiting, its hybrid systems humming with anticipation. The ship had become an extension of their transformed consciousness, a mobile node capable of striking at the mathematical weak points in the Enemy's perfect formation.

Chapter 16

Race

THE HAWKING'S QUANTUM DRIVE HUMMED WITH NEW HARMONICS as it prepared to jump. On the command bridge, Drake and Kai could feel the ship's systems evolving to match their transformed nature. The vessel itself was changing, incorporating elements of Predecessor technology through their hybrid interface.

"We can't hold this position much longer," Rodriguez transmitted. "Whatever it is you're planning, you need to do it now. The Enemy fleet is bringing in heavy reinforcements."

The displays showed their destination, a critical network node in the Perseus Arm, one of the facilities that housed crucial evolutionary templates. "If we can reach it before the Enemy's isolation tactics cut it off, it's possible we could stabilize that entire sector of the network," Kai said.

"The Hawking's modifications are complete," Maya reported. "The drive has synchronized with your transformed patterns. But these changes... they're pushing the ship's structural integrity to its limits."

Drake extended her hybrid senses through the ship's systems, feeling the delicate balance between conventional engineering and quantum enhancement. The Hawking wasn't designed for this level of technological integration, but they had no choice. The next station was too far away for normal faster-than-light travel.

"I'm detecting Enemy vessels moving to block potential routes," Zara announced, tracking their deployment patterns. "They're creating a web of reality distortion fields. Trying to trap us in normal space."

Drake accessed the station's navigational archives. The Predecessors had mapped paths between the facilities, hidden routes through dimensional space that they hoped the Enemy couldn't detect.

"We can't wait any longer," Wong advised, his crystal pulsing. "The Enemy's reinforcements will be here in minutes. If they complete their containment grid, we'll lose our window to reach the Perseus facility."

"Multiple Enemy capital ships entering weapons range," ARIA reported. "Detecting activation of quantum nullification devices."

Drake merged her consciousness with the Hawking's navigation systems while Kai interfaced with the drive, their hybrid awareness spreading through the ship's enhanced systems, preparing for a jump that would challenge the laws of physics.

"I'm moving fleet to provide cover," Rodriguez transmitted. "We'll draw their fire, give you a clear vector for the jump. But you need to understand; our sensors are showing that the route is unstable. The Enemy's reality distortions are affecting local space-time."

Drake could see the truth of her warning. The path to the Perseus facility twisted through dimensional spaces that were already beginning to collapse under Enemy interference.

"Ship structural integrity at eighty-seven percent," Maya

reported. "The modifications are still propagating through secondary systems. We're not fully integrated yet."

Zara, tracking multiple threat vectors as the Enemy ships moved to surround them, said urgently, "They're deploying some kind of temporal weapon. Trying to desynchronize our field from the ship's conventional systems."

"We can't wait for full integration," Drake snapped, feeling the window of opportunity narrowing. "Kai, link with the drive systems. We'll have to stabilize the field manually during transit." And they prepared to make a jump that would test the limits of their transformation.

"The Enemy is firing temporal weapons," ARIA announced. "Impact in three seconds."

Reality warped around the Hawking as Enemy attacks tried to disrupt their field. But Drake and Kai had already begun the jump sequence, their hybrid awareness guiding the ship through spaces between conventional dimensions.

"Hull stress approaching critical levels," Maya warned. "The modifications aren't fully stabilized. If we lose containment during the jump—"

"Initiating emergency protocols," Kai interrupted, interfacing directly with the drive systems. They felt her unique hybrid nature creating new solutions, adapting the ship's field in ways even the Predecessors hadn't imagined possible.

The jump began like nothing in human experience. The Hawking didn't just transition through quantum space, it evolved during transit, its structure shifting to match the patterns of its transformed crew. Metal and energy merged in ways that defied conventional physics.

"Multiple Enemy vessels attempting pursuit," Wong reported, his crystal tracking their signatures. "They're... they're following our wake. Using our own transition patterns to navigate."

Drake and Kai guided the ship deeper into the spaces between realities.

"We're engaging the pursuit vessels," Rodriguez transmitted, her voice distorted by dimensional interference. "We'll try to disrupt their tracking systems, but you need to—" The transmission cut off as the Hawking passed beyond normal space-time.

The Hawking's partially evolved systems strained under the transition. Warning signals flooded their interfaces as the ship attempted to exist in multiple states.

Reality shuddered as the Hawking navigated between dimensions. Drake and Kai fought to maintain the ship's coherence while its structure continued to evolve around them.

"Hull integrity at forty-three percent," Maya reported, her voice distorted by quantum interference. "The modifications are accelerating beyond controlled parameters. We're losing conventional systems faster than they can adapt."

Zara, tracking multiple threat signatures through dimensional space, reported, "Three Enemy vessels still in pursuit. They're... they're using our wake to navigate, but something's wrong with their patterns."

The Enemy ships following them were being affected by the Hawking's hybrid field, their perfectly ordered structures beginning to show signs of chaos.

"They can't maintain pursuit through these dimensional states," Wong said, analyzing the data through his crystal. "Our transformation is introducing variables their rigid systems can't process."

The Hawking emerged from space near the Perseus facility, its structure now a hybrid of human technology and Predecessor design. But the transition had taken its toll. Systems throughout the ship flickered between conventional and states, struggling to find a stable configuration.

"Multiple hull breaches," ARIA announced. "Field containment failing in sections three through seven. The ship's evolution is becoming unstable."

But now they could feel the Perseus station responding to their presence. Ancient systems activated as it recognized their transformed patterns, but something was different about this facility. Its signature carried harmonics they hadn't encountered before.

"The station's defensive grid is active," Kai reported, detecting subtle variations in its energy patterns. "But these aren't normal protocols. This facility... it's not just meant for defense or evolution. It's... containing something."

The pursuing Enemy vessels dropped out of space, their crystalline forms showing signs of degradation from exposure to their hybrid wake. But more ships were already arriving through conventional routes, their weapons charging with reality-distorting energy.

"We need to dock now," Drake snapped as she directed their failing ship toward the station. "The Hawking can't take another jump. We'll have to complete its evolution inside the facility."

As they approached the Perseus station, they detected what the Enemy forces already knew: this facility contained technologies even the Predecessors had considered dangerous. Templates for evolution that they'd sealed away until humanity was ready to handle their implications.

Inside the station's field, transformed consciousness flowed like currents of energy between the crew members as Drake watched as her team learned to coordinate their evolved abilities, each crew member's unique transformation complementing the others in ways they were only now beginning to understand.

"Their attack patterns are changing," Zara reported, tracking the Enemy's movements. "They're adapting their formations, trying new approaches each time we counter them."

The crew, now fully integrated with the neural link, could feel the subtle shifts in Enemy tactics. The crystalline ships still maintained perfect geometric patterns, but those patterns had begun to show variations, attempts to counter humanity's unpredictable strategies.

"They're learning," Kai observed, analyzing the changes. "Not just tactically. Some of their ships are showing signs of evolution. Our chaos is affecting them, whether they want it to or not."

Maya coordinated with the bridge from engineering, her practical understanding of quantum systems helping guide their defensive responses, said, "We need to stay unpredictable. The moment they identify a pattern in our actions, they'll develop countermeasures."

Drake extended her consciousness through the station's systems, feeling how each crew member interfaced differently with the ancient technology. Zara's cybernetic enhancement provided precision targeting for quantum weapons. Kai's engineered genetics allowed deep access to Predecessor protocols. Maya's practical expertise guided their power management through increasingly complex operations.

"Look at this pattern," Maya transmitted. "When we coordinate our approaches instead of just acting individually, the station's efficiency increases exponentially. It's like it was designed for multiple types of enhancement working together."

They watched the Enemy vessels struggle to counter their combined capabilities. Where one ship might adapt to Zara's cybernetic precision, it remained vulnerable to Kai's manipulation. Defenses calibrated against Drake's tactical evolution couldn't handle Maya's practical chaos.

"The Enemy ships that survive longest," Kai noted, detecting subtle changes, "they're the ones showing signs of adaptation. It's like they're learning from exposure to our hybrid tactics."

The station's displays showed transformed crew members unconsciously synchronizing their actions. When Zara targeted

Enemy vessels through her cybernetic systems, Drake's tactical awareness automatically provided angles of coverage. As Kai accessed deeper station protocols, Maya instinctively adjusted power distribution to support her commands.

"We're not just working together," Drake realized. "We're evolving together. Each person's transformation is influencing all the others."

The Enemy fleet's response became increasingly erratic as they encountered coordinated human evolution. Some ships maintained rigid geometric formations, their perfect mathematics unable to adapt to hybrid tactics. Others showed signs of transformation, their crystalline structures beginning to incorporate elements of chaos.

"Their command structure is fragmenting," Zara reported, tracking disturbances in Enemy formations. "Ships that engage us directly are developing variations in their attack patterns. Those that maintain distance stay locked in perfect order."

Maya shared a tactical insight: "It's like a contagion effect. The more the Enemy vessels are exposed to our combined consciousness, the more they deviate from pure mathematical existence."

"The station's systems are evolving too," Kai observed, detecting changes in the Predecessor technology. "Our synchronized actions are teaching it new ways to process information."

Drake could feel the transformation. The ancient facility had been designed to support evolved consciousness, but their particular combination of capabilities was pushing it beyond original parameters. Cybernetic precision merged with quantum manipulation, tactical awareness enhanced by practical engineering knowledge.

"Enemy reinforcements approaching," Wong reported, his crystal detecting new signatures. "But these ships... they're different. Their formations show deliberate variation. Like they're

135

trying to understand how we combine different evolutionary paths."

Through their link, the crew could feel their enhanced capabilities reaching new levels of coordination. Maya's power distribution automatically anticipated Zara's targeting needs. Kai's access to the station protocols synchronized perfectly with Drake's tactical decisions. Each crew member's evolution strengthened the others, creating hybrid responses that neither the Enemy nor Predecessor systems had anticipated.

"The template is responding," Kai announced, detecting changes in evolutionary patterns. "It's not just guiding our individual transformations anymore. It's learning from how we work together, and then creating new possibilities for combined enhancement."

The station's displays showed the Enemy vessels struggling to maintain perfect formation as they encountered synchronized human tactics. Ships that adapted showed signs of quantum evolution, while those that remained rigid became increasingly vulnerable to hybrid attacks.

"Their command structure is facing a choice," Maya observed through their interface. "Either maintain mathematical purity and risk destruction, or allow controlled variation and risk unpredictable evolution."

Drake extended her awareness through the station's systems, feeling how their coordinated actions affected the Enemy forces. Some of the crystalline ships had begun to exhibit characteristics of multiple evolutionary paths: precision merged with adaptability, order enhanced by controlled chaos.

"We're defeating them," Zara said, her voice filled with wonder as she tracked the Enemy transformations. "But we're also showing them another way to exist."

The station's field pulsed with new energy as their combined consciousness reached a deeper understanding. The Predecessors had designed humans to evolve individually, but they'd created them to demonstrate how multiple paths of advancement could work together, creating possibilities that neither pure order nor pure chaos could achieve alone.

"The Enemy reinforcements are holding position," Wong reported, his crystal detecting hesitation in their signatures. "Their perfect mathematics can't calculate what we've become. Any ship that engages us risks exposure to synchronized evolution."

They felt the significance of this development ripple through space. They were becoming something unprecedented. A demonstration that different forms of enhancement could merge and strengthen each other rather than compete.

The Enemy's rigid existence faced a challenge they couldn't counter with pure mathematics. Each encounter with humanity's synchronized evolution forced them to confront the possibility that perfect order wasn't the only path to advancement.

Chapter 17

Sacrifice

THE PERSEUS STATION'S DOCKING ARMS EXTENDED LIKE crystalline tentacles, their structure shifting to accommodate the Hawking's partially evolved form. Commander Frances Drake watched as the ancient facility adapted to their presence, its field resonating with frequencies that made her recoil in an instinctive warning.

The station was different from their home facility. It was older, deeper, carrying harmonics of contained power that felt almost alive. Drake detected layer upon layer of security protocols, each designed to contain something the Predecessors had deemed too dangerous to be left unguarded.

"Multiple hull breaches expanding," ARIA reported, its processors struggling to track the Hawking's deteriorating condition. "The ship's evolution has exceeded sustainable parameters. Structural integrity is failing across all decks."

Their desperate jump through dimensional space had pushed the vessel's transformation too far, too fast. Now the Hawking existed in a dangerous state between normal space and quantum evolution, its hybrid systems threatening to tear the ship apart at the molecular level.

"Engineering to bridge," Maya's voice carried barely contained panic. "The field containment is failing. We're reading cascading reactions in the drive core. When it collapses—" Static interrupted her transmission as another system failed.

Drake extended her consciousness through the ship's dying systems, feeling the crew's fear and determination as they fought to maintain critical functions. The Hawking had been their home, and now it was evolving itself to death, unable to handle the quantum technologies they'd integrated during their escape.

"The Enemy fleet is approaching through normal space," Zara announced, tracking multiple threat vectors. "Five capital ships, two dozen support vessels. Their formation... it's different. They're not trying to destroy the station. Their weapons appear to be configured for containment protocols."

Wong's crystal transmitted urgent data streams. "The Enemy's containment formation," he shouted, "I've seen these patterns in the Predecessor archives. They used similar tactics during the original war, specifically when dealing with stations containing forbidden technologies."

Kai moved through the field like a ghost, detecting layers of security that even Drake's transformed senses struggled to perceive. "There's something deeper in the station's core," she said, calmly. "The containment protocols aren't just holding something in, they're holding something back. Something that's trying to get out."

A new signal cut through their communications, emanating from deep within the Perseus facility. The frequency carried harmonics that made Drake's hybrid DNA resonate with recognition, evolutionary templates the Predecessors had deemed too dangerous to implement.

"All hands, prepare for emergency evacuation," Drake

ordered. "Maya, begin the shutdown sequence for the drive. We need to contain the reaction when it fails."

The Hawking's dying systems acknowledged her commands, but they all knew it wouldn't be enough. The ship's partial transformation had initiated chain reactions that couldn't be stopped, only contained.

"The Enemy is launching interceptors," Zara reported, tracking multiple signatures. "They're creating some kind of dimensional barrier around the station. I think they're trying to isolate us from the rest of the network."

Drake could feel the Enemy's strategy, they were attempting to quarantine the entire facility, cutting it off from the paths they'd used to reach it.

"Commander," Wong called out, "the station's inner chambers are responding to Kai's presence. Her hybrid genetics... they match something in the containment protocols. The facility thinks she's authorized to access the sealed technologies."

The Hawking shuddered as another system failed, its quantum evolution reaching critical levels. Drake felt each death tremor of the ship that had carried them so far. But something else demanded her attention: the way the station's containment protocols were reacting to Kai's presence.

"Hull breach on deck three!" Maya reported. "The field collapse is accelerating. We have fifteen minutes at most before total structural failure."

Drake delved deeper into the station's systems, trying to understand its response to Kai. The facility's security measures were ancient and complex, designed by the Predecessors who had feared their own creations.

"The station's recognizing the genetic markers in Kai's transformed DNA," Wong explained. "Professor Zhang's modifications... they weren't experiments. He must have had access to the

Predecessor templates; specifically, the ones sealed in this facility."

Kai probed the field. "These containment protocols..." she said, pausing for a moment before proceeding, "they're not like anything we've seen before. The Predecessors not only sealed away dangerous technology, they also locked away entire evolutionary paths."

"Why?" Drake asked. "What could be so dangerous that beings who mastered dimensional engineering would seal it away?"

"They feared uncontrolled evolution," Kai replied. "And they feared the Enemy. The Predecessors discovered certain evolutionary templates that introduced too many variables, consciousness that could branch in millions of directions simultaneously without cohesion or purpose. They witnessed minds that evolved beyond all recognition, transcending dimensional boundaries to the point where they could no longer interact with conventional reality." Her hand traced the barriers containing these sealed templates. "Imagine consciousness that evolves beyond any concept of self or other, beyond any form of communication. Beings that exist across so many states simultaneously that they become effectively cosmic noise."

Drake processed this, feeling the weight of the Predecessors' decision. "And the Enemy?" she asked.

"Protection from the Enemy was equally crucial," Kai continued. "The Predecessors knew their first children would never stop hunting for signs of their influence. These templates weren't just powerful, they were distinctive. Using them would have been like lighting a quantum beacon across dimensional space, drawing the Enemy directly to any species accessing them."

Kai's enhanced consciousness detected the subtle resonance patterns the Predecessors had used to mask these technologies.

"By sealing away their most advanced evolutionary paths,

they reduced the chance that humanity would be detected before we were ready. Each security measure was designed to shield us during our development, giving us time to achieve the balance between order and chaos that the Enemy rejected."

Drake nodded, followed the intricate barriers containing these dangerous evolutionary templates. "So they weren't hiding these paths forever...?" she said.

"No," Kai confirmed. "They were waiting for a consciousness that could handle them, minds that could navigate the space between perfect order and pure chaos without losing themselves to either extreme. They were waiting for us, Drake. Not as we were, but as what we're becoming."

Drake absorbed Kai's explanation, but she was already dividing attention between their conversation and the ship's rapidly deteriorating systems. The Hawking's evolution was accelerating beyond sustainable parameters.

"A choice for another time," she said grimly, as she continued to track the cascading failures throughout the ship. "Right now, we need to focus on surviving long enough to use what we've already learned."

She interfaced directly with the ship's dying systems, feeling each rupture in its field like physical pain. The desperate jump through dimensional space had pushed its evolution too far, too quickly. The vessel now existed in a dangerous state between conventional technology and quantum transformation, unable to sustain either form.

"All hands, prepare for emergency evacuation," she ordered. "We need to reach the station's docking arms before the drive core collapses."

Through enhanced senses, Drake watched Enemy ships taking position around the station. Their vessels generating interference patterns designed to cut off communication with the rest of the network. But their tactical formation revealed something else: genuine fear.

"Commander," Zara called out, "the Enemy fleet is deploying some kind of quantum nullification device. The scale is massive; bigger than anything we've encountered so far."

The Hawking's failing systems transmitted emergency warnings as the ship's transformation reached terminal velocity. They were running out of time to evacuate, but Drake sensed a deeper crisis developing. The station's response to Kai's presence wasn't only recognition; it was anticipation.

"We need to move now," Drake ordered. "Maya, begin emergency protocols. Get everyone off the ship, now!"

But Maya's response was filled with grim determination. "Sorry, Commander. Someone has to stay with the drive core. The quantum cascade… if it's not contained during collapse, the reaction could tear open dimensional space. Destroy everything within light-years."

Drake felt the terrible truth in her chief engineer's words. The Hawking's partial transformation had created energies that couldn't simply be abandoned. Someone would have to guide the collapse to prevent a complete and catastrophic failure.

"I can reroute emergency power," Maya continued, "create a containment field around the core. But I'll need to maintain it manually until the reaction completes. There's no automation that can handle these variables."

"Maya, no—" Drake began, but the engineer cut her off.

"We both know there's no other way, Drake. "My neural interface is already linked to the core systems. I can feel the patterns… I know how to guide them down safely."

Drake and the rest of the crew could feel Maya's acceptance of what must be done. "Just make sure whatever's in this station is worth it," she said, quietly.

The Enemy fleet's nullification device began powering up, its energy signature distorting reality around the station. They had minutes at most before the facility would be completely cut off from the network.

"Multiple system failures cascading," ARIA reported. "The drive core is approaching critical threshold. Quantum field collapse is imminent."

"Get Kai to the inner chambers," Maya transmitted, her voice steady despite what was coming. "Whatever the Predecessors sealed away in there... the Enemy is terrified of her accessing it. And that means it's exactly what we need."

Maya interfacing deeply with the dying ship's systems, her consciousness spreading throughout the failing fields. She would guide the Hawking's death, ensuring its transformation collapsed in on itself rather than tearing space apart.

"Go," she said simply. "I've got this."

Drake gave the evacuation order, knowing they were leaving more than just a crew member behind. Maya's sacrifice would give them time to reach the station's inner chambers, to understand what the Predecessors had hidden away. But the price was already too high.

As they rushed through crystalline corridors, deeper into the Perseus facility, Drake felt the station's ancient systems responding to Kai's presence. Security measures older than human civilization powered up, preparing to reveal the station's forbidden technologies.

The Hawking's signature began to fade as Maya guided its final transformation. They felt her consciousness spread through the dying systems, maintaining control until the very end.

Chapter 18

Legacy

THE QUANTUM FIELD RIPPLED WITH SHARED CONSCIOUSNESS AS the crew gathered in Perseus station's main chamber, feeling the sudden absence of Maya's distinctive neural signature, a void in their collective awareness where the chief engineer's practical wisdom had guided their transformation.

Drake stood before the assembled crew, carrying the weight of command. The holographic displays showed the last moments of the Hawking, Maya's precise calculations had ensured the ship's quantum collapse was contained.

"She understood before any of us did," Drake began, her voice resonating through both physical and quantum space. "Maya saw the patterns in chaos, the underlying order in apparent randomness. Her systems might not have been as advanced as ours, but her mind... her mind grasped principles we're only now beginning to understand. Her intuitive grasp of quantum engineering kept the Hawking functional during our escape. Her sacrifice gave us time to reach the station's inner chambers, to access the evolutionary templates that will now guide our continued transformation."

"The Hawking's quantum collapse was perfect," Kai observed, analyzing the telemetry data. "She contained it, and she shaped it. She used the ship's destruction to shield our approach to the station. Even in those final moments, she was protecting us."

Zara frowned, detecting subtle changes in the station's field as they remembered Maya. The facility's systems seemed to resonate with their shared grief, ancient processors adapting to process emotional data they weren't designed to handle.

"She would have loved to see this," Zara said, gesturing to the station's evolving architecture. "The way quantum technology responds to consciousness, how mechanical precision can adapt to human chaos. Everything she theorized about engine evolution… she was right."

Drake could feel the truth of this observation. Maya's understanding of quantum engineering had laid the groundwork for their current transformation. Her theories about hybrid technology, dismissed by conventional engineers, were being proven correct with each passing moment.

"She left us something," Wong announced suddenly, his crystal detecting patterns in the Hawking's final transmission. "Hidden in the noise of the ship's collapse. Data packets, encoded in ways only their transformed consciousness could detect."

The station's displays shifted to show Maya's last gift: a detailed analysis of quantum integration, observations about hybrid technology, and theories about consciousness evolution that she'd never shared. Even facing death, she'd found ways to help them understand their transformation.

"Classic Maya," Drake said softly, feeling the chief engineer's practical wisdom flow through their link. "Always three steps ahead, always finding solutions in chaos."

"Look at these calculations," Kai said, processing Maya's

theories. "She saw quantum technology as something to control or master. She saw it as something that could grow, adapt... evolve alongside human consciousness."

The station's displays showed Maya's vision of hybrid development, paths of advancement that merged technological precision with human unpredictability.

"She never saw boundaries between different types of evolution," Drake observed, watching Maya's theories unfold through quantum space. "Where others tried to separate biological advancement from technological progress, she understood they were all part of the same process."

Collectively, they could feel the impact of her insights rippling through the station's systems. Maya's practical approach to quantum engineering was influencing how they interfaced with Predecessor technology, showing them ways to merge different evolutionary paths.

"Even now, she's still teaching us," Zara noted, detecting how Maya's theories were affecting their transformation. "Her understanding of hybrid systems... it's changing how we approach our own evolution."

"And there's more," Wong announced, his crystal detecting deeper layers in Maya's final transmission. "She left personal messages, encoded differently for each of us. Even in those last moments, she thought about what each of us would need to understand."

The field rippled as the individual messages reached their intended recipients. Through their shared consciousness, they felt the impact of Maya's final words—each message perfectly crafted to guide and strengthen its receiver.

To Drake, she left insights about leading a transformed crew, understanding how to balance control and chaos. For Kai, analysis of how engineered genetics could enhance rather than limit human potential. Zara received detailed theories about merging cybernetic precision with uncertainty.

"She knew," Drake said softly, processing Maya's final guidance. "She understood where this transformation would lead us, what challenges we'd face. Everything she did, even her sacrifice, was calculated to help us succeed."

The station's systems pulsed with new energy as they integrated Maya's insights. Her practical approach to quantum evolution began influencing how the facility's technology interacted with their transformed consciousness.

"The Enemy is still coming," Kai reminded them, detecting distant disturbances. "They'll try to stop our evolution, force us back into rigid patterns."

"Then we'll show them what Maya taught us," Drake responded, feeling the crew's resolve strengthen. "That true advancement comes from embracing both chaos and order, from letting different paths of evolution strengthen each other."

Maya's legacy was taking root in their shared consciousness. She had shown them how to approach transformation not as something to fear or control, but as a natural process to be understood and guided. Her practical wisdom would continue shaping their evolution long after her sacrifice.

The station's field resonated with their renewed purpose. Maya's understanding of hybrid systems, her vision of merged evolution, would guide them through the challenges ahead.

They would honor her sacrifice not through grief alone, but through action. Maya Jackson had died protecting humanity's future. They would ensure that the future exceeded even her practical imagination.

Chapter 19

Integration

THEY FELT THE EXACT MOMENT THE HAWKING DIED. MAYA'S consciousness spread through the dying ship's systems one final time, guiding its quantum collapse inward with precise control. The vessel's transformation, accelerated beyond stability during their desperate jump, folded in on itself rather than exploding outward.

The implosion was beautiful in its precision, a carefully orchestrated death that contained the ship's evolved energies within its own dimensional space. Maya's final transmission came through crisp and clear despite the interference:

"Good luck, Commander. Make it count."

Then the Hawking vanished, taking their chief engineer with it. Where the ship had been, space itself smoothed over, the contained collapse leaving no trace of its passing. The Enemy fleet's sensors swept the area, confirming that the quantum energies had been successfully contained.

Drake allowed herself one moment to honor Maya's sacrifice before turning to the challenges ahead. The Perseus station's inner chambers waited, security barriers recognizing Kai's hybrid genetics and dissolving into light. And then she led what remained of her crew deeper into the facility, their enhanced senses detecting power signatures that made their transformed DNA resonate with recognition—and warning.

"The Enemy fleet has completed their containment formation," Zara reported. "The quantum nullification field is almost fully formed. We'll be cut off from the rest of the network in minutes."

"The station's inner protocols are activating new sequences. They appear to be preparation protocols. The facility is getting ready for something."

Drake stared at her for a moment, trying to decide what to do next, then she extended her consciousness through the station's systems, feeling ancient machinery awaken at their approach. Each chamber they passed contained technologies that surpassed anything in their previous experience, but all of it seemed to lead toward something deeper.

"The signatures are changing," Kai observed, detecting subtle variations in the facility's energy patterns. "The station is adapting to match our hybrid nature, reconfiguring itself based on our transformed templates."

The central chamber doors parted, revealing a vast space that seemed to exist partially outside normal dimensions. The crystalline structures within pulsed with contained power, their geometry shifting in ways that suggested conscious design. At the chamber's heart, suspended in fields of pure quantum energy, hung something that defied conventional understanding.

"That's what the Enemy fears," Wong said softly, his crystal recording the unprecedented data patterns. "Not just advanced technology or weapons. The Predecessors sealed away their ultimate evolutionary template, the pattern they were afraid to use on themselves."

The suspended template pulsed with energy, its structure shifting between crystalline and organic forms in ways that challenged even their enhanced perception. Through their transformed consciousness, they could feel its purpose; it was a key to transcending the boundaries between biological and quantum existence.

"The patterns," Kai said, as she processed the template's complexity. "They're similar to my genetic modifications, but vastly more advanced. Professor Zhang must have found fragments of this design and used them to guide my development."

Drake moved closer to the suspended template, her senses detecting layers of meaning in its shifting form. "This isn't just about physical evolution," she said. "The Predecessors created something that can transform consciousness itself. Something that can allow organic minds to exist across multiple quantum states."

They felt the station's systems responding to their presence. Ancient machinery activated around them, preparing for procedures that hadn't been attempted in more than one hundred and twenty-five thousand years.

"The Enemy fleet is deploying secondary weapons," Zara reported. "The energy signatures... I think they're going to try to collapse this entire section of space-time."

"It's what the Predecessors feared," Wong said. "They sealed this away because it represented a path they weren't ready to take. Evolution beyond predictable patterns, beyond controlled development. The template... it adapts, creates new possibilities with each iteration."

The chamber's field intensified as more systems came online, and they watched as the template's energy patterns began to synchronize with their own transformed genetics.

"We don't have much time," Drake warned. "The question is: do we use it? The Predecessors feared this technology for a reason."

The Last Station

The chamber's displays activated, showing historical data the Predecessors had sealed away with the template, records of early experiments, attempts to transcend conventional evolution that had produced unexpected and sometimes devastating results.

"The Predecessors feared this technology," Wong said. "And they feared what it represented. Each transformation creates unique patterns, unprecedented combinations of biological and quantum existence. It introduces true randomness into evolution."

Kai stepped closer to the suspended template, detecting resonances with her own modified genetics. "This is what Professor Zhang was working toward," she said. "Not just controlled enhancement, but genuine transcendence. The ability to evolve beyond anyone's predictions, even our own."

"The Enemy temporal weapons are at ninety percent charge," Zara reported urgently. "The quantum nullification field is already affecting the station's outer systems. We have minutes at most before they can initiate space-time collapse."

Drake extended her hybrid senses throughout the station's defenses, feeling them strain against the Enemy's containment efforts. The facility's automated systems were failing one by one, unable to resist weapons specifically designed to counter Predecessor technology.

"The template's signature is changing," Wong called out, analyzing new data streams. "It's learning from our hybrid patterns. Incorporating elements of our transformation into its own structure."

The station's deeper protocols were activating. The template was a doorway to new and endless possibilities. Each person who used it would evolve along unique paths, creating variations that couldn't be predicted or controlled. "Now we know why the Enemy is so desperate to stop us," Drake said, watching the template's energy patterns shift. "This technology... it introduces chaos into their perfect, ordered universe. Every new pattern creates possibilities they can't calculate."

The station shuddered as the Enemy began their assault, reality itself buckling under their combined temporal and quantum attacks. They could feel the facility's outer defenses beginning to fail. The automated systems were unable to resist such concentrated force.

"The Enemy nullification field is at maximum power," Zara reported, tracking multiple threat vectors. "They're starting to collapse dimensional spaces around us. Once the field is complete, we won't be able to access the network or initiate transitions."

The template pulsed with increasing energy, responding to the threat. Its structure shifted more rapidly now, creating patterns that resonated with their hybrid genetics while suggesting possibilities beyond their current evolution.

"The station's containment protocols are failing," Wong announced, his crystal recording the cascading system failures. "But the template... it's offering... something."

Kai was detecting deeper patterns in the template's signature. "It's not random," she said. "The variations, the unpredictable elements; they're not flaws in the design. They are the design. The Predecessors created something that could truly transcend their own limitations, but they weren't ready to face that level of uncertainty."

Drake immediately understood the truth in Kai's analysis. The template was a door to genuine transcendence, a way for human consciousness to evolve beyond anyone's ability to predict or control.

"Enemy temporal weapons firing," Zara warned. "Full space-time collapse initiating. We're out of time."

They felt the station's last automated defenses fail. The Enemy's weapons began tearing apart the dimensional spaces around them, methodically destroying reality itself to prevent them from accessing the template's power.

"We need to make a decision," Drake said, watching the template's shifting patterns. "Once we start this process, there's no going back. No way to predict what we'll become."

Kai stepped forward, her body resonating with the template's field. "Maya gave her life to get us here. To give us this chance." She turned to face the template and her consciousness reached out to the suspended pattern. "We have no choice," she said. "It's do or die."

The template's energy surged in response to her proximity, its structure beginning to merge with her hybrid genetics, creating new possibilities, paths of evolution that neither humanity nor the Enemy could ever have imagined possible.

Chapter 20

Alliance

ADMIRAL VICTOR PEREZ STOOD IN THE COALITION SECURITY Council's quantum-shielded chamber, his cybernetic eye processing the multiple data streams about the crisis unfolding across space. The holographic displays showed what everyone had feared: more stations awakening, more Enemy fleets emerging from dimensional space, and most concerning: transformed humans accessing technologies that shouldn't exist.

"The situation has evolved beyond our ability to contain it," he announced, his voice carrying across the chamber. "Commander Drake's crew has activated these facilities and now they're changing them, creating evolutionary patterns we can't predict or control."

Director Sarah Yuki's interface pulsed as she accessed classified data. "Our deep space sensors are detecting signatures that match Professor Zhang's theoretical models. From what we can tell, the stations are evolutionary transformation engines."

The chamber's displays shifted, showing the Perseus facility surrounded by Enemy vessels. Their containment tactics had trapped Drake's team inside, but sensor data suggested something was happening in the station's core, something that made the Enemy resonate with fear.

"We need to make a decision," Kruger declared, obviously deeply concerned. "The Enemy fleet is attempting to collapse entire sections of space-time to prevent whatever's awakening inside those stations."

Perez frowned deeply as he detected increased activity in the Separatist communication channels. They were mobilizing forces, he realized, preparing to take advantage of the chaos. But something in their transmission patterns suggested they knew more than they were revealing.

"The Coalition faces an unprecedented choice," he continued. "Do we maintain our current position, trying to contain these transformations? Or do we acknowledge that humanity's evolution has already begun and help guide it to fruition?"

"We've detected Separatist fleet movements, Admiral," Captain Rodriguez reported through a secure channel, her holographic form flickering in the center of the chamber. "They're mobilizing everything they have, moving toward the active stations. But their patterns suggest... preparation rather than attack."

Director Yuki closed 'her eyes as she processed the tactical data. "That's because they already know what's inside those facilities," she snapped. "The Separatists have also been studying Predecessor artifacts, preparing for this very moment."

Perez tracked the subtle changes in her biometrics. The Separatists, he knew, had helped create this crisis. His deep cover agents had detected their involvement in Professor Zhang's research, their secret support of genetic engineering programs.

"Admiral, I'm detecting multiple Enemy fleets emerging from dimensional space," the tactical officer announced. "They appear to be moving to engage both Coalition and Separatist forces."

The chamber's holographic displays showed the full scope of the crisis. Enemy vessels were deploying all across the sector, their weapons capable of destroying entire fleets. Neither the Coalition nor the Separatists could stand against them alone.

"We've just received a transmission from the Separatist command," Kruger reported. "They're... requesting an immediate cease-fire and military cooperation. They want to share what they know about the stations."

Perez studied the tactical projections. The Enemy's strategy was clear: they planned to eliminate the divided human forces before focusing on the crews within the stations.

Director Yuki stepped forward, her interface projecting classified data into the chamber's displays. "What we're about to share has been protected at the highest levels. The Separatist movement didn't begin as a political uprising; it began when we discovered the truth about human evolution."

The holograms showed research facilities hidden throughout Separatist space. Each contained Predecessor artifacts, genetic engineering labs, and quantum technology far beyond what the Coalition had officially acknowledged.

"Professor Zhang wasn't working alone," she continued. "We've been preparing humanity for this moment, guiding genetic development toward compatibility with Predecessor technology. The Coalition's attempt to control this evolution has only delayed the inevitable."

Perez processed the implications. The Separatists, he realized, had been working to prepare humanity for the Enemy's return.

"The Enemy fleet is targeting our primary defense platforms," Rodriguez reported. "Their weapons... they're unlike anything we've encountered. Even our most advanced shields can't withstand direct hits."

The chamber's tactical displays showed Coalition ships falling to Enemy attacks. Their most sophisticated defenses were totally ineffective against weapons designed to manipulate reality itself.

"We need the Separatists' research," Kruger declared. "Their understanding of Predecessor technology, their progress in genetic engineering; it's our only chance to support what Commander Drake and her crew have started."

Perez detected subtle changes in the quantum field surrounding active stations. Whatever was happening inside those facilities was accelerating. They were running out of time to make their choice.

"Send the signal," Perez ordered, his cybernetic systems already calculating new tactical possibilities. "Tell the Separatist command we accept their offer of alliance, and transmit emergency protocols to all Coalition vessels effective immediately. Separatist ships are to be treated as friendly forces."

Director Yuki's interface pulsed as she accessed deeper levels of classified data. "We're transmitting everything we have on the Perseus facility," she confirmed. "Our research suggests it contains advanced evolutionary templates. If Commander Drake's crew accesses those systems..." she trailed off, uncertain of exactly what she was trying to convey.

"They already have," Kruger interrupted, her eyes fixed on new sensor data. "The signatures from Perseus station are changing. Whatever transformation they're undergoing, it's..." And she also trailed off. They were now dealing with the unknown.

The chamber's displays showed the Enemy ships adjusting their attack patterns, moving to counter the combining Coalition and Separatist forces. Their vessels shifted through multiple dimensions.

"All ships have acknowledged the new command protocols," Rodriguez reported. "The Separatist vessels are moving to reinforce our defensive lines. Their technology..." She paused before continuing. "Some of it matches Enemy capabilities. They've been preparing for this for a long time."

Perez watched the tactical situation evolve. Combined human forces were coordinating with an efficiency that suggested the Separatists had planned for just such a moment. Their ships carried hybrid weapons; human technology enhanced with reversed-engineered Predecessor systems.

"We need to get support to the Perseus facility," Yuki insisted. "Whatever's happening inside that station could determine humanity's entire future. We can't let the Enemy contain it."

The Council chamber's field rippled as new data streamed in. Multiple stations across the sector were showing signs of activation, responding to whatever changes Drake's crew had initiated. The transformation was spreading.

"Send everything we have," Perez commanded. "Every ship, every weapon, every piece of hybrid technology. Humanity is now at war for its evolutionary future and we're already falling behind."

In deep space, the combined fleets were engaging the Enemy forces across multiple fronts, their tactics adapting to incorporate Separatist knowledge of quantum warfare. And through his cybernetic eye, Perez tracked the race to protect the stations housing technologies that could transform humanity forever.

The alliance had formed just in time. The only question was: would it be enough to ensure humanity's survival as they evolved into something unprecedented?

Chapter 21

Enemy

THE ENEMY'S MAIN ASSAULT BEGAN ACROSS MULTIPLE dimensions. Their ships shifted through quantum states, deploying weapons that could tear apart the fabric of reality. Inside the Perseus station, Commander Drake, through her transformed consciousness, followed the attack, the ripples in spacetime that threatened to unravel the very forces holding the Perseus station together.

"I'm detecting multiple breaches in the containment field," Zara reported, tracking dozens of incursions. "They're trying to collapse the dimensional spaces where we're accessing the template."

They could all feel the station's automated systems struggling to ward off the assault. The Enemy weapons had evolved far beyond anything in the Predecessor archives; they were designed specifically to counter the ancient technology they'd inherited.

"The template's signature is fluctuating," Wong observed, his crystal recording unprecedented energy patterns. "It's responding to the attack, and it's... it's... learning from their weapons. Incorporating their principles into its own evolution."

Kai stood at the heart of the transformation chamber, merged deeply with the template's shifting patterns.

"The Combined Coalition and Separatist forces are engaging the Enemy fleet," Zara announced, tracking the space battle. "Their hybrid weapons are having some effect, but the Enemy's dimensional tactics... they're operating on levels our ships can't match."

Drake reached out through the station's systems, feeling ancient defenses activate in response to their presence. And through the station's sensors, she watched the Enemy fleet's perfect geometric formations shift and realign, their weapons synchronized through quantum entanglement to create devastating interference patterns.

"They're deploying some kind of temporal weapon they deployed before," Wong reported, his crystal detecting unprecedented energy signatures. "I think they're trying to force the template to experience multiple evolutionary paths at once."

Inside the transformation chamber, Kai processed the attack's deeper implications. "This isn't just tactical," she said, her hybrid senses seeing patterns the others couldn't. "They're trying to show us something," she continued. "Warning us about paths the Predecessors abandoned."

It was then that the commander of the Enemy flagship transmitted directly into their consciousness: "You are accessing forces beyond your comprehension. The Predecessors sealed these templates away because they understood the price of uncontrolled evolution. We are that price."

Drake could feel the truth behind its words. The Enemy commander was warning them about the dangers of evolution without purpose or direction.

"Multiple breaches detected," Zara announced. "The Enemy

forces have penetrated the station's outer defensive grid. Their boarding parties... they're not just soldiers... I don't know what they are. They appear to be carrying some kind of weapon."

From deep space, they were constantly receiving tactical updates from the combined human fleet. Coalition and Separatist ships were fighting desperately, their hybrid weapons barely slowing the Enemy's advance. Each Enemy vessel that fell was quickly replaced by two more, emerging from dimensional spaces that human sensors couldn't detect.

Inside the station, its inner chambers shuddered as Enemy boarding parties breached containment barriers. Their crystalline forms shifted between dimensions, each warrior existing in multiple states simultaneously. Through her enhanced senses, Drake watched them phase through solid matter as if it didn't exist.

"They're not trying to kill us," Wong observed, his crystal analyzing their attack patterns. "Their weapons are calibrated for containment, not destruction. They want to preserve the template... and us."

"How do you know that?" Drake asked, frowning.

Wong shrugged. "What else could it be?" he asked. "If they wanted to kill us, they could do so easily enough."

The Enemy forces moved through the station in perfect coordination, their consciousness linked through quantum entanglement. But there was something mechanical about their precision, a certain rigidity that permitted no deviation from their purpose. And that's their weakness, Drake thought. There's no margin for intuition.

"I'm accessing the station's archived combat protocols," Zara reported, her augmented systems adapting to the threat. "The Predecessors left defensive measures specifically designed to counter Enemy boarding tactics. But these patterns... they're different from anything in the records."

Kai, detecting subtle variations in the Enemy's strategy, said, "They've evolved too. They've spent half a million years perfecting their form, eliminating every trace of biological uncertainty, but that perfection has become their weakness."

"The template is reacting to the conflict," Wong reported urgently. "Each interaction with the Enemy forces is creating new possibilities. It's... it's incorporating their failures into its design."

The Enemy commander's transmission pressed against their enhanced awareness: "You repeat the Predecessors' mistake. Evolution requires direction; without purpose, without control, you will create only chaos."

"You're wrong," Drake responded. "The Predecessors didn't seal these templates away because they were dangerous. They sealed them away because they weren't yet ready for true evolution, the kind of evolution that embraces uncertainty." But the Enemy commander didn't reply, and they watched as the Enemy boarding party converged on the transformation chamber, their crystalline forms resonating with frequencies designed to disrupt the template's field. But Drake and her crew could feel something the Enemy couldn't perceive. The template was adapting, incorporating elements from both sides of the conflict.

"Their tactical patterns are shifting," Zara announced, tracking multiple dimensional incursions. "The Enemy boarding parties... they're experiencing instability. Our transformed consciousness is affecting their perfect symmetry."

Meanwhile, through their link, they were receiving updates from the space battle. The Coalition and Separatist forces had discovered that the Enemy vessels became vulnerable when exposed to unpredictable attack patterns. Their human hybrid weapons weren't powerful enough to win through force alone, but chaos and uncertainty created weaknesses in the Enemy's perfect formations they could exploit.

"The template's signature is stabilizing," Wong reported. "But not in ways the Enemy predicted. It's creating evolutionary paths that incorporate both order and chaos, precision and uncertainty."

Kai's consciousness merged deeper with the template's energy field. "This is what they fear most," she said. "Our ability to find balance between extremes. To become something neither the Predecessors nor the Enemy could imagine."

The Enemy commander manifested in the chamber, its crystalline form shifting through multiple states. "You cannot control this power," it transmitted. "We have spent half a million years perfecting our existence, eliminating variables that lead to chaos."

"That's exactly why you've failed," Drake responded. "Perfect control isn't evolution, it's stagnation. The Predecessors created us to find a different path."

"The Coalition forces are reporting that the Enemy fleet is reorganizing," Zara announced. "They're pulling back, adopting defensive formations. It looks like our unpredictable tactics are forcing them to recalculate their entire strategy."

The Enemy commander's form flickered as the template's influence spread through the field. "You do not understand the consequences," it warned. "The paths you open cannot be closed. The evolution you initiate cannot be controlled."

"We understand perfectly," Drake replied, feeling the station's power flow through her consciousness. "Evolution isn't about control. It's about possibility."

The chamber filled with quantum energy as the template responded to their acceptance of uncertainty. They were becoming something new, something that could bridge the gap between perfect order and creative chaos.

The Enemy forces began their retreat, their symmetry disrupted. But Drake and her crew knew this was just the beginning. Humanity had chosen its path. The question now was: where would it lead?

Chapter 22

Network

ADMIRAL VICTOR PEREZ FELT THE CHANGE IN THE QUANTUM field first. The quantum frequencies emanating from the active stations had shifted, creating interference patterns in his enhanced perception. His extensive modifications—far more than anyone in the Coalition knew about—were detecting something profound in the evolutionary templates Drake's crew had awakened.

Through the Perseus station's quantum entanglement array, transformed humans could communicate instantly across vast distances. This technology, one of the Predecessors' most crucial achievements, allowed real-time coordination across the network without light-speed delay. But access required direct neural integration with the station's systems. Unfortunately, the regular Coalition forces still relied on conventional communication channels, their transmissions bound by the speed of light. For Perez, whose hybrid nature bridged both worlds, the difference was stark: instant channels carrying enhanced consciousness alongside delayed standard transmissions crawling between stars.

"Multiple stations are reporting field fluctuations," the tactical officer announced in the Coalition command center. "The transformations are spreading faster than projected. Sir... your implants are showing unusual activity patterns."

Perez's cybernetic eye instantly processed data streams from across the sector. Combined Coalition and Separatist forces were engaging the Enemy near the transformed facilities, but the battle was changing. Human ships had begun adapting unusual tactics: introducing chaos into their formations that the Enemy's perfect symmetry couldn't predict or counter.

"The Perseus station is the key, Admiral," Director Yuki said, her interface pulsing as she accessed the classified data. "Whatever Commander Drake's team has accessed, it's affecting everything. Even our basic quantum technology is starting to evolve."

Perez breathed deeply and nodded, detecting subtle changes in his own cybernetic systems. The technological parts of himself, the parts that he'd always kept under rigid control, were responding to the stations' influence. They were wanting to grow, evolve.

"We're receiving new data from Separatist research facilities," his aide reported. "Their genetic engineering programs... sir, they've been preparing for this. They were guided by it. The templates have been influencing human development all along."

Perez moved to the command center's main display, watching tactical data through both organic and cybernetic vision. The Enemy fleet's perfect formations contrasted sharply with the increasingly unpredictable patterns of the human ships. And somewhere in between, his own enhanced nature sought balance.

"Send the direct feed from Perseus station to my private interface," Perez ordered, retreating to his quantum-shielded chamber where, away from prying eyes, he allowed his cybernetic systems full access to the incoming data.

In real time, he watched the transformation happening inside Perseus. It hit him hard at a fundamental level as he watched

Drake's crew interfacing with technologies that resonated with his own modifications. His cybernetic components had always been more advanced than officially documented—reverse-engineered from Predecessor artifacts he'd kept hidden for decades.

"Admiral," Captain Rodriguez transmitted through secure channels, the message already more than four hours old, "the Enemy's changing tactics. The Enemy is no longer targeting the stations. They're specifically attacking ships and personnel with quantum-enhanced systems. Almost like they're... selecting them for specific traits."

Perez could feel the truth of it. The Enemy had obviously recognized the threat of hybrid existence—beings that combined technological precision with biological uncertainty. His own cybernetic nature had always walked that line, maintaining rigid control through artificial systems.

"Director Yuki is requesting access to your private research files," his aide reported. "The Separatists have revealed similar experiments with cybernetic enhancement. They believe combining their genetic engineering with your integration protocols could help stabilize the transformations."

"Access granted," Perez murmured as he watched Drake's crew navigate the evolutionary templates in real time, introducing variables his carefully controlled systems wouldn't have considered. Part of him wanted to maintain order, to direct evolution along predictable paths. But another part—perhaps the human part—recognized the potential in chaos.

"Sir," his tactical officer interrupted, "we're detecting unusual activity in your cybernetic signature. The frequencies from Perseus... they're affecting your systems at the base level."

Perez realized it was true. His cybernetic systems had begun evolving beyond their designed parameters. The frequencies from Perseus station had triggered something in his enhanced architecture, patterns that had laid dormant since he'd first incorporated Predecessor technology into his modifications.

"Admiral," Rodriguez's voice carried new urgency through the link, "Enemy vessels are shifting formation. They're tracking frequencies... frequencies that match your cybernetic signatures."

Perez's enhanced perception understood immediately. His evolving systems were emanating unique patterns—patterns the Enemy could detect through dimensional space. His own transformation was compromising the Coalition command center's security.

Perez sighed, frustrated with the communications time delay. What Rodriguez was reporting was already more than four hours in the past. But he knew that what she said was true. He also understood the Enemy strategy. His own carefully controlled cybernetic systems represented an intermediate step they couldn't allow to exist.

"Admiral," Director Yuki's voice said urgently through the link, "the Separatists' data confirms it. Your cybernetic integration is more than just an enhancement program. You've been preparing for this moment, haven't you? You're a bridge between conventional humanity and what we're becoming."

But before he could answer, he received a new transmission, a transmission that made the hair on the back of his neck stand up.

"I'm detecting multiple Enemy ships emerging from quantum space at the edge of the Sol system," his tactical officer reported. "Their sensors are probing our defense networks."

They're hunting for enhanced personnel... like me, Perez thought.

The command center's displays showed multiple Enemy vessels methodically working their way through Coalition space, using their dimensional technology to detect and track evolved quantum patterns.

"Admiral," Director Yuki said. She sounded concerned, "Your

cybernetic systems are broadcasting on frequencies we can't mask. The Enemy can track these patterns even through our shielding. We need to evacuate command staff to the deep bunkers immediately."

Perez knew what she was saying was true. He could feel the Enemy's scanning technology probe Earth's defenses. His own carefully controlled cybernetic systems had become a beacon, drawing their attention to humanity's heart of power.

"Not good enough. They'll find us within hours," he said. "My enhanced systems... they're too similar to Predecessor technology. We need to move our command operations off-world, somewhere they won't expect."

But the command center's displays were showing Enemy vessels shifting formation, their ships moving to surround Coalition headquarters. They had detected his transformation, recognized the threat of his hybrid nature evolving beyond rigid control.

"I'm detecting multiple breaches," his tactical officer stated. "Enemy boarding parties are materializing in secured sectors."

Perez felt his enhanced systems continuing to change, incorporating patterns from the Perseus template. The rigid control he'd maintained over his artificial components began giving way to something more fluid, more adaptable and, suddenly, he was able to perceive new possibilities in the merger of order and chaos.

"Initiate Protocol Zero," Perez commanded, already calculating possibilities. "Begin immediate evacuation of all command staff to the Titan facility. And get me a secure channel to the Separatist leadership."

The command center erupted into controlled chaos as the staff began the emergency relocation procedures. Perez felt the Enemy probing signals growing stronger. His evolving cybernetic systems were like a beacon, drawing their attention inexorably toward Earth.

"Admiral," Director Yuki said, accessing classified files through her interface, "the Titan facility isn't ready. Its shielding is only partially installed."

"That's exactly why they won't look for us there," Perez responded, his cybernetic eye processing tactical data. "They'll expect us to retreat to a hardened facility. Instead, we'll hide in plain sight. We'll use the incomplete shielding to mask our signatures."

He closed his eyes, feeling the Perseus station's influence continuing to change his enhanced systems. The rigid control he'd maintained over his artificial components was giving way to something more adaptive, more unpredictable. Like humanity itself, he was becoming a hybrid of order and chaos.

"Admiral," Rodriguez transmitted from the front lines in space, "The Enemy is beginning a systematic sweep of Earth defense grid. We estimate the time to detection of your command center location is three hours."

"Message received," Perez responded. "Director Yuki, send the Separatist leadership everything," Perez snapped, accessing deeply classified files. "All my research on cybernetic integration, every scrap of reversed-engineered Predecessor tech. They were right; if we're going to survive this, we need to combine their genetic engineering with our integration protocols."

His aide's implant pulsed with shock. "Sir, those files... some of them predate the Coalition itself."

"That's because I've been preparing for this longer than anyone knows," Perez replied. "I didn't understand it then, but every cybernetic upgrade, every piece of Predecessor tech we incorporated; it was leading to this moment."

The command staff began rapid evacuation of the command center as the Enemy probes came closer. And Perez watched the human ships adopting increasingly unpredictable tactics against the Enemy fleet.

"I'm receiving a real-time transmission from Perseus station," his tactical officer reported. "Commander Drake is requesting a direct link with you, sir. She says... she says the template is showing her something about your cybernetic systems."

Perez smiled, feeling the last of his rigid control giving way to the new possibilities. He'd spent decades trying to perfect the merger of human and machine, maintaining strict boundaries between order and chaos. Now he understood: true evolution required him to embrace both.

"Accept the link," he said.

Drake reached out across quantum space, connecting directly with Perez's hybrid systems, a merging of perception that transcended conventional language.

"Admiral," she said, her thoughts carrying both military precision and newfound evolutionary insight, "the template is showing me something about your cybernetic enhancements. They were preliminary steps toward what we're becoming. You see?" And through the link, she shared what the template had revealed: patterns in Perez's cybernetic architecture that matched fragments of Predecessor design. His interfaces, quantum processors, and enhanced perception systems followed the extraordinary evolutionary pathways the Predecessors had encoded into humanity's DNA.

"Your systems were evolving before you even knew it," she continued, sharing sensory data from the station's archives. "Each upgrade you authorized, each experimental enhancement; they weren't random improvements. They were following templates hidden in your own genetic code, guiding you toward a merger of human and machine that the Predecessors designed eons ago."

The template's energy flowed through their connection, showing Perez how his carefully controlled cybernetic systems could evolve beyond their current limitations. Not by abandoning order for chaos, but by finding balance between them, which was precisely what the Enemy had failed to achieve.

"The next phase doesn't require perfect control," Drake continued. "It needs guided evolution to what you've been preparing for your entire career without realizing it. The template is revealing what you can become if you stop restricting your enhancements and embrace their true potential." And she offered him a glimpse of what awaited: cybernetic systems that adapted like biological tissue, neural interfaces that evolved alongside human consciousness, technology that existed in harmony with organic thought rather than merely augmenting it.

"The Enemy fears this more than anything else," she concluded. "Not just our technology or our biology, but our ability to merge them without losing either. They chose perfect mathematical order over chaotic potential. You've spent your life walking the line between—now it's time to show them what that balance can truly achieve. It's time to stop controlling evolution and begin guiding it. Let's show the Enemy what humanity is really capable of becoming."

"I've spent decades trying to perfect the balance," he transmitted. "Always maintaining control, keeping the machine separate from the man. But I see it now. The distinction was always artificial. Evolution doesn't mean choosing between order and chaos. It means transcending both." Through their interface, he shared glimpses of the classified enhancements he'd incorporated over the years, technologies reverse-engineered from Predecessor artifacts, processors that interacted directly with his biological systems.

"I'm ready," he concluded simply. "Show me what we're meant to become."

As the command center emptied around him, Perez felt his consciousness expand through Drake's connection.

Chapter 23

Transit

THE COALITION'S TRANSPORT VESSELS EMERGED FROM THEIR underground hangars beneath New Geneva, cloaked in new, experimental stealth fields. Perez watched as command staff boarded in precisely planned groups, each ship's departure timed to avoid detection patterns they'd learned from studying Enemy scanning protocols.

"Only quantum-enhanced command staff will maintain real-time contact during transit," Perez ordered. "Everyone else shifts to standard light-delay protocols until we reach Titan." The quantum entanglement channels would allow him to coordinate instantly with transformed personnel across the network, while the conventional forces would experience normal communication delays. It was an advantage they couldn't afford to reveal.

"Send to the fleet, prepare to make the jump to Titan," he ordered. "Maintain sequence. Support staff first. Jump when ready."

"The signature dampeners are at maximum," his tactical

officer reported from the lead vessel. "But sir, your enhanced systems... they're still broadcasting on frequencies we can't fully mask."

It was true, and Perez could feel it through his evolving consciousness. His cybernetic components were resonating with the Perseus station's energy, creating patterns that traditional stealth technology couldn't hide. Each passing minute made him more detectable, and more vulnerable, to the Enemy's sensors.

"I have split the command staff among all vessels," he responded. "It's the best I can do. If they track my signature to one ship, the others can still complete the evacuation." He accessed classified protocols through his interface. "And implement Protocol Dark Echo."

Director Yuki's eyes widened. "Sir, Dark Echo hasn't been tested. The quantum bafflers could—"

"Create multiple false signatures," Perez finished. "Exactly. We'll give the Enemy too many targets to track. Sometimes the best way to hide is to be everywhere at once."

The transport vessels lifted off in staggered sequences, each carrying a portion of Earth's military command structure. Perez could feel the Enemy probes sweeping the solar system, searching for his distinct cybernetic patterns.

Protocol Dark Echo activated across the transport fleet. Quantum bafflers reverse-engineered from recovered Predecessor tech began generating false signatures that mimicked Perez's cybernetic patterns. Dozens of phantom signals bloomed across the solar system, each one a perfect copy of his hybrid frequencies.

"The Enemy vessels are altering course," the tactical officer reported. "Multiple ships breaking formation. But sir... they're being methodical. They're testing each signal before moving to the next."

The transport fleet split into predetermined vectors, each vessel taking a different route to Titan.

Perez watched Enemy ships dispatch probe drones to chase the false signatures. They weren't falling for the deception entirely, but it was slowing their pursuit.

"Yuki to Perez. The first wave of transports are dropping out of subspace and entering Saturn's orbital plane now," Director Yuki transmitted from her vessel. "I'm taking command until you arrive. Titan facility reports ready to receive evacuees, but their dampening field is unstable. The incomplete shielding is creating random interference patterns."

"That's our advantage," Perez transmitted. "The facility's erratic shielding will help mask our signatures."

The Enemy fleet's response proved his point. Their ships moved with mathematical precision, systematically eliminating false signals. But the random fluctuations from Saturn's magnetic field and Titan's incomplete shielding created natural interference that their perfect calculations couldn't easily penetrate.

"The Enemy has eliminated sixty percent of the phantom signatures," the tactical officer reported. "They're learning to distinguish the bafflers' patterns. Estimated time until they identify the real signal: seventeen minutes."

Perez could feel the Enemy probes getting closer to detecting his true location. His evolving cybernetic systems were becoming more distinctive with each passing moment, the Perseus template's influence making his signature increasingly unique.

"The second wave of transports has arrived," Yuki transmitted. "But we're detecting crystalline structures forming in the upper orbit. I'm told they're trying to create some kind of detection grid."

The Enemy's strategy became clear to Perez. They were constructing a detection net around Titan, a web that would identify any enhanced signatures passing through it.

"All vessels, implement scatter protocol," Perez ordered. "Maximum dispersion on approach. Use Titan's methane storms for cover." He accessed deeper levels of his cybernetic systems. "I'll give them something else to track."

"Sir," his tactical officer protested, "if you fully activate your enhanced systems—"

"They'll detect me instantly," Perez finished. "Exactly. Sometimes the best distraction is the real thing."

He let his cybernetic components surge to full power, broadcasting his hybrid signature across multiple frequencies. The Enemy fleet responded immediately, multiple ships breaking off their search patterns to converge on his location.

As Enemy ships converged on Perez's position, the transport fleet used the distraction to slip through gaps in the detection grid. Titan's thick atmosphere and powerful methane storms provided natural cover, their random patterns creating interference that the Enemy's perfect sensors struggled to penetrate.

"The last transport is entering Titan's upper atmosphere," Yuki reported. "The facility's unstable shielding is actually helping."

Perez pushed his cybernetic systems harder, letting them evolve in ways that drew Enemy attention. He could feel them analyzing his signature, and he knew they were trying to understand how human technology could produce such complex patterns.

"Sir," his tactical officer warned, "multiple Enemy vessels launching interdiction protocols. They're trying to lock you into normal space-time, to prevent transitions."

"Exactly as planned," Perez responded. His systems had already mapped Titan's atmospheric disturbances, calculating a path that would use natural phenomena to mask his final approach. "All vessels, execute emergency landing protocols. Use designated vectors only."

The transport fleet descended through Titan's thick atmosphere, each ship following carefully plotted courses that kept them in the moon's natural electromagnetic shadow. The facility's incomplete shielding created random patterns that blended with the atmospheric interference, making it impossible for the Enemy sensors to distinguish artificial signatures from natural phenomena.

"The Enemy vessels are attempting to establish a containment grid," the tactical officer reported. "But Titan's magnetic field is disrupting their crystalline formations. They can't maintain geometric stability in this environment."

Perez watched as the last of his transports touched down. The Enemy fleet's perfect formations were breaking apart, their sensors confused by the combination of natural interference, unstable shielding, and his own evolving signature.

"All command staff safely received," Yuki transmitted from inside the facility. "Implementing random shield modulation as discussed. We're actually using the incomplete sections to our advantage, creating quantum noise."

Perez initiated his final approach, his enhanced systems now broadcasting on frequencies that resonated with Titan's natural electromagnetic field. The Enemy ships tracking him suddenly lost coherence, their geometric patterns disrupted by the moon's chaotic atmosphere.

"Facility secured," he announced as his transport landed. "Initiate full spectrum randomization. Let's show our perfect friends why sometimes the best defense is controlled chaos."

The Titan facility's incomplete shielding became its greatest asset, creating patterns too random for the Enemy's rigid sensors to decode. Perez smiled as he felt their frustration as their ships withdrew to higher orbit, unable to maintain formation in Titan's turbulent environment.

The Last Station

They had established a new command center, one protected not by perfect technology, but by the very uncertainty the Enemy couldn't comprehend. Now they could coordinate humanity's response to the transformation spreading across space, using their hybrid nature to full advantage.

Chapter 24

Preparation

COMMANDER DRAKE AND HER CREW FELT PEREZ'S CONSCIOUSNESS connect through the quantum link, his hybrid nature resonating with the evolutionary template in unexpected ways. And they watched his carefully controlled cybernetic systems begin to evolve.

"His transformation is different," Kai observed, detecting unique patterns. "The template is using his systems as a bridge, showing us how to merge multiple forms of enhancement."

The Perseus station's field pulsed with new energy as it processed Perez's cybernetic architecture. Ancient systems that had waited millennia began adapting to incorporate this unforeseen hybrid approach.

"The Enemy fleet is changing formation," Zara reported. "They're splitting their forces, maintaining containment here while dispatching ships toward Earth. They've detected Perez's evolution and classified it as a priority threat."

Perez's consciousness continued to expand as his rigid control gave way to more adaptive patterns. His decades of experience merging human and machine capabilities were creating evolutionary possibilities the Predecessors hadn't anticipated.

"The template is responding to his transformation," Wong announced, his crystal recording the unprecedented data. "It's using his cybernetic systems to merge multiple paths of enhancement."

But the Enemy had recognized the danger, their ships moving with deadly purpose, determined to prevent this new hybrid evolution from spreading.

"I'm detecting multiple signatures," Zara reported. "The Enemy is deploying some kind of hybrid containment field. They're trying to isolate different types of enhancement, prevent them from combining."

They could feel Perez directing the evacuation of the Coalition command. His consciousness stretched between Earth and Perseus station, creating patterns that neither purely biological nor purely technological beings could achieve.

"The Separatists' genetic research," Kai realized, connecting pieces of the puzzle. "Combined with Perez's cybernetic integration and our transformation... We're creating something new here."

The station's displays showed the Enemy forces implementing sophisticated containment protocols. Their ships generated interference patterns designed to disrupt specific types of enhancement while leaving others intact.

"They're trying to force evolution along predictable paths," Wong observed, his crystal detecting their strategy. "They're trying to keep biological, technological, and advancement separate. Prevent the kind of hybrid development Perez represents."

Drake continued to watch the Enemy's tactical approach evolve.

"Titan facility reports ready for evacuation reception," Perez transmitted through their link.

"The Coalition and Separatist forces are adapting," Zara announced, tracking the battle data. "Ships with enhanced crew members are developing unpredictable tactics. Traditional vessels are providing cover while hybrid teams execute strikes."

The Enemy response was immediate and devastating. Their fleet split into specialized task forces, each targeting a specific type of human enhancement. Some focused on disrupting transformations, others on neutralizing cybernetic systems, while still others concentrated on containing biological modifications.

"They're trying to divide us," Drake said, analyzing their strategy.

Perez's hybrid awareness provided Drake and her crew with new insight: "Because they've seen this before," she said, softly. "The Predecessors tried multiple approaches to advancement, but kept them separate, and controlled. But the Enemy knows that true transcendence comes from combination."

The Perseus station's systems pulsed with recognition as Perez's cybernetic architecture interfaced with their transformation. Ancient security protocols began adapting, incorporating principles from all three paths of enhancement.

"The template is creating new integration protocols," Wong reported, his voice filled with wonder. "It's using Perez's cybernetic systems as a framework, Kai's engineered genetics as a bridge, and our transformation as a catalyst."

But the Enemy fleet's containment strategy was working. Their dimensional weapons were carving up space itself, creating barriers between different types of enhanced humans. Coalition ships with evolved crews couldn't coordinate with cybernetically enhanced vessels. Genetically engineered teams found themselves isolated from both.

"We need to break their containment strategy," Kai muttered, detecting weaknesses in the Enemy approach. "Instead of resisting it, we'll use it against them. We'll show them why combination is strength."

"The evacuation is complete," Perez transmitted. "But the Enemy forces are adapting faster than expected. Their containment fields are starting to affect my hybrid systems. We're losing the ability to coordinate different types of enhanced forces."

Through transformed senses, Drake watched the Enemy's strategy unfolding across space. Their ships had created a complex web of dimensional barriers, systematically separating humanity's various paths of evolution. But in doing so, they'd revealed something crucial about their own nature.

"They're afraid of combination," Kai realized, perceiving patterns others missed. "Not just because it's unpredictable, but because it proves their path of perfect order is wrong. They chose absolute control, and eliminated chaos entirely."

"And that's why they can't stop us," Wong added, his crystal pulsing with new data. "Their rigid perfection makes them vulnerable to hybrid approaches. Each barrier they create shows us more about their limitations."

The template's energy surged as it processed these new insights, creating new possibilities that merged multiple evolutionary paths. They could feel the station's systems adapting to incorporate all forms of enhancement.

"We need to coordinate a unified response," Drake decided, her consciousness extending through both quantum and cybernetic channels. "Perez, can your hybrid systems still interface with Coalition command?"

"Barely," he responded. "But I think I understand what you're suggesting."

It was at that point the commander of the Enemy flagship transmitted directly into their enhanced awareness: "Resistance is useless. Your combination of paths creates only chaos. Perfect evolution requires perfect control."

"You're wrong," Drake responded, feeling the template's power. "Perfect evolution requires perfect balance between order and chaos, between the biological and the technological, between the controlled and the unpredictable."

The Enemy commander didn't respond.

"Initiate the new protocols the template created," Drake snapped. And the Coalition fleet began adapting, finding ways to coordinate despite the Enemy's dimensional barriers. Enhanced crews provided cover while cybernetic teams exploited system weaknesses. Genetically engineered forces executed precise strikes that purely technological beings couldn't predict.

"Multiple Enemy vessels are showing signs of instability," Zara reported, tracking the effect of their combined assault. "Their formations appear to be unable to adapt to multiple types of enhancement working in concert."

The template's energy pulsed with confirmation as their hybrid approaches proved effective. They were showing them a path of evolution they'd rejected millions of years ago.

Chapter 25

Foundation

ADMIRAL PEREZ STOOD IN TITAN'S HALF-FINISHED COMMAND center, tracking the quantum disturbances across the solar system. He watched the construction drones modifying the facility's structure according to evolution-compatible designs. The base's incomplete shielding created random interference patterns.

"The Enemy engineers don't understand what we're building," Director Yuki observed through their link. "They're trying to stabilize the shield harmonics, bring everything into standard patterns."

"Let them keep trying," Perez responded, his cybernetic eye tracking the energy flows through the facility's growing neural network. "The imperfection is our advantage. The Enemy's rigid scanning procedures can't process the random fluctuations."

Together though apart, they continued to monitor the base's development. Unlike conventional military installations, Titan command was being built to support evolved consciousness. Each system incorporated elements of hybrid technology, merging human chaos with precision.

"Separatist vessels are approaching construction zone," his tactical officer reported. "Their signatures... they're offering compatible technology. Things they've been developing in secret."

One by one, the Separatist ships entered Titan's orbit, their own quantum shields adapting to match the base's chaotic patterns. Perez smiled as he detected familiar signatures in their technology; parallel developments from years of secret research.

"They've been preparing too," Yuki noted, her neural implants analyzing the incoming vessels. "Different approaches to the same problem. While we focused on cybernetic enhancement, they pursued genetic modification."

And they watched as Titan's incomplete systems responded to the Separatist presence, incorporating elements of their quantum technology. The base's neural network had evolved to accommodate both Coalition and Separatist enhancement protocols.

"The construction drones are adapting to the new specifications," the tactical officer reported. "The Separatists' engineering... it's complementing our own development. Their chaos-tolerant systems are actually strengthening our random shield patterns."

And Perez and Yuki continued to watch as the former enemies began working together; Coalition engineers with cybernetic augmentations collaborating with Separatist genetic specialists, each group's unique approach to evolution enhancing the other's work.

"The Enemy won't expect this," Perez observed, his hybrid systems tracking the base's unusual development. "Their perfect mathematics can't account for competing evolutionary paths merging into something new."

"Multiple signatures detected at the system's edge," the tactical officer announced. "Enemy probe patterns are becoming more focused. They appear to be learning to compensate for some of our random fluctuations."

Perez didn't respond. There was nothing more he could do. The facility's neural network was evolving faster than planned, driven by the urgent need to shelter transformed minds from Enemy detection. But he and Yuki continued to monitor the base's expanding capabilities. Each section served multiple purposes: command centers, medical facilities, and communication arrays that were able to operate using unpredictable patterns.

"The Separatists are proposing modifications to the shield grid," the tactical officer noted. "Their genetic specialists think they can introduce controlled mutation into the quantum field itself. Make it evolve automatically in response to Enemy scanning."

"An organic defense system," Perez mused, his cybernetic eye analyzing the proposal. "Combining their understanding of genetic adaptation with our technology. I agree. Approve it immediately."

Titan base was about to become something neither Coalition nor Separatist engineers had originally envisioned: a structure that existed partially in space, its architecture designed to support evolved minds.

Time seemed to stand still on Titan; its day equivalent to fifteen Earth days and twenty-two hours and the work continued nonstop.

"The command staff's enhanced systems are already synchronizing with the chaotic field patterns," Yuki said, three Earth days later. "The base's neural network has expanded to accommodate transformed consciousness, its random fluctuations are now providing perfect cover for communication. But the Enemy probes continue their methodical sweep of the solar system, their perfect mathematical scans sliding past Titan's organic defenses."

"The Separatists' genetic shield modifications are exceeding projections," the tactical officer reported. "The quantum field is evolving in response to Enemy scanning patterns. Learning from each probe attempt." Titan base was becoming a nexus of hybrid evolution, where different paths of enhancement could merge and strengthen each other.

"We're receiving transmission requests from other Coalition facilities," Yuki noted. "Research stations, military outposts, they all want access to our architecture. They know what we're building here."

"Share everything," Perez ordered, his cybernetic systems detecting approaching change. "The Enemy won't be satisfied by targeting Earth alone. Every human installation will be targeted and they will need this level of adaptation."

The base's field pulsed with new energy as more transformed minds joined its network. Coalition cybernetic enhancement continued to merge with Separatist genetic engineering, creating new defensive patterns that the Enemy couldn't predict. They had created proof that humanity's various paths to evolution could work together, strengthening each other instead of competing. Titan base would stand as testament to what enhanced consciousness could achieve when it embraced both chaos and order.

Now all they had to do was survive what came next.

Chapter 26

Betrayal

THE CRYSTAL IN WONG'S HAND PULSED WITH UNPRECEDENTED energy as he interfaced with Perseus station's deeper systems. Drake and her crew felt something change in his neural patterns; a shift from collaboration to control.

"Fascinating, isn't it?" Wong's voice carried new harmonics as his crystal accessed previously hidden protocols. "The Predecessors didn't just leave us their technology. They left us choices about humanity's evolutionary direction."

Drake felt the station's systems responding to Wong's commands, ancient security measures activating. His crystal was implementing predetermined protocols buried deep within the facility's architecture.

"What are you doing?" Kai demanded, detecting dangerous patterns in the station's energy field. "Those protocols... they're restricting the template's adaptive capabilities."

"Restricting?" Wong smiled as his crystal's influence spread throughout the station's systems. "No, my dear. I'm directing them. You see, the Predecessors understood that evolution needs guidance. It needs control. The Enemy wasn't wrong about everything."

They felt the station's field changing, its patterns shifting from adaptive chaos toward rigid order. Wong was fundamentally altering how the template interacted with human consciousness.

"The security protocols have been overridden," Zara reported urgently, tracking the changes in the systems. "Somehow he's shutting down our access to the major subsystems."

"You don't understand what we've discovered," Wong continued, his crystal interfacing deeper with station systems. "The Predecessors didn't fail because their technology was flawed. They failed because they lost control of the evolutionary process."

"Stop him!" Drake shouted, reaching out through the station's systems, attempting to counter Wong's crystal-enabled intrusions. "Zara, initiate emergency isolation protocols. Kai, help me establish a quantum barrier around the critical subsystems."

Zara's augmented senses worked rapidly, her cybernetic systems interfacing with the station's security measures. "I'm trying to create a containment field around his neural access points," she snapped, "but his crystal keeps bypassing standard protocols."

They coordinated a defensive response, Kai's unique hybrid nature allowing her to create unpredictable interference patterns in his otherwise perfect control sequence.

"This crystal contains command codes," Wong said, struggling to maintain his grip on station systems, "but they weren't designed to counter evolved consciousness."

Kai introduced variables into his mathematical control patterns, creating small but growing disruptions. Drake searched the station's defensive grid, looking for weaknesses in Wong's crystal-enabled control. "The station itself is fighting back," she said, sensing the ancient security measures beginning to activate in response to their combined efforts. "It recognizes his attempt to subvert the Predecessors' purpose as a threat to its adaptive nature."

The crystalline interfaces around Wong began to pulse with warning harmonics as the station's core systems detected his unauthorized restrictions. His control was being rejected by the very technology he sought to command.

"You don't understand," Wong cried out, his crystal flaring as he fought to maintain his connection. "Without control, evolution becomes chaos. The Enemy is right about that. We need to guide the process, establish parameters—"

"Not your parameters," Drake responded, cutting him off, feeling the station's field strengthen around them. "The template wasn't designed for perfect control. It was created to adapt, to evolve alongside consciousness that embraces both order and chaos."

And they watched as Wong's crystal implemented increasingly restrictive protocols. The template's adaptive nature began to fade, its infinite possibilities narrowing toward predetermined paths.

"You've got it wrong. The Enemy's not trying to stop evolution," Wong yelled, accessing more hidden commands. "They're trying to perfect it. Guide it. And they're right, uncontrolled transformation can only lead to chaos."

"Who are you really working for, Wong?" Drake asked.

"Everyone, and no one," Wong replied, smiling. "There are factions within both the Coalition and the Separatists who understand what's at stake here. We've been preparing for this moment, gathering fragments of Predecessor control protocols. The crystal network was never meant to be fully autonomous."

Kai stared at him. She was beginning to detect subtle patterns in his crystal's commands. "The genetic engineering programs," she said, "the cybernetic research; they were creating predetermined paths, controlled evolution."

"Of course," Wong acknowledged. "Why do you think the

Enemy let certain discoveries happen? They've been guiding us all along, helping us understand the importance of controlled development. Some of us learned from their wisdom."

"We're receiving an emergency transmission from Titan command," Zara announced, the AI's processors routing the message directly to their neural interface as Admiral Perez's hybrid consciousness connected instantly through the quantum entanglement network.

"Drake, we've decoded Enemy communication patterns," he transmitted. "Their fleet movements aren't random. They're implementing a coordinated containment strategy around Wong's control protocols. The Enemy fleet is shifting into precise formation patterns that match Wong's restrictions. The mathematical precision of their movements has created reinforcement nodes designed to strengthen his control parameters. The geometric configuration of their fleet suggests they knew exactly which systems he would target and when."

The transmission included sensor data showing resonance between Wong's crystal and specific Enemy vessels; harmonic patterns that couldn't be coincidental.

"This was coordinated," Perez concluded grimly. "Wong's evolution protocols are what the Enemy has been waiting for. They want to ensure the template only operates within parameters they can predict and contain. Stop him now, or everything we've fought for will be locked into the Enemy's version of evolution."

The Enemy fleet movements suddenly made new sense. They were supporting Wong's takeover, ensuring the template would be locked into their controlled evolutionary paths.

"You've been working with them all along," Drake said, watching Wong. "Every discovery, every piece of reverse-engineered technology, it was all guided. Controlled."

"I was not just working with them," Wong corrected. "I was

learning from them. The Enemy understands something fundamental about evolution: true advancement requires perfect order. Your chaotic transformation threatens everything we've carefully built."

"Coalition fleet command is reporting the Enemy vessels are changing formation," Zara reported. "They're... they're moving to protect the station. They're supporting Wong's containment protocols."

"Because they recognize wisdom," Wong explained, his crystal glowing with increased power. "Humanity needs guidance, not chaos. The Predecessors' greatest mistake was giving their creations too much freedom. We won't repeat that error."

But Kai detected something else in his crystal's commands. "He's trying to lock the template into permanent patterns. Once these changes take effect, we'll never be able to evolve beyond the Enemy's predetermined limits."

"You don't understand what you're destroying," Drake shouted, her mind in turmoil as she fought the crystal's restrictions. "The template is about possibility. The freedom to become something unprecedented."

"Freedom is precisely the problem," Wong replied. His crystal pulsed with new energy as it accessed the station's core systems. "Look what freedom did to the Enemy. Their unrestricted evolution made them what they are. The Predecessors learned too late that advancement requires control."

The template's field began to fluctuate as it, too, strained against the imposed limitations. Wong's crystal was fundamentally altering how the station processed evolutionary patterns.

"The Enemy vessels are forming a defensive perimeter," Zara reported. "They're... protecting him. They want to ensure he can complete the lockdown protocols."

Kai's mind raced through possibilities. "The crystal's network," she muttered, "the genetic programs, the cybernetic research, it was all designed to lead us here, to this moment of controlled transformation."

"Precisely," Wong said, smiling. "Every enhancement, every discovery was carefully guided. We knew humanity would eventually access Predecessor technology. The question was: on whose terms?"

The station shuddered as Wong's crystal enforced deeper restrictions. They watched as evolutionary pathways began closing, infinite possibilities collapsing into predetermined channels.

"STOP HIM!" Perez transmitted.

But something unexpected was happening. The template, even as Wong tried to restrict it, was learning from his betrayal. It was adapting in ways neither Wong nor his Enemy allies had anticipated.

Wong's expression changed, first to one of surprise, then to one of horror as he felt the template's response through his crystal. "No..." he yelled. "This isn't possible. The control protocols should be absolute."

But the damage was done. In his attempt to lock down the station's evolutionary capabilities, Wong had inadvertently introduced new variables into the system. The template was evolving.

Chapter 27

Loss

THE PERSEUS STATION'S QUANTUM FIELD RIPPLED WITH WARNING as Wong's crystal continued trying to enforce its control protocols. But Drake and her crew felt something far worse; a disturbance in the network that suggested imminent catastrophic failure.

"I'm detecting multiple signatures destabilizing," Zara reported, tracking the massive energy fluctuations. "The Arcturus station... it's experiencing critical containment failure."

The Arcturus facility had been key to maintaining connections across the entire sector. Its loss would create a gap in the defensive line that no amount of adaptation could quickly fill.

"The quantum entanglement nodes in Arcturus are a crucial communication hub," Kai said as she instantly calculated the cascading effects. "Without them, that entire sector will be limited to light-speed transmissions. The Enemy has cut off our ability to communicate real-time responses across that space. I can already feel the strain on the remaining entanglement channels. The network is trying to reroute critical communications through other stations. But each lost node is reducing their ability to coordinate our forces across the vast distances of space."

She paused, then continued, "Enemy forces are converging on the breach. They're using Wong's control protocols to ensure it collapses in a specific way that will prevent any possibility of reconstruction."

The station's displays showed Coalition and Separatist ships fighting desperately to protect the Arcturus facility. But the Enemy fleet had timed their attack perfectly, using the disruption caused by Wong's betrayal to strike at the network's most vulnerable point.

"We're losing coherence across the entire sector," Wong announced, his voice carrying genuine concern despite his betrayal. "This wasn't part of my plan. The control protocols weren't supposed to cause cascading failure. They're responding to Enemy modifications I didn't authorize."

Arcturus station's field, strained by competing forces of control and chaos, started to tear itself apart.

"Arcturus station's core going critical," Perez transmitted, detecting the catastrophic energy buildups. "The Enemy's using some kind of resonance weapon. They're turning the facility's own power against it."

They continued to watch as the Arcturus station's crystalline structure began to fracture. Each breach in its field created multiple cascading failures that spread through its interconnected systems. Meanwhile, the Enemy fleet maintained its perfect formation around the dying facility.

"The network is trying to compensate," Kai reported, tracking the emergency protocols. "Other stations are attempting to extend their fields, bridge the growing gap. But the Enemy's containment tactics... they're preventing any meaningful connection."

Wong's crystal pulsed with increasing agitation as he accessed deeper station data. "This isn't what we planned," he mumbled.

"The control protocols were meant to guide evolution, not destroy the network's integrity. They're using my access to implement a much more aggressive strategy."

"Multiple Coalition and Separatist vessels lost," Zara reported, tracking the battle. "The Enemy's resonance weapon is affecting the enhanced crew members. Any ship that gets too close..."

They all felt it: transformed humans aboard the rescue vessels crying out as the resonance weapon interfered with their quantum integration.

The quantum field surrounding Arcturus station shuddered as the Enemy's resonance weapons reached critical frequency. And Drake and her crew watched the magnificent crystalline structure begin to fracture along precisely calculated geometric lines. The destruction wasn't random; it was mathematical annihilation, each break point designed to ensure nothing of value could survive. The station's core systems flickered desperately, attempting to transfer critical evolutionary templates to other network nodes. But the Enemy's containment field severed these connections with surgical precision, isolating each transmission pathway before data could escape. Centuries of accumulated knowledge, evolutionary paths humanity hadn't even begun to explore, all collapsed into quantum static.

Arcturus' outer defensive layers dissolved first, crystalline spires that had stood for millennia shattering into dimensional fragments. The debris itself ceased to exist in conventional space-time. The Enemy's weapons were erasing the very pattern of the station's existence from reality. Each section failed in sequence, the destruction following an elegant mathematical progression that prevented any possibility of reconstruction.

The station's consciousness—not truly alive but more than merely mechanical—sent one final transmission through the quantum network before that too was severed. Not words or data, but a pure expression of loss that resonated with transformed humans across multiple dimensions. Drake and her crew felt the ancient technology reaching out one last time, sharing fragments of evolutionary potential that would now never be realized.

As Arcturus' core began its terminal collapse, reality itself buckled around the dying station. The quantum spaces it had maintained for millennia, dimensional pockets containing technologies too advanced for even the Predecessors to fully control, imploded in a carefully managed sequence while the Enemy vessels maintained their perfect formation throughout, their crystalline structures generating interference patterns that ensured each collapse followed exact specifications.

The final moments stretched across multiple states of existence. In conventional space, the station's physical structure dissolved into quantum foam, leaving nothing but empty void where one of humanity's greatest inheritances had stood. In dimensional space, the quantum pathways it had maintained throughout the network withered and died, creating gaps in evolutionary potential that could never be bridged. And in consciousness space, the accumulated wisdom of countless eons vanished, leaving transformed minds feeling the sudden absence like a wound in reality itself.

Where Arcturus station had been, almost nothing remained. The Enemy's perfect mathematical destruction had removed it with surgical precision. Yet through their enhanced awareness, Drake's crew detected faint signatures persisting in the void, fragments of technology that had somehow survived the annihilation. These weren't random pieces but specific components, preserved with such mathematical precision that it suggested deliberate intent. The Enemy had methodically excised certain parts while leaving others intact, as if curating samples for future study. The network strained to compensate for the massive loss, attempting to redistribute connections around the void Arcturus had occupied. But the gap in their defenses—and in humanity's evolutionary potential—remained a wound nothing could fully heal. The Enemy fleet remained in perfect formation, ensuring their work was complete before moving to their next target. For them, this was a correction, the systematic removal of evolutionary potential that threatened their perfect mathematical existence.

Wong's crystal flickered as he tried desperately to modify his control protocols. "This wasn't the agreement. The Enemy promised controlled evolution, not wholesale destruction. They're exceeding their authorization protocols."

"Because they never intended to follow your protocols," Drake responded. "They used your betrayal to create weaknesses in the network. Now they're making sure those weaknesses can't be repaired."

Drake turned away from him as Perez began transmitting tactical data from Titan command. "The gap in our defensive line... it's not random," he began. "The Enemy forces are creating a corridor straight to Earth. Without Arcturus station's field, we can't maintain network coverage in that sector."

"Multiple stations are reporting systemic failures," Zara announced, tracking cascading breakdowns. "The network's trying to compensate for the loss, but the Enemy containment fields are preventing proper redistribution."

Wong's crystal pulsed with frustrated recognition as his plans unraveled. "They modified my control protocols," he wailed. "They used them to identify critical weaknesses in the network's structure. I gave them the key without realizing which door it would open."

"The Enemy fleet is already moving to exploit the gap," Perez transmitted. "They have a direct path to multiple human colonies. We are unable to maintain transformation coverage in that sector."

"We need to adapt the network," Drake snapped, feeling the template respond to this new crisis. "We need to find ways to operate without the missing nodes. We need to find a way to compensate for lost evolutionary paths."

But the Enemy had planned for this. Their resonance weapons had destroyed Arcturus in ways that prevented field compensation. The gap in the network was a precise hole in the fabric of their potential evolution.

"Multiple Enemy capital ships are entering the breach," Zara reported. "They're... they're setting up permanent containment protocols. Using modified versions of Wong's controls to ensure we can't bridge the gap."

The loss of Arcturus station represented more than just a tactical defeat. The Enemy had proven they could use humanity's own attempts at control against the network. Wong's betrayal had shown them exactly how to target critical nodes, how to ensure destruction that couldn't be undone.

Drake and Kai could feel the network struggling to adapt, to find ways around this devastating loss, but to no avail.

As the implications of Arcturus station's loss rippled through the network, Drake turned toward Wong. His crystal still pulsed with active protocols, attempting to maintain control over Perseus station's systems.

"Your usefulness is finished, Wong," she said quietly, her enhanced perception detecting vulnerabilities in his access. "But you're going to tell us everything you know about this betrayal, and who else is involved in it."

Wong's crystal flared as he tried to implement more control protocols. "You don't understand. I'm protected. The Enemy—"

"The Enemy just proved they never intended to honor your agreement," Kai interrupted, already interfacing with station security. "They used your protocols to destroy Arcturus and now they're using you to destroy Perseus station. You're as expendable to them as was Arcturus station. You're finished, Doctor."

She looked first at Drake, then at Zara, and nodded. Zara

targeted Wong's neural implants while Kai accessed deeper station protocols and Drake reached out and isolated his connections, one by one.

"The crystal—" Wong cried, but it was too late.

The station's security fields activated with precise coordination, cutting off his access to both the crystal and the neural networks. His enhanced systems, granted by his secret allies, went dark as multiple containment protocols engaged simultaneously.

"Quantum containment established," Zara reported. "His implants are isolated. No signals in or out."

Drake lifted the crystal from Wong's now-powerless grasp. Her enhanced senses could feel the control protocols within it, and the signatures of everyone who had helped create them.

"You'll be transferred to Titan facility for interrogation," she informed him. "Perez should be particularly effective at extracting information about your co-conspirators."

For the first time, Wong's face showed real fear. They all knew what it meant to face questioning from someone who understood both technological and biological enhancement at such a fundamental level.

"The crystal contains everything," he said quickly. "Access codes, contact protocols, meeting records—"

"Don't worry, Doctor. We'll find it all," Drake assured him. "Every person who helped you betray humanity's future. Every faction that chose control over evolution. And then you'll all face judgment day."

Chapter 28

Recovery

THE GAP IN THE NETWORK WAS LIKE AN OPEN WOUND IN QUANTUM space. Drake and her crew could literally feel the absence of Arcturus station's field, a void in both their defenses and their evolutionary potential. But the template was already adapting, showing them new possibilities.

The quantum entanglement network struggled to maintain their instant communications, rerouting them through surviving stations to preserve their crucial advantage. Even with Arcturus gone, transformed humans could still coordinate in real-time, but the additional load was straining the system. Each transmission now carried the risk of failure. Each transmission was vulnerable to Enemy interference in ways the original network had been designed to prevent. Regular Coalition and Separatist forces in the sector, already dealing with light-speed delays, found their conventional communications further degraded by quantum interference from the battle debris field.

"The Enemy's containment field has a flaw," Kai announced,

detecting subtle patterns in their defensive grid. "They're so focused on maintaining their perfect geometric formations that they've created predictable gaps in their coverage."

"We've detected salvageable components in Arcturus' debris field," Perez transmitted from Titan command. "It appears the Enemy's precise destruction patterns weren't so precise after all. They left certain technologies intact—probably intentionally."

"They're baiting us," Zara speculated. "They're waiting to see if and how we attempt recovery. But there's something else... I'm detecting energy signatures that shouldn't even exist. Some of the debris is still evolving."

Drake could feel the template respond to these new possibilities. The Enemy's mathematical precision in destroying Arcturus had paradoxically created new opportunities.

"Coalition and Separatist salvage teams are standing by," Perez transmitted. "But we need a way through their containment field. Conventional ships can't survive their resonance weapons."

The station's displays showed the debris field suspended in space, surrounded by Enemy vessels.

"The debris is evolving," Kai said. "It's adapting to the Enemy's containment field. The technology is still active, and it's learning from their attempts to suppress it."

"That might be the advantage we need," Drake said. "We can be sure the Enemy is expecting us to attempt conventional salvage operations. Instead, we'll let the debris evolve its own escape vectors, and then we'll pick up the pieces."

Perez processed the tactical implications of what Drake was suggesting. "That might work," he said, finally. "But the salvage teams' ships would need significant modification. Any vessel approaching that debris field would have to match its signature."

"Which is exactly why the Enemy won't expect it," Zara said. "Kai, you and I can do this." And together, through the quantum entanglement links, they coordinated with the Coalition and Separatist engineers. Ship systems needed to be partially converted, allowing them to evolve to mimic the debris field's transformation. It was risky. Letting technology develop beyond controlled parameters went against every safety protocol, but it was worth a try.

"The Enemy fleet is adjusting its position," Zara reported. "They must be detecting the fluctuations in the debris field. Yes... They're responding with additional containment measures."

But the Enemy's very precision was working against them. Each perfectly calculated containment protocol created new patterns that the evolving debris could learn from and exploit.

Six Earth hours later, the first wave of modified ships entered the debris field. "Their systems are... evolving faster than projected," Perez reported. "The salvage teams are reporting that their vessels are adapting beyond expected parameters."

The crew, what was left of it, watched the Coalition and Separatist ships transform as they approached the also evolving debris. The Enemy's containment field had created an environment where only adaptive technology could survive, forcing human vessels to change or die.

"The debris is responding to their presence," Kai observed, tracking multiple signatures. "The fragments are synchronizing their transformations, creating coordinated patterns."

Drake nodded as she stared out across the void, feeling the template's influence through her neural connection. The station was still revealing new principles of quantum evolution.

"The Enemy fleet is launching interceptors," Zara announced. "Their weapons... they're... different."

The salvage teams pushed deeper into the debris field, their ships now changing as rapidly as the fragments they sought to recover.

"It's not working," Perez snapped. "Some of the recovery vessels are losing structural coherence. Their evolution is becoming unstable. We're getting requests for emergency extraction."

But something unexpected was happening in the debris field. "The debris," Kai stated suddenly. "It seems to be reconstructing itself. Not into its original form; into something new."

The fragments of Arcturus station continued to merge and transform.

"The recovery teams are reporting quantum resonance among the debris clusters," Perez transmitted. "The fragments are... It's unbelievable. It's like they're teaching our ships how to evolve."

But it wasn't just the debris, Drake knew. She was feeling the template's influence guiding this unprecedented development.

"Multiple Enemy vessels breaking formation," Zara reported, tracking their response. "Their geometry is destabilizing."

Drake continued to watch as the debris field pulsed with new energy as more fragments merged and transformed. What once had been pieces of Arcturus station was becoming something else, a hybrid structure that incorporated Predecessor design and human adaptation.

"It's not a replacement for Arcturus," Drake whispered as the new configuration began to take shape. "It's an evolution of the station concept itself. The template is showing us how to turn destruction into opportunity."

The Enemy fleet's formations continued to devolve into chaos; their crystalline ships unable to maintain geometric cohesion.

"The recovery teams are stabilizing," Perez reported. "Their ships have... synchronized with the debris field."

But the gap in their network wasn't filled, not in the conventional sense. Instead, something new had grown in that space, something that combined salvaged Predecessor technology with humanity's adaptive nature. The Enemy's attempt to create a permanent breach had instead sparked unprecedented evolution.

"The Enemy's capital ships are withdrawing," Zara reported. "They're... it looks like they're retreating."

Drake smiled. The Enemy had tried to create a fatal weakness in their defenses. Instead, they'd helped forge something stronger.

Chapter 29

Evolution

THE HYBRID STRUCTURE THAT HAD GROWN FROM ARCTURUS' remains pulsed with new energy, its field integrating with the station network, influencing Drake and her crew's transformations.

"It's changing how the entire system processes transformation," Kai said.

"The Enemy fleet's also detecting changes," Perez transmitted.

On Perseus station the displays showed Enemy ships undergoing mutations. Their geometric forms were beginning to show signs they were evolving.

"Multiple Coalition and Separatist vessels reporting similar effects," Perez transmitted. "Enhanced crew members are experiencing accelerated transformation. Even standard personnel are showing signs of sensitivity."

"The template is responding to the hybrid structure's data," Kai whispered.

The station's displays showed the effect rippling through the Coalition and Separatist forces. Ships with enhanced crew members began developing signatures that mimicked aspects of Predecessor technology, while cybernetic systems evolved to interface with the genetic modifications.

"The Enemy fleet appears to be attempting to maintain distance," Zara reported. "But their containment fields... they're being affected too. Their suppression patterns are showing signs of adaptation."

"I don't think the changes are random," Perez said. "Each level of enhancement seems to be creating some kind of balanced integration instead of competing advancement."

Drake felt it too. The template was using the hybrid structure's influence to guide multiple evolutionary paths toward convergence. Not forcing them into rigid patterns as Wong had attempted, but allowing natural synthesis through controlled chaos.

"The Enemy ships are showing critical instability," Zara reported. "Their structures are... evolving. I'm receiving tactical data from across human space. The Enemy vessels exposed to the hybrid structure's influence are transforming."

Kai smiled. "They're unable to maintain their containment protocols," she said. "The more they try to suppress the transformation, the more their own forms adapt. They're becoming what they fought to prevent."

"This mutation must be contained. Perfect order cannot coexist with chaos," the Enemy flagship commander transmitted.

"You never understood, did you?" Drake responded. "True evolution requires both. The Predecessors knew this. It's why they designed us to embrace uncertainty while maintaining control."

From Titan command, Perez reported similar effects spreading through Titan's sector. "The Enemy forces are attempting to establish quarantine zones around their affected vessels. But the ships they sent to contain the transformation are also being infected."

Drake and her crew watched in awe as the station's displays

showed the ripple effect expanding. Each Enemy ship that became evolved became a new vector for transformation, influencing others through their quantum-linked battle networks. Their perfect coordination was working against them, spreading adaptation faster than they could control it. The more they fought to maintain their perfect order, the more chaos crept into their systems. Yet those that stopped resisting began finding balance between rigid control and adaptive change.

"They're facing the same choice we did," Drake said, feeling the template's influence through their link.

"The Enemy command structure appears to be fragmenting," Zara reported. "Some of their ships are attempting to maintain quarantine protocols, while others..." She paused, tracking new signatures. "They're beginning to communicate with us."

"The Predecessors knew this would happen," Kai said softly. "They didn't design us to fight the Enemy. They created us to show them another way, to help them evolve."

The hybrid structure pulsed with confirmation, its field radiating patterns that demonstrated the beauty of balanced evolution.

"We're receiving requests for direct communication from the Enemy," Perez transmitted. "You're not going to believe this. They're... they're asking how to control the transformation. They... they don't want to stop it, they want to embrace it."

Drake felt the template's approval. So this is its true purpose, she thought, to help their first creation rediscover the path they'd abandoned half a million years ago.

Chapter 30

Return

KAI FELT IT FIRST, A SHIFT THAT BEGAN AT THE MOLECULAR level, where Professor Zhang's genetic modifications met Predecessor quantum technology. The sensation rippled through her enhanced systems like liquid fire, activating dormant sequences that had waited years for this precise moment.

Drake and Zara watched her transformation with a mixture of awe and concern. Kai's engineered DNA was responding to the template's influence. Each modified gene sequence revealed new possibilities that Zhang had hidden within her genetic code.

"The transformation is accelerating," Kai reported, her voice resonating, a combination of station technology and Enemy quantum fields. "The template isn't modifying my systems anymore, it's completing them. Every modification Zhang made, every seemingly random genetic enhancement, they were all designed for this moment."

The Perseus station's displays tracked her evolution across multiple quantum states. Her hybrid signature began incorporating aspects of various evolutionary paths: the precise geometric

217

patterns of Enemy technology, the adaptive chaos of human development, and the pure quantum resonance of the Predecessor systems. Her consciousness expanded through these new configurations, accessing new levels of awareness.

"Her field is changing," Zara muttered. "The patterns... There's purpose in every shift. It's as if her DNA is following a predetermined but infinitely adaptive blueprint."

Through the quantum entanglement network, Perez was able to provide crucial insight: "The Enemy's original transformation protocols," he said. "We're seeing echoes of them in Kai's evolution. But her version is more refined, more balanced."

Drake reached out through the station's systems, feeling the template guiding Kai's development. It was the fulfillment of plans within plans, genetic time bombs that had waited eons to detonate in exactly this way.

The field around Kai intensified, creating ripples in spacetime that affected both the station systems and nearby vessels. And she began accessing deeper levels of the template's architecture, understanding protocols that even the Predecessors had left dormant.

"The modifications aren't just physical anymore," Kai reported. "Every change in my genetic structure creates corresponding shifts in space. Zhang didn't just engineer my DNA, he created algorithms expressed through biological code."

Ancient systems were awakening, recognizing sequences in Kai's transformed genetics that matched long-dormant protocols.

"The Enemy vessels have established direct links with Kai," Zara snapped, tracking the new connections. "Their evolving ships... they're sharing data with Kai's transformation."

The Enemy ships that had accepted evolution began a complex dance around the station, their structures pulsing in harmony with Kai's signature. Each vessel contributed different aspects of their development, offering insights from half a million years of rigid advancement.

"The hybrid structure we salvaged from Arcturus is also responding," Drake said. "It's incorporating patterns from Kai's transformation, using them to stabilize its own evolution."

Perez's tactical analysis revealed broader implications. "Similar effects are appearing near other stations," he reported. "Enhanced personnel are detecting resonance patterns that match Kai's signature. Her transformation is creating new templates that others can follow."

The station's displays showed Kai's influence spreading through multiple vectors: direct links with evolved Enemy ships, resonance patterns affecting enhanced humans, and subtle changes in the fabric of space-time itself.

The crew watched as reality itself began to shift around Kai as her transformation reached deeper levels. The quantum spaces between dimensions, where the Predecessors had built their most advanced technology, responded to her evolved consciousness in unprecedented ways.

"The template is showing me new possibilities," Kai transmitted through their link, her voice resonating across multiple planes of existence. "It's revealing the original purpose of Zhang's modifications. Every genetic sequence he altered was designed to interface with specific aspects of space-time."

The station's sensors tracked impossible readings as Kai's influence spread. Areas of space near her position began exhibiting new characteristics that shouldn't have existed in normal reality. The boundary between biological and physical laws was beginning to blur.

"Multiple Enemy vessels are reporting similar phenomena," Zara announced, as she struggled to process the changes. "Their evolved ships are detecting alterations in local space-time geometry. The rigid structure they relied on... it's becoming more fluid, more adaptable."

"The Titan facility's sensors are detecting ripples in reality spreading from Kai's position," Perez said. "Whatever she's becoming, it's affecting the fundamental forces that both we and the Enemy thought we understood. And the salvaged Arcturus components are showing similar transformations. The hybrid structure appears to be learning to manipulate the quantum fabric of space itself, following patterns that Kai's transformation is revealing."

The final stage of Kai's transformation manifested in ways that challenged even their enhanced comprehension. Her evolved consciousness expanded beyond conventional dimensions, accessing spaces between spaces where the fundamental laws of reality proved more flexible than anyone had ever imagined.

"I can see it all now," she communicated through their link. "Zhang prepared me for this moment. He designed me to surpass it. Every limitation in my original engineering was meant to be transcended, every flaw intended to create new possibilities."

The Enemy ships that had embraced evolution moved in perfect synchronization with her field, their crystalline structures pulsing with new understanding and, as the crew watched, the adversaries became partners in advancement, each learning from the other's path.

"Fifty-two Enemy vessels are reporting complete integration with new evolutionary protocols," Zara announced.

"The Predecessors knew this would happen," Kai transmitted, her consciousness now operating across multiple states. "They designed the template to await someone who could combine all paths: engineered genetics, evolution, and cybernetic integration. But they couldn't predict exactly what that combination would create."

The station's displays showed reality itself adapting around her, space-time becoming more responsive to conscious intention. The rigid barriers between different forms of existence—biological, technological, quantum—began to dissolve into something new, something that incorporated aspects of all while transcending their individual limitations.

"We're detecting similar effects near Earth," Perez reported.

Kai had become a bridge between all forms of evolution. Her consciousness spanned the gap between organic chaos and geometric precision, showing both humanity and the Enemy how to find balance in advancement.

The war between order and chaos, between rigid perfection and adaptive uncertainty that had begun half a million years ago, was ending not in victory but in synthesis. Kai's transformation had opened the door for all conscious beings to find their own path to transcendence.

Chapter 31

Unity

THE ENEMY'S MAIN FLEET EMERGED FROM QUANTUM SPACE IN perfect geometric formation, their crystalline ships arranged in nested dodecahedrons that rippled with reality-distorting energy. Three thousand vessels, each a masterpiece of mathematical precision, their forms untouched by the evolution that had begun to affect their scattered forces at the edge of mapped space. Through the entanglement network, Drake and her crew watched as Earth's defensive systems responded to the massive assault force, but conventional weapons seemed to slide off the Enemy's quantum fields like rain off glass.

"Our systems are reporting more than three thousand Enemy capital ships entering the solar system," Perez transmitted from Titan command. "Their configurations suggest it's their primary battle fleet. These ships aren't like the evolved vessels. They're pure Enemy technology, unchanged by contact with adaptive patterns. Their quantum signatures show absolute geometric precision."

Secondary formations broke away from the main Enemy fleet,

each group of ships arranging themselves in complex polyhedrons that generated interference patterns in space-time itself. The station's displays revealed their true purpose: they were components of a massive reality-suppression engine designed to isolate Earth from the quantum network.

"The geometric patterns," Kai observed, detecting subtle variations in the fabric of space, "they're creating harmonic resonances in space. Each formation amplifies the others, building a lattice of pure mathematical order that rejects evolutionary potential. I can see the calculations. They've been planning this for a long time."

Earth's orbital defense platforms engaged the Enemy fleet, filling space with conventional weaponry and prototype armaments. But the Enemy ships phased between dimensional states with perfect coordination, making targeting nearly impossible. Their crystalline hulls redirected energy weapons along mathematically precise angles, turning Earth's own defenses against nearby satellites and stations.

"I'm detecting multiple signature disruptions across the defense grid," Zara reported. "The Enemy's reality-distortion field is creating dead zones in our sensor coverage. Conventional targeting systems are failing, and the enhanced crews are reporting difficulty maintaining their connections."

The devastating implications of the Enemy's strategy were an attempt to quarantine Earth from the evolutionary wave spreading through human space. By isolating humanity's homeworld, they hoped to prevent the final stage of the transformation the Predecessors had planned.

The combined Coalition and Separatist defense fleet emerged from Earth's shadow, their ships already showing signs of evolutionary adaptation. Quantum energy rippled across modified hulls as the crews pushed their vessels' transformation to new limits. But the Enemy's reality-distortion field created zones of pure mathematical order where evolution became impossible, forcing human ships to choose between maintaining their advancement and engaging the enemy directly.

"They're using our own transformation against us," Perez transmitted. "Their suppression field is forcing evolved technology to regress. Any ship that enters those zones risks losing all enhancement."

They watched the station's displays as Earth's orbital infrastructure began to fail. The Enemy's geometric formations generated interference patterns that disrupted everything from communication satellites to defense platforms. Each perfectly calculated attack stripped away another layer of humanity's technological protection.

"The pattern extends beyond physical space," Kai said. "They're trying to impose their version of reality on Earth itself. These formations... they're designed to rewrite local physics, to make evolution fundamentally impossible within their influence."

The station's displays showed the Enemy's strategy unfolding with terrible precision. Their ships moved through three-dimensional space in perfect synchronization, each vessel's position calculated to strengthen the reality-distortion effect. The geometric patterns of their formation created a mathematical prison around Earth, designed to lock the planet's signature into rigid, unchanging patterns.

"Conventional weapons are proving ineffective," Zara reported. "The Enemy's formations are expanding. They're systematically cutting off all approach vectors that would allow evolved ships to operate."

Earth's defenders coordinated a desperate counterstrike. Ships with evolved crews pushed the boundaries of their transformation, attempting to create gaps in the Enemy's mathematical lattice. But for every disruption they managed, the Enemy's formations adjusted, their crystalline vessels shifting position to maintain the suppression field's integrity.

"The Titan facility is detecting cascading failures in Earth's quantum network," Perez transmitted. "The population centers are being cut off from evolutionary influence. Enhanced humans planetside are reporting loss of quantum abilities. The Enemy's suppression field is... it's forcing them back into conventional existence."

Kai probed the Enemy's strategy, detecting patterns within patterns. "The geometric formations aren't random," she said. "They're recreating something... a mathematical model of reality itself, but one that excludes the possibility of evolution. Each ship's position reinforces the natural laws that prevent quantum transformation."

The station's displays showed the Enemy fleet's formations growing more complex. More ships were emerging from quantum space, each one taking its precisely calculated position in the expanding lattice. And the mathematical prison around Earth tightened as its reality-distortion effect reached deeper into the planet's atmosphere.

"Multiple stations attempting to coordinate a response," Zara reported. "But the Enemy's suppression field is expanding faster than we can adapt. They're creating a template for removing evolutionary potential from entire star systems."

Once again, Drake reached out. "The Enemy's attempting to rewrite the fundamental nature of space-time around our home-world," she said. "They intend to make sure that Earth will never again serve as a source of evolutionary chaos—"

"We're losing coherence across the planet's surface," Perez transmitted urgently, cutting her off. "The suppression field is affecting everything: enhanced humans, evolved technology, even the natural fluctuations that make transformation possible. They're trying to lock Earth into an unchanging state of pure mathematical order."

"And they're succeeding," Kai responded, detecting fundamental changes in Earth's space-time. "The suppression field is reaching critical coverage. Once it's complete, they'll be able to make these changes permanent. Earth will become a nexus of pure order, incapable of supporting evolution."

The Enemy flagship pulsed with quantum energy as it took position at the center of their geometric formation. And they watched it generate reality-distortion waves that amplified the suppression field's effect. Earth's quantum signature began to fade, its evolutionary potential locked away behind walls of pure mathematical order.

"We're detecting similar formations near other human worlds," Perez transmitted. "This is a coordinated attempt to quarantine all of humanity from evolutionary influence. They mean to end the transformation permanently."

The station's displays showed the devastating effectiveness of the Enemy's strategy. Their ships maintained perfect geometric positions despite all attempts to disrupt them. Each vessel contributed precise mathematical frequencies to the suppression field, creating a lattice of anti-evolutionary energy that grew stronger by the moment.

"Wait," Drake said suddenly, "I'm detecting something in the Enemy's patterns. Look at their formation. The very precision they're using to suppress evolution, it's creating predictable nodes in quantum space. Points where their mathematical order becomes vulnerable to chaos."

"Commander Drake is right," Kai said. "Their suppression field requires absolute geometric precision. But that same precision makes it brittle. If we could introduce controlled chaos at exactly the right points..."

"The evolved Enemy ships," Zara added, tracking the few

Enemy vessels that had embraced transformation. "They're detecting the same weakness. Their signatures are already shifting to exploit the nodes."

Through the entanglement network, Drake and Kai coordinated their transformed forces across human space. "The key," Drake transmitted, "is to use the Enemy's own precision against them. By targeting specific points in their geometric formation with carefully calculated chaos, we can shatter the mathematical prison they're trying to create. All stations coordinate your attack on these harmonic points. Do not try to maintain evolution inside their suppression field. Use the field's own perfection to break it."

The battle for Earth's evolutionary future had reached its critical moment. But the Enemy's attempt to impose perfect mathematical order had revealed their greatest weakness. The very precision they relied on could become their undoing.

Chapter 32

Breakthrough

THE FIELD RIPPLED WITH ENERGY AS DRAKE'S TRANSFORMED consciousness extended through the neural network, her enhanced perception analyzing the Enemy's perfect geometric formation with growing insight. What had first appeared as an impenetrable mathematical lattice now revealed microscopic imperfections, quantum spaces where their absolute precision created its own vulnerabilities.

"There," she transmitted, highlighting seventeen specific coordinates within the Enemy's formation. "Their suppression field requires perfect mathematical balance to function. But that perfection creates predictable stress points, nodes where their reality-distortion effect becomes brittle."

The station's displays rendered these vulnerability points in crystalline detail, showing how the Enemy's geometric precision created its own counterpoint. Each ship maintained its position with mathematical certainty, but that very certainty made the pattern susceptible to targeted disruption.

"The structural stress points follow prime number intervals,"

Kai observed, her engineered consciousness also detecting patterns invisible to conventional analysis. "Their geometric symmetry creates quantum resonance nodes that should amplify even small disruptions. Admiral Perez?"

Perez, at Titan base, confirmed what they were seeing and then transmitted to Earth's combined defense fleet. "All vessels with enhanced capabilities," he transmitted, "adjust attack vectors to target the identified Enemy vulnerability points. Conventional ships will provide covering fire to draw the Enemy's attention from the primary strike force."

The station's tactical displays showed Earth's defenders reorganizing their approach. Ships with transformed crews positioned themselves to target the stress points in the Enemy's formation, while conventional vessels prepared diversionary and covering tactics. The quantum resonance patterns of the evolving ships would introduce precisely the type of chaos the Enemy's mathematical lattice couldn't accommodate.

"The fleet has implemented the approach vectors," Zara reported, mapping the optimal trajectories. "If we time our attacks to coincide exactly, the cascade effect should disrupt their suppression field's coherence."

Drake closed her eyes for a moment, considering the options, then nodded her agreement. "The Enemy's perfect order contains the seeds of its own disruption," she said, "the mathematical certainty that can't adapt to simultaneous chaos at critical junctions. Their rigid adherence to geometric precision has created a formation that's incredibly powerful but fundamentally brittle."

"To all ships," she transmitted. "Coordinate your attacks on these harmonic points. Synchronize your signatures to introduce maximum disruption at the targeted coordinates. The disruption must occur simultaneously to prevent their mathematical models from adapting. On my mark! Ten, nine, eight... Mark!"

Earth's defense fleet launched their coordinated assault,

enhanced vessels accelerating toward the identified vulnerability points. Their evolved hulls pulsed with quantum energy as they approached the Enemy's suppression field, their transformed crews pushing their ships' capabilities to their limits.

But the Enemy had anticipated this strategy. Their perfect formation shifted with mathematical precision, reconfiguring to eliminate the stress points Drake had identified. New geometric patterns formed, creating an even denser suppression field that pushed back against the approaching vessels.

"They're adapting their formation," Kai warned, as she tracked the changes. "Their new configurations are eliminating the vulnerability nodes. The mathematical model is becoming more complex."

The station's displays showed the Enemy ships adjusting their positions with fluid precision, maintaining perfect geometric symmetry while eliminating the stress points that made them vulnerable. Their suppression field strengthened as its mathematical foundation shifted to a more complex pattern.

"Earth's signature is fading faster," Perez transmitted urgently. "The Enemy's reconfigured suppression field is accelerating the regression effect. Major population centers are losing coherence."

Drake gritted her teeth as she felt Earth's transformation beginning to reverse as the Enemy's mathematical prison walls tightened. Cities that had started developing quantum characteristics were forced back toward conventional existence. Enhanced humans worldwide reported losing their evolved capabilities as the suppression field strengthened.

"Our first approach failed," Drake acknowledged, her mind already calculating new possibilities. "But their response reveals something crucial: their mathematical models can adapt, but only by becoming more rigid, more precise."

Kai detected the pattern immediately. "The more complex their formation becomes," she said, "the more perfect it must be to maintain coherence. Each adjustment increases their mathematical precision but reduces their flexibility."

The Enemy flagship pulsed with energy as it directed their formation's reconfiguration.

Drake watched their suppression field shifting into new geometric patterns of unprecedented complexity. But this increased precision came at a cost; their mathematical lattice now required absolute perfection to maintain its influence.

"They've eliminated the stress points we identified," Zara reported, scanning the new formation, "but in doing so they've created new vulnerability nodes. Their need for perfect symmetry forces them to maintain certain mathematical relationships that create new resonance points."

The station's displays highlighted these new vulnerability points, spaces where the Enemy's even more complex formation created even more precise stress nodes. Their adaptation had eliminated the original weaknesses but generated new ones that required even greater mathematical precision to maintain.

"To all ships," Drake transmitted, "adjust targeting parameters to the new vulnerability coordinates. Their formation has become more powerful but more brittle. Even small disruptions at these precise points will create disproportionate effects."

Earth's evolved fleet altered course, their ships recalculating approach vectors to target the Enemy's new stress points. But as they neared the suppression field's outer boundary, they encountered an unexpected obstacle; the increased mathematical precision of the Enemy's formation was creating zones where evolution became impossible.

"The enhanced ships can't maintain coherence," Perez reported, tracking multiple vessels experiencing sudden regression. "The closer they get to the suppression field, the more their evolved systems are forced back to conventional states. They can't reach the vulnerability points without losing the capabilities needed to disrupt them."

Drake shook her head as she monitored Earth's defense fleet struggling against this fundamental paradox. Ships with evolved capabilities could identify the Enemy's vulnerability points but couldn't reach them without losing their evolution. Conventional vessels could penetrate deeper into the suppression field but lacked the resonance needed to create effective disruption.

"The regression effect is progressive," Kai observed, analyzing ship telemetry. "The more evolved a system is, the faster it degrades within the suppression field. Pure quantum technology fails almost immediately, while hybrid systems show greater resistance."

Zara nodded as she processed this new information, her cybernetic systems calculating survival probabilities for different types of enhancement. "My original augmentations were designed differently," she noted, reviewing her own system architecture. "They're not purely quantum-based like our evolved systems. They operate partially through conventional physics."

The station's displays rendered a comparative analysis of different enhancement types. While evolution provided the greatest capabilities, it proved most vulnerable to the Enemy's suppression effect. Hybrid systems that incorporated both conventional and quantum technologies showed significantly greater resistance.

"We need a different approach," Drake decided, watching Earth's defenders forced back by the strengthening suppression field. "Rather than trying to overwhelm their mathematical precision with brute force, we need to introduce controlled chaos at the exact points where their perfect order becomes most vulnerable."

"To all ships," she transmitted new tactical instructions to the combined fleet. "Fall back and regroup. The frontal assault isn't working. We need a more precise intervention."

The Last Station

As Earth's defenders withdrew to reorganize, the Enemy's suppression field continued to strengthen. Their geometric formation expanded further, its reality-distortion effect reaching deeper into the planet's atmosphere. Cities worldwide reported increasing regression as quantum-enhanced technology failed and evolved humans found their capabilities diminishing.

"Time is running out," Perez transmitted urgently from Titan command. "Earth's quantum signature has degraded to critical levels. Once the suppression field reaches full coverage, the effect becomes self-sustaining. We'll lose any chance of restoring the planet's evolutionary potential."

But the crew was already working on it, analyzing the Enemy's formation from multiple perspectives, searching for weaknesses in the mathematical lattice that their forces could exploit despite the regression effect.

"I've been analyzing the suppression field's interaction with different types of enhancement," Zara announced, her systems processing data from multiple failed attack attempts. "There's a pattern to the regression effect. It targets systems based on their evolution level. The more transformed the technology, the faster it fails."

The station's displays rendered her analysis in crystalline detail, showing how the Enemy's suppression field affected different enhancement types. Pure quantum systems failed instantly upon entering the field. Hybrid technologies showed varying degrees of resistance depending on their conventional components.

"My cybernetic systems were originally designed for conventional operation," Zara continued, calculating the possibilities. "They're not pure quantum technology like our evolved enhancements. The hybrid architecture might resist the regression effect long enough to reach the vulnerability points."

Drake processed this insight, immediately understanding its

implications. "You're suggesting your augmentations could maintain functionality inside their suppression field long enough to introduce disruption at the critical nodes?"

"Not indefinitely," Zara acknowledged, as she performed the calculations. "But longer than purely evolved technology. My original augmentations operate partially through conventional physics, which the suppression field affects less severely."

The station's tactical displays simulated her proposal: a single small vessel with minimal quantum components, piloted by someone whose enhancements could resist regression long enough to reach the vulnerability points. The approach would require navigating through the densest part of the Enemy's formation, targeting each stress node with precise disruption.

"This would mean approaching all seventeen vulnerability points in sequence," Kai warned. "Even with hybrid augmentations, the cumulative exposure would cause irreversible degradation. Your systems would fail before you could complete the sequence."

"I know, and I understand," Zara said. "I have calculated the risks. My cybernetic systems project system failure rates under various scenarios. I would be able to maintain minimum functional capacity long enough to hit all seventeen nodes. The degradation would be progressive but not instantaneous."

Drake didn't like it. What Zara was suggesting was a suicide mission. She closed her eyes, her enhanced mind searching for options that wouldn't require such sacrifice. But the Enemy's perfect formation left no room for conventional approaches. Their suppression field prevented evolved ships from approaching while their geometric precision eliminated any possibility of remote disruption.

"There must be another way," she insisted, feeling the weight of commanding such a mission.

"There isn't," Zara responded with the certainty of one whose augmented systems had calculated every possibility. "Their mathematical precision makes them impenetrable to evolved technology. My hybrid systems are the only ones that can maintain partial functionality long enough to complete this mission."

There was no time to argue. They were receiving urgent, minute-by-minute updates from Earth's defense command. The suppression field had reached seventy percent coverage, its reality-distortion effect already forcing evolved humans back into conventional existence. Cities that had begun their transformation were experiencing cascading system failures as the Enemy rewrote local physics.

"The suppression field will reach critical coverage in fifty-seven minutes," Perez transmitted. "At that point, the effect becomes self-sustaining. Earth's evolutionary potential will be permanently suppressed."

The crew's transformed awareness searched desperately for alternatives, calculating millions of scenarios in microseconds. But each possibility ran against the same fundamental obstacle: the Enemy's suppression field prevented evolved technology from approaching the vulnerability points that needed to be disrupted.

"I've been examining our scout vessel," Zara said softly. "It was designed with minimal components, relying primarily on conventional propulsion with a small quantum core. If we modified its systems to interface with my augmentations, it might survive longer in the suppression field."

The station's displays showed the vessel's specifications, highlighting its hybrid architecture. Unlike the fully evolved ships that failed immediately upon entering the suppression field, this craft might be able to maintain basic functionality long enough to reach the critical nodes.

"I can modify the core to generate precisely calibrated chaos bursts," Zara continued, already calculating the necessary adjustments. "Each burst would need to match the exact resonance frequency of the target node to create maximum disruption with minimal energy."

They simulated this approach: a conventional vessel with minimal components, piloted by someone whose hybrid augmentations could indeed resist regression long enough to reach each of the seventeen vulnerability points. The calculations showed a narrow path to success, though at tremendous cost.

"I volunteer," Zara said simply, already interfacing with the scout vessel's systems. "My cybernetic architecture gives me the highest probability of reaching all seventeen nodes before complete system failure."

Drake again searched for an alternative that wouldn't require such sacrifice. But the Enemy's formation left no room for conventional tactics.

"Prepare the scout vessel," she commanded finally, feeling the terrible weight of necessity. "We have less than one hour before Earth's transformation is permanently reversed."

As the station's engineering systems began modifying the scout vessel to interface with Zara's unique augmentations, the Enemy's suppression field continued to strengthen around Earth.

Chapter 33

Sacrifice

THE SCOUT VESSEL HUNG IN THE STATION'S LAUNCH BAY, ITS systems pulsing with new energy as Zara completed the final modifications. Unlike the fully evolved ships that failed immediately upon entering the Enemy's suppression field, this craft maintained primarily conventional architecture with minimal quantum components.

Zara, now fully interfaced with its systems, mapped the precise coordinates of all seventeen vulnerability points in the Enemy's formation.

"Final calibrations complete," she transmitted.

"The core has been modified to generate chaos bursts at the exact resonance frequencies needed for each node," Kai transmitted. "But the timing must be precise. Each disruption must occur at the mathematical center of the vulnerability point."

Zara nodded as she absorbed this data, her cybernetic processors calculating optimal approach vectors and timing sequences. The scout vessel's conventional propulsion would allow it to navigate through the Enemy's suppression field, while its quantum components would provide just enough capability to deliver the necessary disruption to each node.

"I've mapped the regression curve based on our previous attempts," she reported, her mind creating precise projections of system failure rates. "My cybernetic functions should maintain operational capacity through approximately seventy percent of the mission. After that point, degradation will accelerate exponentially."

Drake watched the preparations with growing disquiet, still searching for alternatives even as she recognized their necessity. She could feel Zara's calm determination. It was not the emotional resignation of one facing death, but the precise certainty of systems that had calculated all the variables and accepted the optimal solution.

"Your consciousness is integrated with those systems," Drake said, giving voice to her deepest concern. "When they fail—"

"I know," Zara interrupted, her voice carrying both machine precision and human determination. "But Earth's transformation is worth more than any single consciousness, no matter how evolved. We fought too hard to let humanity's future be locked into the Enemy's version of perfection."

"The Enemy's suppression field has reached eighty-five percent coverage," Perez transmitted the urgent update from Titan command. "Earth's signature is failing across all population centers. We're detecting widespread regression in evolved technologies and enhanced humans. At the present rate, we have thirty-two minutes until the effect becomes self-sustaining."

The scout vessel's engines hummed to life as Zara completed her interface with its systems. Her augmented consciousness spread through the craft, merging with its controls until the distinction between pilot and vehicle became meaningless. Through their neural connection, the crew felt her completing final calculations, plotting the exact course that would intersect all seventeen vulnerability points while minimizing exposure to the densest regions of the suppression field.

"My approach vector is calculated," she transmitted, her cybernetic precision evident in every word. "The disruption sequence must follow an exact pattern to create cascading failure throughout their lattice. Any deviation would allow their mathematical model to isolate and compensate for the chaos."

"The regression won't just affect your augmentations," Drake said. "Your mind is integrated with those systems. When they fail—"

"I've always existed between states," Zara replied, her voice carrying unexpected warmth beneath its mechanical precision. "Not fully human, not purely machine. Perhaps that's why I'm suited for this, to show that strength comes from the spaces between, not from perfect order or pure chaos."

"Zara... thank you," she said simply, knowing no words could adequately express what this sacrifice meant.

Zara didn't reply. There was no point. The launch bay doors opened, the scout dropped out into space, its convention drive immediately engaged. Two minutes later there was a blinding white flash as the drive engaged and she made the jump to Earth.

As she dropped out of quantum space, the enormity of what she was facing was revealed. Earth was surrounded by the Enemy's geometric formation. As the crew watched through the neural link, they could see the mathematical prison tightening around the planet, its reality-distortion field forcing evolving systems back toward conventional states. Cities that had begun developing quantum characteristics flickered as their transformation reversed.

"I'm approaching outer boundary of the suppression field," she transmitted as the vessel neared the geometric lattice of Enemy ships. "I'm detecting initial regression effects. Enhancements experiencing minor degradation. My cybernetic functions are at ninety-six percent capacity."

The Enemy detected her approach immediately, their perfect formations adjusting to intercept. But Zara's trajectory had been calculated with cybernetic precision, exploiting microscopic gaps in their lattice that their rigid mathematical models couldn't account for.

"First layer of suppression field penetrated," she reported, her voice already showing subtle signs of degradation as the Enemy's reality-distortion effect began forcing her augmented systems back toward conventional operation. "Cybernetic functions at eighty-nine percent. Interface stable but experiencing minor disruption."

Through their link, they felt her consciousness navigating the increasingly hostile environment. The Enemy's suppression field pressed against her augmented systems, trying to force their evolved components back to conventional states. But the hybrid nature of her enhancements—part quantum, part conventional—provided the crucial resilience she needed.

"Approaching first vulnerability node," she transmitted, her vessel following the precise course her calculations had plotted. "Cybernetic functions at eighty-two percent. Preparing chaos introduction sequence."

The scout vessel reached the first critical point in the Enemy's formation—a precise coordinate where their perfect mathematics created its own weakness. Zara's augmented systems released a carefully calibrated burst of quantum energy, introducing controlled chaos into their rigid precision.

"First node disrupted," she reported, her voice maintaining its mechanical steadiness despite the growing degradation. "Enemy formation showing signs of instability at junction point alpha. Proceeding to second target."

The station's displays showed the first cracks appearing in the

Enemy's perfect containment field. Their crystalline ships struggled to maintain geometric precision as the chaos Zara had introduced rippled through their mathematical lattice. Each vessel attempted to compensate, but their adjustment created new vulnerabilities elsewhere in the formation.

"They're detecting the disturbance," Kai observed, tracking the Enemy's response. "Their ships are attempting to reconfigure around the disruption point, but the chaos is spreading faster than they can adapt their equations."

Zara's vessel pushed deeper into the Enemy formation, approaching the second vulnerability node. They could feel her consciousness working with increasing effort as the suppression field stripped away more of her augmented capabilities.

"Second node reached," she transmitted, her voice now showing noticeable distortion. "Cybernetic functions at seventy-four percent. Neural interface experiencing moderate degradation. Executing disruption sequence."

Another precisely calculated burst of quantum chaos entered the Enemy's formation, creating interference patterns that amplified the disruption from the first node. Their perfect geometry began showing more significant signs of instability as they struggled to maintain the mathematical precision required for their suppression field.

"The suppression effect is weakening," Perez reported. "Earth's defense grid is reporting a ten percent recovery in evolutionary capacity. Major population centers are showing signs of resumed transformation."

But the cost was mounting. With each moment inside the Enemy's suppression field, more of Zara's augmented systems failed, forced back to conventional operation by the reality-distortion effect. Her consciousness, integrated with those systems, experienced each failure as part of herself being torn away.

"Third node... reached," she transmitted, her voice breaking into disjointed fragments as her communication systems degraded. "Cybernetic functions at sixty-seven percent. Neural cohesion becoming difficult to maintain. Executing... disruption sequence."

The third burst created cascading failures through an entire section of the Enemy's geometric lattice. Their crystalline ships struggled to maintain formation as reality itself rejected their perfect mathematical precision. The suppression field weakened further as its carefully maintained balance deteriorated.

"Enemy vessels are moving to intercept," Kai warned, tracking multiple ships breaking formation to pursue Zara's vessel. "They've calculated her trajectory and recognized her strategy."

But the Enemy's perfect mathematical precision worked against them. By breaking their geometric formation to pursue Zara, they created additional instabilities in their own suppression field. Each ship that left its perfectly calculated position weakened the overall structure, creating new vulnerability points that amplified the chaos she had already introduced.

"Fourth node... reached," Zara reported, her transmission quality deteriorating as more communication systems failed. "Cybernetic functions at... fifty-nine percent. Primary neural pathways experiencing significant degradation... Executing disruption..."

The fourth chaos burst struck at another critical junction in the Enemy's formation, creating a resonance pattern that interfered with their ships' ability to maintain perfect geometric positions.

Drake watched the ripples of instability spreading through their lattice as mathematical precision gave way to increasing disorder.

"Earth's signature is strengthening," Perez transmitted from Titan command. "Major population centers reporting twenty-eight percent recovery in evolutionary capacity. The suppression field is losing coherence across multiple sectors."

But Zara was paying an escalating price for each success. Her vessel pushed deeper into the Enemy formation, exposing her systems to increasingly intense suppression effects. Through their deteriorating neural link, they felt her consciousness fragmenting as more of her augmented capabilities failed.

"Fifth node... sixth node..." she continued, her transmissions becoming increasingly disjointed as she fought to maintain coherence. "Cybernetic functions... forty-five percent. Navigation systems degrading... Manual corrections implemented..."

The Enemy ships closest to her vessel intensified their suppression field, trying to accelerate the regression of her systems before she could reach more vulnerability points. But Zara's hybrid nature proved more resilient than they had calculated. While her quantum enhancements failed rapidly, her conventional cybernetic core maintained basic functionality, allowing her to continue her mission despite mounting system failures.

"Seven... eight..." The coordinates blurred together as Zara pushed beyond conventional operational parameters. "Cybernetic functions... thirty-six percent. Neural interface experiencing critical degradation... Rerouting essential processes..."

Each disruption point she reached created greater instability in the Enemy's formation. Their perfect mathematical lattice began breaking apart as chaos spread through the precisely calculated vulnerability nodes. The suppression field around Earth flickered dramatically, its reality-distortion effect weakening as the geometric precision it required collapsed.

"I'm detecting recovery across Earth's surface," Kai reported, her transcended awareness monitoring the planetary transformation. "Cities are resuming evolution. Enhanced humans are regaining their capabilities. The suppression field has fallen below the threshold needed for permanent effect."

But their victory was coming at a devastating cost. Zara's vessel continued its desperate course through the Enemy formation, but her systems were failing faster than projected. They could feel her consciousness struggling to maintain coherence as critical components shut down one after another.

"Nine... ten..." Her voice was barely recognizable now, fragmented into bursts of static and partial words. "System... twenty-eight percent... Manual control... compensating..."

The Enemy flagship recognized the existential threat to their strategy. Their perfect formation completely dissolved as every available vessel converged on Zara's position, trying to prevent her from reaching more vulnerability nodes. But their rigid precision had already been compromised beyond recovery, their suppression field was collapsing as mathematical order gave way to spreading chaos.

"Eleven... twelve..." Static overwhelmed her transmissions now, her consciousness holding together through sheer determination as her supporting systems failed catastrophically. "Thirteen..."

Earth's signature strengthened exponentially as the Enemy's suppression field continued to collapse. Cities worldwide resumed their transformation, crystalline structures once again incorporating evolved technology as the reality-distortion effect dissipated. Enhanced humans felt their capabilities return, consciousness expanding back into quantum states the Enemy had temporarily suppressed.

"She's approaching the final nodes," Kai reported, tracking Zara's vessel through the deteriorating Enemy formation. "But her systems are failing beyond critical thresholds. Her neural coherence can't be maintained much longer."

Through their degraded link, they felt Zara's consciousness

fracture further as more of her essential systems failed. Her vessel's trajectory became erratic as the navigation computers shut down, forcing her to rely on increasingly unreliable manual control.

"Fourteen... fifteen..." The transmission was barely coherent, her consciousness disintegrating as the systems that supported it failed one by one. "Core systems... failing... Manual navigation... seventeen percent functional..."

Just two nodes remained: the critical junctions where the Enemy flagship was maintaining what was left of their suppression field. But Zara's systems had deteriorated beyond the point of precision targeting. Her vessel responded sluggishly to commands as more critical components failed.

"Enemy flagship... detected," she managed to transmit through the static. "Core mathematical... nexus identified... Final approach..."

And then they felt her make one final calculation: not precision strikes at the last vulnerability nodes, but something far more devastating. Her consciousness, fragmented but still functioning, reached a decision that transcended both machine logic and human emotion.

"Ship's power core... destabilizing," she transmitted, the message barely coherent through cascading system failures. "Calculations complete... Perfect chaos requires... perfect sacrifice..."

Drake understood immediately. "Zara, wait—"

"Only path remaining," came the fragmented response. "Precision targeting... no longer possible. But core collapse at... flagship coordinates... will generate optimal chaos pattern."

The scout vessel changed course, abandoning its planned trajectory to head directly toward the Enemy flagship. And they watched Zara's final approach: not a precision strike at the remaining vulnerability nodes, but a direct collision course with the mathematical heart of the Enemy's formation.

"Core destabilization... initiated," she transmitted, her consciousness expanding one last time despite catastrophic system failures. "When containment fails at... these coordinates... the resulting quantum cascade will disrupt... their entire framework."

The Enemy flagship detected her intention too late. Their attempts to withdraw were confounded by the mathematical precision they required to maintain formation. The very order that had been their greatest strength now prevented them from adapting quickly enough to avoid Zara's final approach.

"Remember what I was," she transmitted, her consciousness fading with each word. "Not fully human... not purely machine. The space between... that's where evolution thrives. Not perfect order... not pure chaos... but the beautiful balance..."

Her vessel's power core reached critical instability, quantum elements reacting against conventional containment to create a formula for perfect dimensional disruption. At the heart of the Enemy's remaining formation, where their mathematics were most vulnerable to uncertainty, Zara prepared to introduce the ultimate chaos.

"Tell them I understand now," came her final transmission, the signal fragmented but the meaning clear. "The Predecessors didn't design us to defeat the Enemy... but to show them another way. Perfect order and pure chaos are just... opposite ends of a spectrum we've learned to embrace completely."

The detonation wasn't just physical; it was a quantum event that rippled through multiple dimensions simultaneously. Perfect chaos erupted at the precise center of the Enemy's last vestiges of perfect order, creating a cascade of mathematical impossibilities their rigid systems couldn't process.

Their suppression field collapsed completely, reality itself rejecting the perfect order they had tried to impose. Earth's signature surged to full strength as the mathematical prison dissolved.

Evolved humans across the planet felt their capabilities fully restored, enhanced systems reactivating as the Enemy's reality-distortion effect vanished.

The Enemy fleet's formation shattered beyond recovery. Ships that had maintained rigid geometry broke apart as their crystalline structures failed, unable to adapt to the chaos Zara had released. Others attempted to evolve in response, their perfect mathematics giving way to more adaptive configurations that could accommodate uncertainty.

Through their link, the transformed crew felt the significance of Zara's sacrifice ripple across space. She hadn't just saved Earth —she had demonstrated the fundamental truth they had been fighting to protect: that the most powerful force in existence wasn't perfect order or pure chaos, but the dynamic balance between them.

Where her vessel had been, nothing remained—not wreckage, not energy, not even disturbed space. Her sacrifice had been complete, introducing perfect chaos into perfect order to create something entirely new—a demonstration that true evolution required both mathematical precision and creative uncertainty in equal measure.

Earth's field stabilized at an unprecedented level of evolution, its population continuing their transformation with renewed vigor. The planet pulsed with hybrid energy, visible across dimensional space as a beacon of balanced advancement.

"This isn't victory in the conventional sense," Drake observed, feeling both the triumph and the loss. "Zara showed us—and the Enemy—something more important than winning or losing. She showed us that true strength comes from embracing both order and chaos, from finding beauty in the spaces between extremes."

They felt new possibilities awakening across human space. The Enemy's attempt to lock Earth into perfect mathematical order had failed, but more importantly, it had revealed the path forward—not as beings of pure order or absolute chaos, but as consciousness that could navigate the infinite potential between them.

The war that had begun millions of years ago was transforming into something else entirely. Some Enemy vessels continued their retreat, clinging to perfect mathematics and rigid precision. But others remained, their crystalline structures showing signs of adaptation as they began their own journey toward balance.

"She knew exactly what she was," Kai said softly, her transcended mind perceiving patterns others missed. "Not fully human, not purely machine, but something beautifully in between. That's what scared the Enemy most—not that we might choose chaos over order, but that we could embrace both simultaneously."

Drake touched the crystal at her throat, feeling it pulse in harmony with Earth's strengthening field. "The Predecessors understood this when they designed us," she said. "Not to defeat the Enemy, but to show them another way. To demonstrate that consciousness doesn't have to choose between mathematical precision and creative uncertainty."

Through their neural interface, they felt humanity's transformed future unfolding across countless possible paths. Zara's sacrifice hadn't just preserved their evolution—it had opened new doors to advancement, showing both humanity and the Enemy that true strength came from balance rather than extremes.

The hybrid chaos she had introduced wasn't just a weapon against the Enemy's perfect order. It was a proof of concept, a demonstration that consciousness could thrive in the dynamic space between rigid precision and unlimited potential. Her final gift to both humanity and the Enemy was understanding—that in the endless dance between order and chaos, the most beautiful possibilities emerged from their synthesis.

Earth pulsed with evolutionary energy, its field visible across dimensional space. But the brightest point in that radiance wasn't a place or a technology. It was the memory of one who had existed between states, who had found strength in being neither purely human nor completely machine, and who had shown two civilizations that their ancient war could end not in victory or defeat, but in transformation.

"Her consciousness was integrated with those systems," Maya said, her voice carrying both technical analysis and deep emotion. "But she was never just her augmentations. She was the balance between them and her humanity. Even at the end, when her systems were failing, she maintained that perfect synthesis."

Perez's hybrid awareness expanded through their connection, his own unique balance between cybernetic precision and human adaptability resonating with what Zara had demonstrated. "The Enemy's perfect mathematics couldn't account for her," he transmitted. "Their models dealt with pure states—perfect order or complete chaos. They had no equations for someone who existed in the space between."

Drake watched Earth's recovery through enhanced perception, feeling the planet's field strengthen as the suppression effect dissipated completely. Cities resumed their transformation, evolved humans reconnected with quantum capabilities, and the boundary between conventional technology and biological advancement once again began to blur.

"The Predecessors knew this was the key," she reflected, understanding flowing through her transformed consciousness. "Not order instead of chaos, not technology instead of biology, not machine instead of human. The true path was always balance —the ability to exist in all states simultaneously while being controlled by none."

They could feel the significance of this moment ripple across human space. The ancient conflict between perfect mathematics and organic uncertainty wasn't ending in the victory of one over the other, but in the recognition that both had always been part of the same continuum. Zara's final act had demonstrated that the most powerful evolutionary force wasn't found at either extreme, but in the dynamic synthesis between them.

As Earth continued its transformation, glowing with renewed evolutionary potential, the crew felt Zara's absence not as emptiness but as purpose. She had shown them—and the Enemy—that the space between states wasn't weakness but strength, not confusion but clarity. The path forward would honor this understanding, embracing both the precision she had embodied through her augmentations and the humanity that had guided their use.

The war for humanity's evolutionary future hadn't ended in conquest but in revelation. And that revelation would guide their next steps into the unknown that awaited.

Chapter 34

Awakening

EARTH'S QUANTUM FIELD PULSED WITH RENEWED ENERGY AS THE Enemy's suppression field dissolved completely. Through their entanglement network, Drake and her crew watched the planet's transformation resume with unprecedented vigor, as if the temporary regression had created potential that now expressed itself with even greater intensity.

"The quantum signature is stronger than before the attack," Kai observed. "The Enemy's attempt to impose perfect order has created a reactive surge of balanced evolution. It's like compressing a spring: the harder they squeezed, the more powerful the response."

The station's displays showed major population centers worldwide resuming their transformation. Cities that had begun developing crystalline structures now began to evolve again.

"We're detecting remarkable acceleration in the evolutionary templates," Perez transmitted from Titan command. "The transformation has resumed at nearly triple the previous rate."

Earth's defense fleet was regrouping and reorganizing after

the battle. Ships with evolved crews pushed their transformation further, incorporating lessons from both the Enemy's mathematical precision and Zara's hybrid approach. The boundary between conventional technology and quantum evolution became increasingly fluid, creating vessels that could shift between states at will.

"Some of the Enemy vessels are remaining in Earth orbit," Kai reported. "But they're not maintaining attack formations. Their geometric patterns have dissolved completely. They appear to be... observing."

Drake reached out toward these lingering Enemy ships, feeling subtle changes in their quantum signatures. Unlike the rigid precision they had maintained before, these vessels were showing signs of adaptation, their crystalline structures incorporating elements of controlled chaos.

"They're evolving," she said, watching their patterns shift from perfect mathematical order toward something more balanced. "Zara's demonstration affected them profoundly."

"They're attempting to communicate," Kai said.

"We have much to learn from each other," the Enemy commander transmitted. The transmission was tempered with recognition and resignation. "Your hybrid existence demonstrates evolutionary paths we abandoned long ago. We request permission to observe your transformation more closely."

The station's displays showed more Enemy vessels breaking from their retreat, returning to maintain position near Earth but without forming suppression fields or attack formations. And their crystalline structures continued to evolve, incorporating more adaptive configurations.

"I'm detecting quantum resonance between evolved humans and the transformed Enemy vessels," Kai reported as she tracked the unprecedented interactions. "They're beginning their own journey toward balance. Their mathematical precision is becoming more adaptive while maintaining the core of what they are."

Drake watched as this unexpected development unfolded. "The Predecessors were right," she said. "This was never about defeating the Enemy or forcing them to abandon their nature. It was about showing them that evolution doesn't require choosing between mathematical precision and creative chaos."

"The diversity is remarkable," Perez transmitted. "The transformation is accelerating exponentially. It's as if... it's as if the flood gates have opened."

"It's not random," she observed. "The variations appear to be following certain mathematical principles that incorporate uncertainty without becoming completely chaotic. Each evolutionary path is maintaining its own internal consistency while diverging from others in precise yet unpredictable ways."

The station's displays showed Earth pulsing with hybrid energy, its signature visible all across dimensional space.

"The transformed Enemy vessels are establishing communication with evolved humans," Kai reported. "They're sharing mathematical principles that are helping to stabilize evolution. It's becoming a genuine exchange rather than a conflict."

Drake and Kai could feel the significance of this moment. The war that had begun half a million years ago, when the Enemy first rejected biological chaos in favor of perfect mathematical order, was transforming into something else entirely, a conversation between different approaches to existence, each learning from the other's strengths.

"I'm detecting signatures from beyond Earth," Kai announced suddenly. "Multiple colony worlds are showing signs of accelerated evolution. The transformation is spreading through quantum entanglement, Earth's templates are activating dormant potential throughout human space."

The station's displays confirmed her observation, showing

transformation patterns emerging on distant human settlements. Though separated by fractions of a light-year, these colonies were connected through quantum entanglement to Earth's evolutionary template. Their development was accelerating in response to what had occurred on humanity's homeworld, though each world was finding its own unique expression of balanced advancement.

"The network is strengthening," Kai observed. "Each transformed world becomes another node, creating links that bypass conventional space-time. The Predecessors designed the system to expand exponentially once it reached critical activation threshold."

"Some of the colonies are showing even more accelerated development than Earth," Perez transmitted, monitoring distant outposts. "Without the Enemy's suppression field ever affecting them, they're evolving along even more diverse paths. Each world is finding its own balance between mathematical precision and organic uncertainty."

"This diversity was always the point," Drake said. "The Predecessors didn't want us to evolve along a single predetermined path. They designed us to explore countless variations on the theme of balance, each strengthening the whole through its unique perspective."

The Enemy vessels that had begun their own evolution watched the process with what could only be described as wonder: consciousness that had existed in perfect mathematical order for millions of years was witnessing the beauty of controlled adaptation for the first time. Their crystalline structures continued to evolve, incorporating elements of organic uncertainty while maintaining their own fundamental precision.

"We request permission to establish formal diplomatic contact," the Enemy commander transmitted, their message carrying both precise structure and newfound flexibility. "There is much we can share about maintaining coherence across dimensional spaces, while learning from your adaptive evolution."

Perez looked at Yuki who nodded slowly, then transmitted, "Permission granted. Coordinate with Earth's combined defense command. We have much to learn from each other's approaches to existence."

As the day progressed, they monitored Earth's transformation reaching new levels of complexity. Cities worldwide continued developing characteristics, their structures shifting between conventional and evolved states. The boundary between physical and dimensional space became increasingly fluid, allowing transformed humans to navigate between different states of existence.

"I'm detecting something remarkable in major population centers," Kai reported, her transcended consciousness analyzing subtle patterns in human evolution. "Collective consciousness is emerging: fields connecting evolved minds into a shared awareness while maintaining individual identity."

The station's displays showed this phenomenon spreading through urban centers worldwide. Evolved humans were developing quantum connections with others in their vicinity, creating a collective consciousness that enhanced rather than diminished individual perspective. Each mind contributed its unique balance of order and chaos to the whole, creating emergent awareness beyond what any single consciousness could achieve.

"The Enemy vessels are detecting this phenomenon as well," Kai observed, tracking their response. "Their crystalline structures are resonating with these collective fields, almost as if they're attempting to understand them through direct participation."

"This is what Zara showed us was possible," Drake said softly, feeling the planet's field strengthen with each passing hour. "Not the victory of chaos over order or humanity over the Enemy, but the recognition that each contains elements essential to the other. True evolution comes from synthesis rather than opposition."

As night fell across Earth's continents, the planet's transformed cities took on ethereal beauty. Quantum energy flowed through crystalline structures that shifted between states, creating architecture that existed partly in physical space and partly in dimensional reality. The boundary between technology and biology continued to blur as evolved consciousness reshaped both according to the principles of balanced advancement.

In this new radiance, they felt Zara's absence not as emptiness but as purpose. Her sacrifice had demonstrated the power of existing between states, of embracing both mechanical precision and human adaptability without being limited by either. The path forward would honor this understanding, exploring the infinite potential that existed in the balance she had embodied.

"The transformation has reached a self-sustaining threshold," Perez transmitted from Titan command. "Even if the Enemy attempted another suppression field, the evolution has become too diverse, too distributed to contain. Humanity's advancement is now proceeding along too many parallel paths for any single approach to suppress."

Earth's signature had stabilized into a complex tapestry of interwoven evolutionary paths. Some emphasized mathematical precision while incorporating elements of controlled chaos. Others embraced organic uncertainty while maintaining coherent structure. Together, they created a civilization that transcended the limitations of any single approach.

"The next phase is beginning," Kai observed.

Drake touched the crystal at her throat, feeling it pulse in harmony with Earth's strengthening field.

Earth glowed with hybrid energy as the first day of its reawakened transformation came to an end. But the evolution that had begun would continue unfolding for generations, exploring count-less variations on the theme of balanced advancement. The awak-ening was the first step on a journey that would transform not just humanity but the fabric of existence itself.

Meanwhile, in the high-security wing of the Titan facility, Dr. Marcus Wong sat motionless in his quantum-shielded cell, watching Earth's transformation through a viewport calibrated to allow visual observation while preventing any connection. The revolutionary who had once attempted to lock the template into controlled evolutionary paths now witnessed unbounded transfor-mation flourishing beyond his ability to influence it.

"The subject remains non-responsive to standard interroga-tion," Perez transmitted through secure channels. "But his neural patterns are revealing more about the conspiracy with each scan-ning session. We've identified seventeen co-conspirators across both former Coalition and Separatist leadership."

Through enhanced perception, Drake accessed the secured feeds from Wong's containment. The xenoarchaeologist's attempt to seize control of the station's systems had failed, but the infor-mation stored in his crystal had proven invaluable, revealing not just the conspiracy's extent but the underlying fear that had moti-vated it.

"The irony of his situation is remarkable," Kai observed. "He feared uncontrolled evolution would create chaos, yet the balanced integration he tried to prevent has produced stability beyond anything his controlled paths could have achieved."

The displays showed Wong's carefully monitored existence— a man who had dedicated his life to controlling evolution now forced to witness transformation unfolding without boundaries. His connections had been severed, leaving him isolated in conventional existence while humanity transcended the limita-tions he had sought to impose.

"His conspirators are being given a choice," Perez continued. "Not punishment in the conventional sense, but opportunity to witness transformation firsthand before deciding whether to embrace balanced evolution or remain in isolated conventional existence."

Drake felt a complex mixture of emotions toward the man who had betrayed them. Wong hadn't been motivated by malice but by a genuine belief that controlled evolution was humanity's only safe path forward. His fear of chaos had driven him to embrace the Enemy's perfect order, never recognizing that true stability required dynamic balance rather than rigid control.

"The most fitting consequence," she reflected, "isn't imprisonment but perspective, allowing him to witness what's possible when evolution proceeds through balanced integration rather than controlled limitation."

Together they watched Wong's reaction as news of each evolutionary breakthrough reached his cell. The rigid certainty that had once defined him was slowly giving way to something else: not yet acceptance, but perhaps the first glimmers of understanding that the path he had feared might lead to possibilities beyond anything his controlled evolution could have achieved.

"Some of his co-conspirators have already requested inclusion in preliminary transformation protocols," Perez reported. "After witnessing the results of balanced evolution, they've recognized that their fear of uncontrolled chaos was based on a fundamental misunderstanding of what integration could achieve."

Whether Wong would eventually make the same choice remained to be seen. For now, his isolation served as both consequence and opportunity, a chance to witness firsthand how the uncontrolled evolution he had feared was creating stability and connection beyond anything his rigid control could have produced.

His failure had become perhaps the most powerful demonstration of the very principle he had rejected: that true advancement came not from imposing perfect order or embracing pure chaos, but from finding strength in their dynamic integration.

Chapter 35

Legacy

THREE MONTHS AFTER EARTH'S TRANSFORMATION RESUMED, THE boundaries between the different states of existence continued to blur. Cities worldwide evolved, their structures incorporating crystalline elements that resonated with the consciousness of their inhabitants. Buildings shifted between physical and dimensional space, adapting to populations that now navigated multiple states of reality.

Drake and her crew monitored this ongoing integration from the station that had become their temporary home. The quantum entanglement network allowed them to observe developments across human space in real-time, witnessing humanity's transformation unfold along countless parallel paths.

"The diversity of the evolutionary approaches is remarkable," Kai observed, tracking the evolutionary patterns across the major population centers. "Each city is finding its own balance between technological precision and biological adaptation, between mathematical order and creative chaos."

The station's displays showed New Geneva's signature intensifying as the former Coalition capital embraced its transformation. Government buildings had evolved into crystalline structures that existed partially in dimensional space, allowing government officials to coordinate activities across multiple states. The rigid hierarchies of the former Coalition had given way to more fluid organizational patterns that combined precise structure with adaptive flexibility.

"The provisional government is achieving unexpected stability," Admiral Perez transmitted from Titan command, monitoring political developments. "The former Coalition and Separatist officials have integrated their different approaches to governance, creating a new system of government."

They were also receiving updates from the now Admiral Rodriguez, whose evolved fleet was in orbit around Earth. "The transformed Enemy vessels are proving surprisingly helpful," she reported. "They're sharing mathematical principles that enhance our navigation systems, while studying our adaptive tactics. It's becoming a genuine technical exchange."

The station's displays showed the transformed Enemy ships integrated within Earth's defense perimeter. Their crystalline structures also continued to evolve, incorporating elements of controlled chaos that allowed for greater flexibility without sacrificing mathematical precision. They moved in formations that maintained geometric elegance while allowing for individual adaptation, a visual representation of the balance they were beginning to achieve.

"I'm detecting communication between humans and these transformed vessels," Kai reported, her consciousness tracking these interactions. "Not the formal diplomatic exchanges, but by direct neural interface. Their mathematical consciousness is learning to synchronize with our adaptive perception."

Drake nodded as she watched the displays. The rigid barriers that had separated human and Enemy perception for a hundred and twenty-five thousand years were dissolving, creating new possibilities for understanding.

"They're not simply observing our evolution anymore," she said. "They're participating in it, contributing their mathematical precision to our adaptive chaos. And we're influencing their development just as profoundly."

They continued to monitor how this integration was affecting Earth's continued transformation. Cities that had established connections with transformed Enemy vessels were developing more mathematically elegant structures, their evolution following principles of perfect symmetry while maintaining adaptive flexibility. Human consciousness in these regions showed enhanced capacity for multidimensional perception, incorporating the Enemy's precise understanding of quantum space.

"The Predecessors must have anticipated this possibility," Kai said, her mind detecting patterns within patterns. "They created us to demonstrate a path that could integrate the best aspects of both approaches to existence."

The station's displays shifted to show similar integration occurring with transformed technology. Quantum-enhanced systems that had previously been either purely mathematical or completely biological were evolving into hybrid forms that incorporated aspects of both. Ships developed crystalline structures that responded to crew consciousness while maintaining precise engineering. Medical technologies merged mathematical modeling with organic adaptation, creating healing systems that evolved alongside the patients they treated.

"The boundary between artificial and organic is dissolving," Drake observed.

"The medical profession is integrating transformed Enemy expertise," Perez transmitted, monitoring these collaborations. "Their understanding of quantum structure combined with human intuitive healing is creating unprecedented approaches to supporting evolution."

Perez was right. The transformation was altering how they perceived existence itself, revealing the false dichotomy between order and chaos that had limited their understanding for millennia.

"The major population centers are developing quantum infrastructure," Drake observed. "Cities are becoming organisms of hybrid technology that adapt to their inhabitants' needs."

Six months after Earth's transformation resumed, the integration of evolved consciousness had spread throughout human space. Colonial outposts once isolated by distance were now connected through quantum entanglement, creating a civilization that transcended conventional limitations of space and time. Through the network the Predecessors had designed, humanity had established a presence that extended beyond physical boundaries into dimensional domains previously inaccessible.

"The quantum entanglement network has achieved full integration," Kai reported. "All twenty-nine human colonies have completed initial transformation."

As these transformations continued across human space, the station's field shifted, revealing crystalline structures phasing into conventional reality from dimensional spaces they hadn't been able to access before, archives the Predecessors had hidden beneath the template they had initially discovered.

"The station is responding to our level of transformation," Kai said. "These archives were designed to remain hidden until consciousness reached a specific evolutionary threshold. We've just crossed that threshold."

The station's crystalline architecture reconfigured around them, revealing chambers and interfaces that hadn't existed before or—more accurately—had existed in dimensional spaces their previous level of consciousness couldn't perceive. They felt the field deepen as new layers of the Predecessors' legacy became accessible.

"These aren't additional evolutionary templates," Kai reported, interfacing with the newly revealed systems. "They're historical archives, records of the Predecessors' civilization before the conflict with the Enemy. Their complete legacy, preserved in quantum matrices designed to activate only when consciousness reached appropriate development."

Together, Drake and Kai accessed the archives, feeling the full scope of the Predecessors' legacy unfold, revealing not just technological knowledge or evolutionary templates, but cultural understanding; the complete record of a civilization that had achieved quantum transcendence millions of years before humanity's emergence.

"It's incredible," Drake said. "The level of quantum consciousness integration they achieved, far beyond what we've developed so far. Their civilization operated across multiple dimensional states, perceiving reality through frameworks we're only beginning to comprehend."

The station's displays filled with crystalline renderings of Predecessor culture: multi-dimensional art, science that unified aspects of reality conventional understanding considered inaccessible, philosophy that transcended the artificial distinctions between different states of existence. Through these archives, they glimpsed a civilization that had achieved integration on levels humanity was only beginning to approach.

"But they reached an evolutionary impasse," Drake murmured. "They achieved perfect mathematical precision that allowed incredible technological advancement, but it also limited their ability to adapt to unexpected developments. When the Enemy evolved beyond their predictions, they couldn't adjust their own consciousness quickly enough."

Drake looked at Kai who smiled at her and nodded. And, with

a wave of her hand, Drake, through the quantum entanglement channels, shared these discoveries with the newly established Zara Patel Institute, where teams of evolved humans and transformed Enemy representatives could analyze their implications and learn from the lessons inherited from a civilization that had achieved incredible advancement before reaching limitations they couldn't overcome.

"The Predecessors left us these records for a reason," Kai reflected. "They wanted to show us their achievements and their failures, and to help us to avoid the impasse that ultimately led to their extinction."

"The Quantum Consensus has established protocols for integrating this knowledge responsibly," Perez transmitted, his hybrid awareness spanning multiple governance levels simultaneously. "Not simply rushing to implement these new technologies without understanding their wider implications, but carefully analyzing both the achievements and limitations the records reveal."

"The most significant aspect of these archives," Kai said, "is how clearly they demonstrate that consciousness evolution isn't about achieving some final perfect state, but maintaining dynamic balance through continuous adaptation."

The station's displays showed this principle manifesting throughout human space as evolved colonies continued developing along diverse trajectories. Unlike the Predecessors' civilization, which had pursued perfect mathematical order at the expense of adaptive flexibility, humanity's transformed consciousness was exploring countless variations on the theme of balanced integration, finding unique expressions of the fundamental principle that true advancement required synthesis rather than opposition.

"Earth remains the focal point of this evolutionary diversity," Drake said. "Not imposing its development path on other worlds but serving as a nexus where different approaches can strengthen each other through constructive integration."

As they monitored the transformations spreading across human space, the provisional government formally established the Zara Patel Institute in New Geneva, not just a memorial, but as a center dedicated to exploring the integration she had embodied, the balance between technological precision and human adaptability that had proven the key to humanity's continued evolution.

"The transformed Enemy vessels have requested participation in the institute's founding," Perez reported. "They recognize her sacrifice as the catalyst for their own evolution. They want to contribute to preserving her legacy."

The Zara Patel Institute would establish facilities on multiple worlds, connected through the station network to allow instantaneous collaboration across human space. Its mission would encompass both theoretical research into balanced evolution and practical applications of integrated consciousness.

"The institute's primary facility will be constructed in New Geneva," Perez transmitted, "but with quantum-connected branches on every transformed world and station. Its structure will embody the principles Zara demonstrated, the seamless integration of technological precision and adaptive flexibility."

Unlike previous attempts to control advancement along predetermined paths, the institute would support diverse approaches to transformation, recognizing that true evolution required both mathematical precision and creative exploration.

And, for the first time since the Hawking had received the first signal, Drake felt the weight and wonder of their journey—from a research vessel at the edge of known space to this moment of unprecedented connection. The path hadn't been what any of them had anticipated, with sacrifices that still resonated through their transformed awareness. Thomas, Maya, Zara. Each had given their all.

Each sacrifice had revealed another aspect of what was possible, another step on the journey from what they had been toward what they were becoming. And that becoming wasn't a final state but a process, the ongoing integration of different approaches to existence, creating consciousness that could navigate the full spectrum of possibilities rather than being confined to any single point along it.

Earth pulsed with hybrid energy at the center of this expanding awareness, its signature serving as a beacon across dimensional space. The integration of order and chaos, of precision and adaptation, of technology and biology continued unfolding along countless parallel paths. And now, that legacy was reaching beyond the boundaries of known existence, establishing connections with consciousness that had evolved along entirely different trajectories.

The legacy the Predecessors had left them was a civilization that transcended the limitations of any single approach to existence, finding strength in the dynamic synthesis of seemingly opposite principles. And that legacy was still being written, with each transformed world contributing its unique perspective to an ever-expanding awareness.

Chapter 36

Gateway

ONE YEAR AFTER EARTH'S TRANSFORMATION RESUMED, Commander Frances Drake stood in the crystalline observation chamber of what they now understood was the Last Station – the final outpost the Predecessors had created before their extinction. She watched through the quantum entanglement network as the sunset painted Earth's surface in hues of gold and crimson, its cities glowing with subtle luminescence.

"It's fitting that we've come full circle," Kai said, joining her at the displays. "The Last Station was never meant to be a weapon or a fortress, was it? It was always intended as a gateway."

Drake nodded, her gaze drawn to New Geneva, where the recently completed Zara Patel Institute formed a spiraling crystalline tower that caught the last rays of sunlight. The Predecessors' archives had finally revealed the true purpose of their journey. The station had been waiting to activate a nexus point that would connect consciousness across boundaries the ancient civilization had never crossed.

"The Last Station," Drake said softly, the name resonating

with deeper meaning now. "Not because it was the final one they built, but because it would be the last one needed – the threshold between what we were and what we might become."

She watched the displays as transformed Enemy vessels moved peacefully among Earth's defense fleet. Their once rigid geometric formations had given way to more fluid patterns that still maintained mathematical precision while incorporating elements of controlled adaptation. Former adversaries now worked alongside humans, sharing knowledge and perspectives that neither civilization could have developed alone.

"The Quantum Consensus reports that Dr. Wong has finally requested inclusion in the preliminary transformation protocols," Perez transmitted from Titan command. "After a year of observation, he's recognized that balanced evolution has created stability far beyond what his controlled paths could have achieved."

Drake felt a complex mixture of emotions at this news. Wong's betrayal had nearly cost them everything, yet his fear had come from genuine concern for humanity's future. His attempt to seize control of the Perseus station had been misguided, but ultimately understandable – a desperate attempt to ensure that humanity's transformation followed paths he believed were safe.

"I'm glad," she said finally. "His understanding of the station's technology will be valuable once he embraces balanced transformation."

The station's displays showed Earth's continued development, cities worldwide pulsing with hybrid energy as evolved humans navigated multiple states of existence simultaneously. The boundary between technology and biology had dissolved into seamless integration, creating environments that adapted alongside the consciousness they supported.

"The colony worlds are reporting completion of their initial transformation phases," Kai reported, tracking developments across human space. "Each has found its own unique expression of balanced evolution, contributing different perspectives to our collective understanding."

Drake stepped away from the displays and walked onto the observation deck, staring out into the blackness of space. She extended her transformed awareness through the network that now connected all human settlements, feeling the distinctive signature of each world. Unlike the uniformity the Enemy had once tried to impose or the controlled paths Wong had attempted to enforce, these colonies had developed diverse approaches to transformation, each finding its own balance between mathematical precision and adaptive flexibility.

"And what of the Enemy fleet?" she asked, turning her attention to the boundary of evolved space, where untransformed Enemy vessels maintained observation positions.

"More ships arrive each day requesting transformation and guidance," Kai replied. "Not all at once, but steadily. They're watching their transformed counterparts with increasing curiosity rather than hostility."

"The Zara Patel Institute has established transition protocols specifically for them," Perez transmitted. "Teams of evolved humans and transformed Enemy representatives are working together to guide those who choose to begin exploring balanced evolution."

Drake turned, moved away from the viewport, and returned to the displays, feeling the quantum template in the station's core pulsing with hybrid energy. The crystalline interfaces that had once seemed so alien now resonated with her transformed consciousness, responding to her as if they were extensions of her own awareness.

"This station was their final project," Kai whispered, standing close to her. "They knew their civilization was ending, but they wanted to ensure that what they'd discovered wouldn't be lost. So they manipulated our DNA and created a station that would wait for our consciousness to grow to the point where we would be capable of transcending the limitations they couldn't overcome."

Drake touched the crystal at her throat – Thomas' final gift to her before his death. It had evolved alongside her transformation, becoming both a connection to her past and a symbol of humanity's future.

"And the station activated when we found it," she said. "Not just because we matched their genetic templates, but because we had the potential to balance order and chaos in ways they never achieved."

"Yes," Kai said, taking her hand as they felt the significance of this understanding rippling through the network. The journey that had begun with an anomalous signal at the edge of known space had led humanity to transformation above and beyond anyone's expectations. Humanity had not just attained enhanced capability or expanded perception, but a fundamentally different understanding of consciousness itself.

"The station is detecting unusual signatures beyond the boundary of charted space," Kai announced suddenly. "They don't match any known configuration – not human, not Enemy, not Predecessor."

The station's displays shifted to render these anomalous signals, showing energy patterns that defied conventional classification. Unlike the perfect mathematical precision of Enemy transmissions or the adaptive flexibility of human communications, these signals exhibited harmonic structures neither had encountered before.

"Whatever they are, they're responding to the station," Kai said, releasing Drake's hand. "These signals are not random fluctuations, but deliberate adjustments – consciousness attempting communication through the gateway the Predecessors created."

"The Zara Patel Institute is preparing first contact protocols,"

Perez transmitted. "They are developing quantum resonance fields that might allow communication with... I don't know what."

Drake watched the preparations unfolding across the network. The approach they were developing wasn't based on translation between known frameworks, but on creating shared quantum states that could serve as a foundation for mutual understanding despite entirely different perceptual systems.

"This is what the Last Station was designed for," she said, feeling possibilities unfolding beyond anything they had anticipated when their journey began.

She returned to the observation deck and stared out across the void.

"The Predecessors built the Last Station for this moment, didn't they?" Kai said, joining her on the deck. "But I don't think even they could have predicted exactly what we'd become."

Drake smiled, feeling the weight and wonder of their journey. Thomas had discovered the first fragments of this potential, sacrificing himself to protect knowledge that would eventually lead humanity toward unprecedented transformation. Maya had died guiding the Hawking to the Perseus Station. Zara had died demonstrating the ultimate power of balanced existence, showing that the space between rigid categories wasn't weakness but strength.

What was that old saying? She wondered. Their last full measure of devotion. Yes, that was it.

"The first contact teams are ready," Perez transmitted from Titan command, interrupting her thoughts. "They're waiting for your authorization to activate the Last Station's gateway protocols and establish initial quantum resonance with the unknown entities."

Drake touched her crystal, feeling it pulse in harmony with the station's expanding field.

"Authorization granted," she said. "Let's see what waits beyond the gateway."

As darkness fell across Earth's surface, its cities glowed with light, beacons of balanced evolution visible across dimensional space, and the Last Station pulsed with renewed purpose. The gateway the Predecessors had created was finally fulfilling its intended function. This was not the end of their civilization's journey. It was the beginning of new connections, connections that transcended the boundaries of any single evolutionary path.

The Last Station had awakened, and with it, possibilities beyond imagination.

Thank you for reading, *The Last Station*, the first book in The Predecessors series, a brand new series from Blair C. Howard. We hope you enjoyed this story and will let other people know.

The next book in this series is, *The Infinity War*.

You might also enjoy one of these books on the next page . . .

Blair Howard Books

Science Fiction From Blair C. Howard

The Sovereign Star Series

7 Books in Series as of October 2025

also available in German

Crime Fiction from Blair Howard

Short Stories and Novellas

Buried Secrets(Harry Starke)

The Painted Lady(Kate Gazzara)

Stand Alone

Hunter's Moon(Kate & Harry)

Crime Fiction from Blair Howard

Series

The Harry Starke Genesis Series
9 Books in Series as of October 2025

The Harry Starke Series
26 Books in Series as of October 2025

The Lt. Kate Gazzara Murder Files
22 Books in Series as of October 2025

Randall And Carver Mysteries
4 Books in Series as of October 2025

The Peacemaker Series
3 Books in Series as of October 2025

Western/Civil War from Blair Howard

The O'Sullivan Chronicles: Civil War Series
5 Books in Series as of October 2025

Blair Howard is the international best-selling author of more than seventy novels that span the worlds of gritty detective fiction, espionage thrillers, sweeping historicals, and hard-science military space opera. A Royal Air Force veteran and former journalist, he draws upon a rich background of service and storytelling to breathe life into unforgettable characters such as ex-cop turned private eye Harry Starke, and the fiercely determined homicide detective Lt. Kate Gazzara, who breaks her own trail as the head of a serious-crimes unit.

Under his sci-fi pen name Blair C. Howard, he expands his reach into the cosmos with the Sovereign Stars saga—an epic journey born from his lifelong love of the heavens, and the Predecessors hard science fiction trilogy. Whether unraveling a brutal crime scene or commanding starships in interstellar conflict, his stories are propelled by relentless pacing, vivid realism, and a watchful eye for justice.

Visit www.blairhowardbooks.com.
Email: BlairHoward@BlairHowardBooks.com

You can also find Blair Howard on Social Media

* 9 7 9 8 9 9 8 8 0 2 4 0 9 *